Riding Dirty on I-95

"*Riding Dirty on I-95* is USDA hood certified."
—Teri Woods, author of *The Dutch Trilogy* and *True to the Game*

"[A] gritty, fast-paced street tale with heart."
—*Publishers Weekly*

Street Chronicles: Tales from da Hood

"Nikki Turner has put together one helluva team for this one. *Street Chronicles* is a joint you need to cop!"
—Thomas Long, author of *Cash Rules*

"*Street Chronicles* is a walk through Anyhood U.S.A."
—K'wan, bestselling author of *Gangsta, Street Dreams,* and *Hoodlum*

The Glamorous Life

"Though hip-hop began in the music industry, Nikki Turner found a creative way to bring the rhythm to print—in fictional novels that give readers a close-up look at urban life."
—*Booking Matters*

"Turner creates colorful, yet emotionally driven characters that captivate. Despite the deceit, cruelty, hatred and unspeakable wrongs, humanity maintains its presence in this glamorous life."
—*Upscale*

"A gritty street tale of a young woman who has to decide which is more important—money or love."
—*The Seattle Skanner*

"One of the premier queens of urban literature presents her latest steamy page-turner!"
—*Black Expressions*

ALSO BY
NIKKI TURNER

Riding Dirty on I-95

The Glamorous Life

A Hustler's Wife

A Project Chick

Girls from da Hood

AS A CONTRIBUTOR

Street Chronicles: Tales from da Hood
(editor, contributing author)

The Game: Short Stories About the Life
(contributing author)

Forever a
Hustler's Wife

ONE WORLD

BALLANTINE BOOKS

New York

· ·

A

NIKKI TURNER

ORIGINAL

Forever a
Hustler's Wife

· · · · · · · · · A NOVEL · · · · · · · · ·

A One World Books Trade Paperback Original

Copyright © 2007 by Nikki Turner

Published in the United States by One World Books, an imprint of The Random House Publishing Group, a division of Random House, Inc., New York.

ONE WORLD is a registered trademark and the One World colophon is a trademark of Random House, Inc.

ISBN 978-0-345-49385-9

Library of Congress Cataloging-in-Publication Data
Turner, Nikki.
Forever a hustler's wife : a novel / Nikki Turner.
p.   cm.
ISBN 978-0-345-49385-9
1. Swindlers and swindling—Fiction.   2. Street life—Fiction.
3. African Americans—Fiction.   I. Title.
PS3620.U7659F67   2007
813'.6—dc22   2006046947

Printed in the United States of America

www.oneworldbooks.net

6 8 9 7 5

THIS BOOK IS DEDICATED TO
ALL THE WOMEN WORLDWIDE
WHO WILL FOREVER BE
HUSTLERS' WIVES.
I FEEL YOU MORE THAN
YOU COULD EVER KNOW!

A Special Message From Nikki Turner to Her Readers

. . . .

Dear Readers,

This past year I was faced with one of the most trying obstacles that I have experienced in a very long time . . . birthing this baby. Although you hold in your hand this beautiful book, it took a lot of blood, sweat, tears, heartache, and pain to produce the sequel to *A Hustler's Wife*.

But before I tell you about the process of writing this book, I have to be *totally* honest with you and come clean about something that I've held in for a long time. My first novel, the book that put me on the map and went on to become a #1 bestseller—*A Hustler's Wife*—was so dear to me because parts of the story were based on actual events in my very own life. There you have it! You heard it here first, straight out of the horse's mouth. *And* . . . if you are a true Nikki Turner fan you'd know that the novel's ending was only a fantasy, my fantasy. It breaks my heart to say that my Des didn't come home, but at that time in my life that was the ending I wished for. I absolutely loved that ending and I know you did, too. I mean, you tell me what girl who has a man behind bars with a sentence equivalent to football numbers wouldn't? But as you know, in life things don't always happen when, where, and how you want them to. I may hold the power in the pen but sometimes no authority in my own reality.

Writing a sequel isn't easy. A part of me wanted to postpone this book because I had another story that I was longing to write—*The Black Widow*—a book that I had on my heart big time! I could easily have written it in sixty days flat. However, I knew it was now or never and I'd given my word to you that the sequel to *A Hustler's Wife* would be my next book, and I don't make promises to break them.

So, I commenced to push this baby out. As I pushed and pushed, it wouldn't come. I mean the story line was there but I just couldn't fully focus to write it. It seemed like every possible curveball was coming my way. I had so much stress and confusion surrounding me. (I'm not going to bore you with the specifics, but don't worry, one day I'll give you the in-depth details between the pages of yet another Nikki Turner Original!)

I was convinced that this was just a storm in my life, and I had to stand the rain. So many nights I cried, asking God when this hurricane was going to leave my world. But I knew good and well that I was a survivor and had made it through much harsher conditions. The bottom line was that I wasn't going to be a casualty of this storm, and I knew giving up wasn't an option. No, not when the e-mails, letters, and calls were pouring in asking for this sequel. The only thing that I was really sure of was that I wasn't going to disappoint my fans. To make a long story short: My back was up against the wall, the clock was ticking, the deadline to turn in my book had passed, and

I needed a plan. There was only one place I could go to seek the right answers. I leaned on the One that I knew wouldn't steer me wrong. I fell on my knees and begged God to remove this madness from my life, but if that wasn't possible, to help it get resolved quickly, or at least remove it long enough so that I could get focused and start this book.

I don't know if y'all are feeling me but if you don't know the power of God, darling . . . let me be the first to share my testimony: After I put it in God's hands, ten minutes later, what seemed to be a routine checkup call from my platonic friend Antonio Tarver turned out to be the answer to my prayer. He invited me to the first two weeks of his training camp in Vero Beach, Florida, to give me the solitude and peace I would need to write. Staying at Antonio's lavish beach house was enough to clear my mind and get me focused so that I could do the damn thing. Two weeks later I returned home with over a third of this book completed, and about twelve pounds lighter thanks to Dudley Pierce, Antonio's strength and conditioning coach. Dudley, if you are reading this you literally changed my life by putting me on the road to eating and exercising right.

But as soon as I returned, *Riding Dirty on I-95* dropped and then the I-95 tour started. Life on the road is always hard and not glamorous at all—don't let anyone tell you different. And living out of a suitcase and promoting from damn near sunup to sundown leaves no time to write. Toward the end of the tour, I ended up getting sick (don't worry, your girl made it through). The doctors sat my butt down, but how could I rest when my editor was calling me every single day, even Sundays, gently asking, "How's the writing coming?"

I had to explain to her that nothing great was ever created overnight. Rome wasn't built in a day, and fine wine only gets better with time. Shoot, it takes a baby nine months to develop and we definitely wanted this baby to meet its full potential. It may have taken thirty-seven days to write the first draft of *A Hustler's Wife,* but it actually took years for the series of events that made up the story to come to a head. I wanted to let this baby go through all its trimesters and a premature birth wasn't an option. My editor agreed with me and when I e-mailed chapters to her, I would title the electronic files as "hardest labor ever," because it was indeed, and also so that she could keep the faith in me and the story. (I'm so glad that I did send the chapters over to her as I wrote them, because if I hadn't, we would've lost the entire book. After I finished the book, my computer crashed, and my backup disk had an error on it. Thankfully, my editor was able to e-mail the chapters back to me. I lost all my information and e-mail addresses. If you haven't heard from me or my fan club in a while it's because I no longer have your e-mail address, so please e-mail me, *Nikki@nikkiturner.com.*) All in all I was glad that I didn't get sidetracked by the chaos or that I didn't force the delivery of this baby. I wanted to feel proud of my creation, and most of all make sure that it was worth your wait. And if it took me another nine months to do it, then so be it! (I'm glad it didn't though.)

I want to thank you so much from the depths of my soul and the bottom of my heart for buying my books. As long as I am a writer, I promise I will continue to push out the hottest Nikki Turner Originals that you've grown to love over the years. My prayer today is that you receive this one as you have all my babies and that you enjoy the fruits of my labor. Having you love this book is enough for me to know in my heart that all the pitfalls and perils that I endured while birthing this book were not in vain.

I can say it a million times over and over again and you will *never* know how much I do love you for changing my life! For saving my life! Thank you for embracing my craft, my talent, and the mere fact that I am able to do what I love to feed my children! And it is all possible because of YOU!

You have no idea, I'm so emotional right now! I'm crying, I'm sweating, my heart is beating fast as I reflect on the love you've given me from DAY ONE when *A Hustler's Wife* was released! Tears are falling on the keyboard! I'm weeping, and my children hear me. They are outside my door knocking and inquiring about what's wrong with me. I think I've written enough. I'm taking a deep breath and making the last push!

Here's my new baby! I hope you love it as much as I do! I present to you the newest member of the Nikki Turner dynasty, *Forever a Hustler's Wife*!

Forever Yours,
Nikki Turner

Forever a Hustler's Wife

CHAPTER 1

A Million Damn Dollars

As Yarni Taylor entered the old courtroom and searched for a seat toward the front, she couldn't help but overhear clients arguing with their attorneys as well as the chitchat of folks·waiting for their loved ones' cases to be heard. "I wish they'd hurry up and get this started, because I got to go to work," one person said. Another asked, "So you think that Boo-boo gon' come to court and testify on Freddie Boy?"

She tried to control the sway of her ample behind as she walked down the aisle, but all eyes were on her. Yarni wasn't sure if it was the confidence she exuded or her exotic looks—almond-shaped hazel eyes, high cheekbones, and caramel skin so smooth you wanted to lick it—which were complemented by her cream-colored Tahari suit that, like a little red Corvette going a hundred miles per hour on the highway, hugged every curve. Diamond studs glistened in her ears, and a huge six-carat rock weighed down her left hand. She wasn't a stranger to the courts. A successful attorney, she had won many cases in the very room in which she was now taking a seat. This time, though, Yarni wasn't there to defend a case.

If it wasn't for all the bad luck, there would be no luck at all, Yarni thought as she sat there trying to be strong, holding back the tears that threatened to spill from her eyes. The system had railroaded her man, Des, once again. The last time was almost fifteen years ago, but no matter the outcome, just like before, she was going to hold her man down through it all: rain, sleet, hail, or sunshine . . . bad, good, happy, or sad . . . win, lose, or draw. One thing was for certain, and two things were for sure: She had Des's back, and he had hers—through hell or high water.

When Yarni first met Des, he was already a street legend, and she was just a high school girl who had been raised by a single mother. Her mother had given Yarni every opportunity that a girl like her could ever want, all in hopes of her growing up to be a strong, independent woman, but once she met Des, Yarni didn't care about anything her mother had given her or instilled in her or any of it. Yarni and Des fell in love with each other hard, but their perfect relationship was put through the test of fire when Des was arrested and convicted for a murder he didn't commit. For ten years after that, Yarni rode for her man, never losing hope, and eventually got his sentence overturned. Yarni later became a lawyer to help other minority men caught up in the wrath like Des had been. And now here they were again, facing another murder rap. Yarni sat on the edge of her seat while waiting for her husband's case to be called. But first, another defendant was up for a bail bond hearing, temporarily distracting Yarni from thoughts of Des.

"Samuel Johnson, you are being charged with three counts of

murder, threatening a witness, tampering with state's evidence, conspiracy to commit murder, shooting in an occupied dwelling, possession of a firearm while a convicted felon," the court clerk stated as she looked up at the man standing in front of her before taking a deep breath and continuing, "use of a firearm in commission of a felony, kidnapping, torture, abduction, malicious wounding, felonious assault, and use of a firearm near a school zone."

Yarni thought the clerk should have taken a bow after putting her vocals through so much work. Instead, the clerk looked out into the packed courtroom, which was so quiet you could have heard a mouse pissing on the carpet. The sheer number of charges forced every single spectator to direct his or her undivided attention to this particular case, curious as to how one person could have so many indictments against him. *Damn, I haven't heard anybody with that many charges since the Briley brothers,* Yarni thought, recalling a 1979 case involving brothers who were sentenced to death for an eight-month string of gruesome murders in Richmond.

"Your Honor, we're here to ask for a bond for Mr. Johnson," the defense attorney said. "He's a father and a Little League coach." The attorney walked around the oak table where he and his client were standing and approached the judge at the front of the courtroom. "He has always lived here. His roots are here, Your Honor."

The judge's hands were folded as he glared at the defendant through his glasses, which sat on the tip of his nose. Samuel Johnson fidgeted in his orange jumpsuit, his eyes never meeting the judge's stern gaze. Just looking at the man, Yarni felt that Mr. Johnson was being taken for a ride. Instead of the nice trim or touch-up on the jailhouse braids most attorneys made sure their male defendants had before appearing in court, Samuel's hair was in a nappylike 'fro. He hadn't shaved, his goatee was raggedy, and it didn't help that his fair skin accentuated his dark shades of hair. He turned around to glance into the audience and to make matters worse, his gray eyes were blinding, like sun rays around his pupils, making him appear almost devil-like.

The first thing I would have done was buy that man a pair of brown contact lenses, Yarni shook her head at her thoughts.

The defense attorney was trying to pretend to have confidence, but because of the number of charges, he knew he really didn't have a leg to stand on. He hadn't even done the proper research to prepare for the hearing. What was the use? "Your Honor, he isn't a flight risk." The attorney went through the motions.

"I beg to differ," the feisty prosecutor interjected, rising from his chair. "These are very serious charges, Your Honor. With serious consequences. There's no reason for the defendant not to run."

The judge looked at the defendant and then at his defense attorney and bluntly said, "No bond. Next case, please."

The defense attorney turned, walked back behind the table, and began gathering his paperwork. "I'm sorry," he said, unable to look his client in the eye. "I did all I could do." When his client did not respond, he shrugged his shoulders and added, "I don't know what you were expecting. With all those charges, you were fooling yourself thinking that a bond would come out of this."

"I was expecting what the fuck you promised," Samuel snapped. "You promised me a bond, motherfucker. You sold me and my girl a fucking dream."

The bailiff was slowly walking over to escort Samuel Johnson out of the courtroom, and before anyone could stop him, Samuel spit on his attorney. Next, he drew back and punched his attorney in the eye. The lawyer fell to the floor holding his face. Snatching up a chair, Samuel screamed, "Succckkk my dick!" and hurled the chair at the judge. It missed, but as the judge was running for his chambers, his black toupee fell on the ground.

For a few minutes the courtroom was completely out of control, and although the deputies were trained to handle situations like this, they were shocked themselves and very slow to react. Two of the three deputies looked like they had been eating a few too many Twinkies, which was probably why they weren't too swift on their feet.

Samuel charged toward his attorney, who had gotten up and was trying to make it to the door. Unfortunately, the attorney wasn't the track star he used to be, so he wasn't fast enough either. Samuel grabbed him by the neck and hit him three times in the back of the head before the deputies got a hold of him and pulled him away. The bystanders were in a frenzy. While Yarni didn't agree with all of the defendant's actions, she could understand his frustration. His lawyer appeared to have given up on him.

There was a brief recess not only to get the courtroom back in order but also to get the judge's toupee back on and straight. Once all was calm, the bailiff announced the next case: "The state of Maryland versus Desmond Taylor."

Yarni's heart raced and skipped a few beats when the deputy sheriff brought in Des. He, too, had on a bright orange jumpsuit, but Des's dark chocolate complexion, compact muscular body, and swagger made him stand out. Yarni's heart melted as her eyes met Des's for the first time in more than three weeks.

The last time she saw him was when he jetted out of the hospital room after the birth of their first child, Desi Arnez Taylor.

"Your Honor, this defendant is being charged with the murder of his former attorney," the prosecutor stated. "We recommend denying bail because this man is a serious flight risk."

"Excuse me, Your Honor, but the prosecutor is mistaken," said Mark Harowitz, Des's new high-profile attorney. He was a commanding presence in his custom-made navy pinstripe suit and elaborate bow tie. His cockiness let everyone in the courtroom know that he was not some public pretender who was on the same payroll as the prosecutor. It wasn't hard to imagine that his bank account held quite a few more zeroes than the judge's.

"Desmond Taylor has a stable residence in Richmond, Virginia, where he was born and attended college," Harowitz said.

The prosecutor stood and countered, "And Virginia was the place where he served a ten-year prison sentence for murder, Your Honor."

Harowitz cleared his throat then calmly voiced, while holding his hundred-dollar ink pen, "A murder that he did not commit and for which he received an unconditional pardon." He turned to look at the prosecutor. "He was robbed of ten years of his young life."

"How ironic it is that two years after he is released from prison his attorney, who Mr. Taylor feels railroaded him, is murdered in cold blood," the prosecutor responded. And we have evidence that the defendant was less than forty miles from the scene of the crime on the same day."

Harowitz looked directly at the judge. "Technically this evidence as well as any mention of prior crimes is inadmissible in a bail hearing. We're here only to prove that he isn't a flight risk, which he isn't, and to determine what is a reasonable amount for a bond," he said calmly.

"My client has strong ties to the community. He has a newborn daughter and a large family that loves and supports him. He and his wife have a lucrative luxury-car dealership, which he manages himself. His wife is a very successful attorney, who is here today in the courtroom." He turned and briefly made eye contact with Yarni; she offered a small smile to the judge before looking at Des. Des smiled at her, and her heart melted again.

"We're not here to discuss his wife," the prosecutor said in an irritated voice. "We're here to discuss your client's checkered past."

Harowitz was about to let loose a verbal onslaught on the prosecutor, but the judge finally stepped in. "Sidebar."

Both attorneys approached the judge's bench.

"Fellas, this isn't a boxing match."

"Your Honor." The prosecutor jumped in, determined to have the first say. "I'm making it known that this guy is an ex-offender and doesn't deserve a bond."

"Ex-offender?" Harowitz said. "No. He was railroaded in the previous case, and by law he's indeed innocent until proven guilty."

"Which I intend to do," the prosecution said, lacking conviction.

"I'd like to see that happen when the only evidence you have is a measly gas receipt charged to his company credit card from some station forty-eight miles away from the murder scene. On top of that, any one of his twelve employees could have used the card to purchase gas. Where are your witnesses? Your exhibits?" Harowitz looked at the prosecutor, who seemed to be tongue-tied and unable to respond. "Cat got your tongue? Or better yet, did a law change and someone forgot to send me the memo? My client deserves a reasonable bail."

The prosecutor looked to the judge, his Shriner buddy, for some help. "Your Honor, the only reasonable bail in this case is no bail."

"I hear you both, and you both have good arguments." The judge sighed. "Bail is going to be set at a million dollars."

"Your Honor!" Harowitz exclaimed. "A million dollars? That's a bit excessive, don't you think?"

"That's my ruling. It is what it is. Let's not forget that I'm the judge, and I make the final decisions in this courtroom." With that, he struck his gavel once and signaled with a nod for the attorneys to take their places back behind their tables.

"Thank you, Judge," the prosecutor said as he walked away with a smile of victory on his face and a bounce in his step. Although his Shriner brother had set a bond, he had still, in effect, ruled in his favor. As far as the prosecutor and the judge were concerned, no black man besides an athlete or entertainer could ever make that kind of bail.

Both attorneys positioned themselves behind their respective tables facing the judge. When Des observed the big smile plastered on the prosecutor's face, his first thought was that he was conquered, but his gut told him differently, and his gut was usually right. Harowitz didn't give him any indication of what was said during the sidebar, so Des just focused in on the judge as he began to speak.

"Bail will be set at one million dollars cash."

Chills went up Yarni's spine, but she tried not to let the ruling affect her. She focused only on what the judge had to say.

"The rules on this bail are as follows: You can put up one million dollars cash, or if you own a piece of property valued at least three times the one million dollars, that can be put up to secure your bail."

At least there was a bond, so Yarni knew there was hope. She struggled to hold back her tears. She didn't want to break down, not now at least, not in the courtroom. Des gazed over at her as he whispered in his attorney's ear. Yarni quietly moved her lips to say "I love you," and nodded, offering him a small smile, which Des returned.

Because of the last episode, it seemed the bailiff was moving much faster. Before Des was even finished speaking to his attorney, the bailiff pulled him away. A few minutes later, after Harowitz gathered his case files, he made his way outside the courtroom to where Yarni was waiting.

"So, a million dollars?" Yarni said as he walked over to her.

"I'm sorry, Yarnise. I wish it wasn't so—"

"I know. You did really well in there. We both know that it could have been so much worse."

"The prosecutor is a complete asshole, and he knows he doesn't have a case. The bail is so high only because they're the good ol' boys."

"I kind of figured that." She paused. "For the record, Mark, I will help with any research that you need. I really appreciate this. I can't tell you how much."

"Oh, I know you will, but I'm going to put my best foot forward. I'll handle this. You just take care of that little baby girl of yours."

Yarni's face lit up at the mention of her daughter. "Taking care of my little Desi is mandatory, but I will not kick back and let my husband fall victim to this system again. I can't. I won't," Yarni stated with determination. "I'm simply not going to let that happen."

"I know," Harowitz said, placing his hand on Yarni's shoulder. "We've just got to be on top of everything, and it starts with a million dollars."

"I know." She glanced down and then looked back up at him and repeated, "A million dollars, huh?"

He nodded slowly and echoed, "A million dollars. I know it's a lot of cash, but I think it would help us prepare for the case if Des was out of jail."

"He won't be in jail," Yarni assured Mark.

A million dollars wasn't going to stop Yarni from having Des with her. Des was her all—he was her everything, her world, her heart, her mind, her soul, her husband, her baby's father. A million dollars, though a lot of money, was not enough to stand in the way of her being with her man.

"Keep me posted. I'll call you tomorrow to check on you."

"Thanks, Mark," she said as he started to walk away.

"Oh," he said, snapping his fingers as if remembering something. "Desmond said to tell you to come visit him before you make any moves." The word *moves* sounded funny coming from Mark. "He says he really needs to talk to you."

"Okay. Thanks again for everything."

"I'll be in touch," he said over his shoulder, heading for the elevators.

Yarni went directly to the jail to try to see Des, only to be informed that her visitation rights with him were revoked because years ago she had been a convicted felon. With the help of a lawyer she had worked for, her record had been expunged before she went to law school and now she was a working attorney, but no matter how many ways she tried to explain, they still refused to let her see Des. Yarni finally realized that there was no hope in getting through to them. She didn't want to get all worked up, so she thanked them and left, but she wouldn't give up. She knew that there was always more than one way to skin a cat. And she was about to skin one alive.

Yarni exited the jail and conjured up her plan over a leisurely lunch. The reality was that no man, woman, or child, no bars, walls, or fences, and damn sure no underpaid, paper-pushing deputy sheriff was going to keep her away from seeing her man. She made a few phone calls to kill time until after 2:30 that afternoon, when the shifts changed at the jail. At 3:05, she returned with her briefcase in hand.

"Yes, ma'am," greeted the female guard with short dreads, looking her over. "Can I help you?"

"Yes," Yarni replied. "Attorney visit with Samuel Johnson." She handed the guard her business card.

After looking over the card, the guard said, "Just one moment, ma'am."

Yarni smiled.

"It's nice to see a sistah as an attorney," the guard said.

"Thank you," Yarni said aloud in a gracious tone, but to herself she said, *I am so glad that the new millennium Angela Davis is working today.* She looked up at the ceiling and smiled.

It only took a few minutes for them to point her to the visiting room where Samuel was waiting for her. When she walked into the room, he looked her over and rolled his eyes and asked her with much attitude, "Did that bullshit-ass attorney of mine send you?" He didn't try to hide the attitude in his voice.

"No, he didn't," Yarni answered his question. "Do you really think he's thinking about you right now? I mean really?" Yarni pouted and tilted her head sideways as if he had just made the dumbest comment of the year.

"He just ought to be thinking about my black ass. My peoples paid that motherfucker top dollar."

"You actually paid him money?" She burst into a roar of laughter. "You can't be serious. I would have sworn that he was court-appointed."

He looked up at her and said with hostility, "Well, who the hell are you, and what the fuck do you want?" Still disgruntled, he asked, "You police? Because if you are, I ain't do shit, and I ain't telling a motherfucking thing. So, beat yo' feet, baybee."

Yarni chuckled a bit, but she knew she had to throw professionalism out the window and get straight gully with this guy. "Look, I'm not trying to rob you with or without a gun. I'ma say it like this because Dougie couldn't have said it any better, 'Cut that zero and get with this hero.' "

He laughed. "It's going to take more than a pretty face to beat my charges."

"Look, I'm the cream of the crop. I've worked for and with the best, and have beaten, the best."

Samuel leaned back, looked Yarni up and down, then smacked his lips. "You ain't no lawyer. Shawdy, go 'head wit' dat bullshit and stop playing wit' me."

"It isn't a joke," Yarni said in a very serious tone, leaning forward. "I don't play games. I win games. I had a baby just three weeks ago. You think I got time to come down here and play games with you when I could be at home with my baby?"

Samuel gave Yarni the once-over again and began nodding while tilting back on two legs of his chair. "What can you do for me that the other attorney can't?"

"Can't or ain't? Which one? Because there's a difference," Yarni said.

He looked at her and, without answering, let out a slight chuckle.

"Look, the bottom line is that your attorney is bull-mother-fucking-shit, okay?" She continued to let him know what was real in the field. "All he's going to do is plead you out." She moved her head back and forth and let the words roll off her tongue as if they were a song. "He's going to come to visit you all of a total of thirty minutes, if that, throughout the entire case. He'll spend five minutes talking to the prosecutor, and, before you know it, you gonna be standing in front of the judge, your family, and your loved ones saying the word *guilty* to a lesser charge in exchange for about forty to fifty years."

Samuel was shocked that Yarni was giving him the rundown like she was doing, so he couldn't help but listen as she made him buy into her vision. She saw she had his attention and continued to lay it on thick.

"Then the next thing you know," Yarni continued, "you look at yourself in the mirror and that 'fro you got now will be long processed curls, and you'll be answering to the name Samantha." He was about to say something smart to her, but she cut him off before he could even get started. "I know you ain't going out like that, but, brother man, forty years is a long time for you to try to rumble. You a light-skinned dude, small and frail, too. You know how it goes. You been down before. You're not going to the boot camp this time, so this time it's straight to the big house, my darling."

He nodded and listened to her because he could tell she was a woman who knew some things, most likely some things that could help him.

"And how would you be different?" he asked, still slightly doubtful. "What could you do?"

"I wouldn't take any shit, and I'd come out fighting." She gave him a compassionate stare. "If there is a way for you to be exonerated, I'll find that way."

"Look, I ain't got no mo' money. That other jive-ass lawyer got it all."

"Don't worry about that. You can pay me in another way."

He got quiet and put his chair back down on all fours. "How?" he asked with a confused look on his face. "I just told you I don't have no money."

"I'm going to have you be the go-between for me and my husband. He's the guy whose case was heard right after yours today in court. You're going to need to let him know that I'm your attorney now. Also tell him to make sure that he calls me at eight o'clock tonight. Can you handle that?"

"Yeah, but what about if your husband gets out? Are you going to forget about me?"

"A deal is a deal: My word is law and my word is my bond. And your deal is more than a fair deal."

He thought for a minute before asking, "That's all I gotta do?"

"Yes, that's all you have to do. Now, is it a deal?"

She extended her hand. After hesitating for a moment, he smiled and shook Yarni's hand.

She grabbed her briefcase and stood up. "There's one more thing."

"What is it?" Samuel asked, knowing this was too good to be true.

"I need to know that I can trust you."

"You can, like my life depends on it."

"Don't talk to anyone but me about anything regarding your case. There are a lot of people trying to make deals to get out of jail."

He smiled. "I know what's up."

"Anything we discuss is between us. Don't talk to any cell mates, homeboys, girlfriends, baby mommas—none of that. They're all suspect and can be broken."

"I gotcha."

"Now, let me warn you. This is going to be an uphill battle. I'm going to start by flooding them with paperwork. I'm going to file for a change of venue, as well as a discovery motion, and I'm going to continue to push a ton of paperwork; they are going to get intimidated. They hate that. Prosecutors have small offices and don't have the time to respond to large briefs," Yarni informed her new client. "All in all, if that doesn't stop them, then I'll just put my gloves on and box it out with them."

"I hear you, Layla Ali." Samuel smiled, glad to have this woman as his attorney.

"No, I'm a heavyweight." Yarni winked.

Once their visit was over, she went back to the front desk, where there was now another guard working.

Thinking quickly, Yarni said to the guard, "You can send in my other client now."

"And who is he?" the guard asked, too busy looking at a tabloid magazine to pay much attention to her.

"Desmond Taylor."

"Okay, no problem," he said.

"Thank you," Yarni said, then returned to the room she had just left.

Before long, Des walked into the room. A huge grin swept across his face when he saw Yarni sitting there.

News always traveled quicker than a wildfire in the penal system. Des had heard about her failed first attempt to see him, but he knew that Yarni would figure out a way to come see him somehow. She always did and always would. Yarni stood when she saw Des and ran over to him. He embraced her with a tight hug, and as soon as he did, she couldn't fight her battle anymore, the tears just poured from her eyes and onto his shoulder.

"I love you, baby," Yarni said as Des kissed her on her head and rubbed her hair, trying his best to comfort her.

"I love you, too," he replied, and Yarni lifted her head to look him in his eyes. "Are you okay?"

"Yeah, I'm good, now that I've gotten a chance to talk to you. How are you and my baby girl doing?"

"She's good, just big and fat." Yarni gave a dry chuckle, but Des could tell it was only a way for her to keep from crying again.

"Baby, I'm sorry for leaving y'all like that."

"No problem. I know you're married to the game," she said, unable to resist taking a shot at him for leaving her and their baby at the hospital to take care of business.

He looked into her eyes and grabbed her hands, pulling her even closer to him. "No, baby, I'm married to you and our baby girl."

Yarni sighed and walked away. "Look, baby, this isn't even the time for us to get into this." Frustrated with the whole situation, she put her hand on her forehead. "We'll discuss this when you get out of here. Right now, let's focus on making that happen."

"Look, I know we got over a million stashed," Des said, following her, "but that is what they're waiting for. We ain't giving them no million dollars."

"Oh, I know that," Yarni agreed, letting him know that they were on the same page. "I already made the phone call about the deed."

"I knew you would. That's what I wanted to talk to you about. Look, I got too much at stake here—my baby girl, you, my freedom. Shit, I just did ten years and finally got things falling sweet like I want 'em." He maintained eye contact with her. "And for real, I know you probably think that I had something to do with what they're charging me with—"

"No, baby, and for real, it doesn't matter to me. I'm on your team 'til death do us part." She instinctively placed the palm of her hand over to the left side of her chest. Underneath her hand and the fabric of the designer blouse that she wore was a tattoo of a bejeweled seven-pointed crown, engraved at the top of the headpiece were the words *Death Before Dishonor*. And the inscription at the base was the name of the only man she had ever loved: *Des.*

She knew something wasn't right, and all bulletins were reporting to Des, but whether he did or didn't kill his attorney, that wasn't her issue. She cared only about him and the life they had together. Fuck the evidence, the prosecutor, the crooked judicial system; screw the politics and politricks of it all—he was her only concern.

"I know, but I want you to know I didn't do it."

"I know," she said, nodding. Des caught a brief glimpse of doubt in her eyes and could tell that even though she really wasn't 100 percent sure, she was riding with him anyway.

"Look, like I said, I got too much to lose, and before you sign to get me out, you gotta know that once I walk out of here, it ain't no turning back. They gonna take the house if I can't prove my innocence. I'm not going through what I did the last time."

"I know." Yarni knew that Des would run rather than sit in jail again for a crime he didn't commit. And as a result they would lose their dream house.

"You sure you gon' be able to handle that?"

"Boo, I don't give a fuck about a gotdamn house. We'll just get another one. You know I'm fine as long as we're together. It's just when we're not together; that's when I lose it."

"I'm just saying, we worked hard getting that house built and decorated, and I know how much you love it."

"Fuck that house," Yarni said with sincerity. "It's just a house. Like I said, it can be replaced." She touched his cheek and trailed her fingers down his chin, drawing his face close to her, "But you, my darling . . . you can't."

He nodded and smiled inside. He knew that if anything was stable in his life, it was Yarni.

"Besides," Yarni continued, "if I had to sell ten houses and the clothes on my back, then guess what? I wouldn't leave you in here."

"That's why you're my wife," Des said, planting a kiss on Yarni's lips.

"So we're not going to burn this out," Yarni explained to Des about the visit. "You know I had to finagle my way in here."

"You still want me to call you at eight o'clock?"

"Damn, ol' boy told you already, huh?"

"Which reminds me: What I tell you about bringing stray dogs home?" Des joked.

"You know I'm always trying to fix a wounded puppy."

"I know, and you gon' do it, too. I got confidence."

"Thanks, baby."

"Oh, and he didn't do that shit. His man did it."

"Huh?" Yarni asked, slightly puzzled.

"Your client. He didn't do what they're accusing him of. His man did it."

"For real?" Yarni said, staring at him.

"Jailhouse gossip. He was with the people that did it, but he was passed out drunk in the car. He had nothing to do with it."

"Good looking out." She stood up and gave Des a hug and a quick, juicy kiss. "The paperwork should be done in twenty-four hours, and I'll be back here to pick you up."

"Make sure you bring Desi when you come."

"I will." Yarni smiled as she left Des to go watch the clock and await making his phone call.

Yarni pulled into her long winding driveway at 7:30 P.M. She didn't go by Des's mother's house to pick up Desi because she didn't want to take a chance on being late and missing Des's eight o'clock call. After parking her platinum Bentley coupe in the driveway beside Des's money-green Bentley coupe, she walked into the lavish home she shared with Des and their daughter. Yarni couldn't help but take a moment to admire the columns, the archways, the beautiful decor, and the furniture, knowing that it might all be pulled from under her feet. The more she roamed from room to room, the more the possibility of the loss of her house bothered her. If it came down to doing more time or running, she knew what choice Des would make.

For all the time she had lived in this house, she had taken so much for granted, never really stopping to look at the beautiful original paintings she had purchased from a downtown gallery.

Now, with the chance that she might lose it all, she noticed everything—even the smoke gray tissue-box holder that was in the half bath. When Yarni reached Desi's room, she fell to the floor and began to sob, but as soon as the loud chimes on the huge grandfather clock struck eight, the pity party was over. The phone rang, and she wiped her tears and answered, knowing who awaited her on the other end.

CHAPTER 2

Three Weeks Earlier . . .

"Relax, baby, I'm here," Des said as he caressed Yarni's hand and watched while the doctor lifted the tiny blood-covered baby from his wife's womb. The next thing he heard were cries, first Yarni's and then the baby's.

"It's a girl," the doctor informed everyone in the room.

Des smiled. He was amazed as the new life appeared right in front of his eyes. He had taken a life before, and even spared a few, but to take part in creating life was something that affected him deeply.

"Do you want to cut the cord?" the doctor asked Des.

Without saying a word, Des released Yarni's hand and took a few steps toward the doctor. He took the scissors from the doctor's hand and proceeded to separate his daughter from her mother. He was speechless.

Des followed the nurse and watched like a hawk as she took the baby over to a small table to clean her up and wrap her in a blanket. She looked at Des and extended the baby to him. "Would you like to hold your baby girl, Daddy?" the nurse said, smiling.

Des held out his arms, and the nurse placed the baby into them; he cradled her close to his heart, gazing at her in awe.

"Well, we know she's got some good lungs." Des laughed as the tiny creature began wailing, with not a tear seeping from her eyes. Des looked at his daughter and put his finger in her mouth, and she began to suck on it like it was a pacifier. For the first few minutes of her life, he held her, kissing and hugging her.

Yarni lay there smiling, watching her baby girl connect with her father. It was the greatest moment in her life. A tear ran down her cheek. She could tell that Des wanted to cry, too. When he looked over at her, he swallowed the lump in his throat, and she could see the wonder in his eyes.

"You doing okay, Mommy?" he asked after the nurse had taken the baby from him. He kissed Yarni on the forehead and pushed her sweat-drenched hair out of her face. Yarni just nodded and smiled, still overcome with emotion. "I'ma go tell Gloria and them." Des kissed Yarni on the forehead again and made a beeline for the door. Yarni knew that he just wanted to hurry up and get out of there before he broke down with emotion.

After telling Yarni's mother, Gloria, that she was the grandma to a beautiful, healthy baby girl, Des decided to head outside for some fresh air while he waited for them to get Yarni into her room with the baby. As he walked through the hospital's entryway, he ran into Yarni's sister, Bambi. There was a striking resemblance between the two sisters, except Bambi was dark chocolate to Yarni's caramel complexion. The two sisters have different mothers so they hadn't even known they were related until they were both grown, but now they were inseparable, as if they'd been together since the cradle.

"What's up, Hollywood?" Des beamed, giving her a kiss on her cheek, almost knocking her big Chanel frames off her face. Bambi, as always, was looking stylish. She was sporting a trendy Mohawk with spiked curls, and a short jean skirt hugged her hips.

"Nothing, brother-in-law," Bambi greeted. "I got here as soon as I heard that Yarni was in labor. Gloria just called me on my cell and told me that y'all had a girl."

"Yep." Des smiled proudly.

"I wanted to be here while she was delivering my little niece," Bambi said, pouting.

"Well, you're here now," Des said in an attempt to make her feel better. "How was your flight?" he flipped the subject. "You came in from Paris, right?"

"Good, but it seemed like the damn pilot was taking his sweet time, and I swear to God my luggage was the last to be taken off the plane. I watched everybody else's shit go round and round before mine dropped."

He chuckled a bit. "Well, the party's upstairs—sixth floor, room 633," he said as he turned to walk outside.

"Who she look like?" Bambi stopped him in his tracks.

"Her daddy. Who the hell you think?"

"I know God ain't curse that baby like that," she joked, hitting him playfully on the shoulder before she made her way through the hospital.

Des went to his car to retrieve the very limited edition cigars he had gotten just for this occasion. When he got to the car, he dug under his seat and pulled out the machine-engraved platinum case that housed his cavern-blue, aged Zino Platinum Crown Series cigars. Before heading back into the hospital, he checked the messages on his cell phone. There was only one message he felt obligated to return: that of his dear friend and brother in the game, Rico.

Rico was like Des's brother but from a different mother. They shared no blood, and Rico wasn't even American, but he and Des loved and respected each other all the same. They had been down for each other for over a decade and a half and shared many secrets. Des had even done ten years for a crime that Rico's nephew committed. In exchange for Des's loyalty, Rico had taken care of a major problem for Des. They rolled for each other without question.

Des returned Rico's call. He wanted to be the first to give Rico the good news.

After punching the correct speed-dial code, Des said, "Congratulations, my brother, you are the godfather of a beautiful baby girl."

"Ahhh, congratulations to you, brother," Rico said, his smile evident even through the phone line.

Des could sense by Rico's voice that something wasn't right. "So what's really good? Everything cool?" Des probed.

"I'm not trying to stop your parade, but I'm in a bind—literally between a rock and a hard place."

"Speak about it?" Des asked with concern.

"Two of my children just got exposed to some poisonous weeds while playing around the house. Now the weeds are getting to be a problem. I need someone to extract them." Rico spoke in code.

"I got a little up-and-coming shawty that specializes in these types of problems. I can freelance him out to you," Des offered.

"It's super delicate. Besides, it's not wise for a man in our position to let outsiders near his house. You never let outsiders work on your house, so why would you send an amateur to mine?"

Des phased out for a minute, trying to get his thoughts straight. He stood by the car with the door open, holding the phone with one hand and looking up at the blue sky. He took a deep breath. "A'ight, I'm going to need at least two, three weeks before I'll be able to get it taken care of."

"This weed is growing like a beanstalk," Rico said seriously. "I'm afraid more of my family may get hurt. I need you now. I'll pay you whatever you need to come out after hours and handle this for me. This is urgent."

Des could hear the desperation in Rico's voice. He also knew Yarni would have a fit if he left her and their newborn baby girl alone right now. For Christ's sake, the baby wasn't even two hours old yet. He took a deep breath. "I understand, big bro. I'ma take care of it for you, but understand that it's out of love, not because of anything else, strictly out of love."

"I'll give you the details when I get there with my god-daughter's arrival presents."

"A'ight then, bro," Des said before they ended the call.

Des sat down in the car with the door open and lit a cigar while he analyzed the situation. He knew he had to be his brother's keeper as his brother had kept him for so many years. On the other side of the coin, what kind of father would he be to leave his newborn baby and wife to go and take care of business—someone else's business at that? After deep contemplation and anguish he finally went back into the hospital to enjoy what little time he had to spend with his daughter.

He looked around the hospital sitting area at all the people who filled the room waiting their turn to go in to welcome his daughter into the world. Bambi came over and stood beside him.

"I swear it's too many gotdamn people up in here," Bambi said with a sigh.

"I know," he said slowly.

"But you know like I know it's better to let all these mother-fuckers come here; that way they don't have any reason to come to your house being nosy," Bambi informed her brother-in-law. He looked at her as she stealthily pulled out her cell phone and began to send a text message to someone.

"You know you ain't supposed to use that in the hospital," Des warned her.

"I know." Bambi continued to pound her thumb on the key-pad, typing out her message.

"You betta put that shit away with my daughter at this hospi-tal." Des watched until Bambi did just as he said, but not before she made sure her text had gone through. "Besides, I need a favor from you."

She placed the phone in her Gucci bag and looked up at Des. "Anything for you, brother-in-law."

"I'ma have to go out of town. I don't want to alarm the family, but I'ma need you to hold down the fort for me for about a week."

"I'm not even gon' ask no questions," Bambi said as she put her hands up. "I'ma just hold you down. But I don't know how you plan to run that past my sister. You know she ain't gon' be feelin' that at all."

"I know," Des said, wishing there was another way.

Just then Yarni's mother walked over to Des.

"Des, baby, Yarni was just asking about you," Gloria said, placing her hand on his shoulder and rubbing his back. "Go on and see your wife and baby while I hold all of these folks at bay."

Des looked over at Bambi, who gave him a "nigga, you on your own" look. He then headed to Yarni's room.

"Hey, beautiful," Des said as he walked into the hospital room to find Yarni sitting up with her hair slicked back in a ponytail and her lips lined in dark plum and filled in with a clear lip gloss. She hadn't wasted any time at all getting back to look- ing at least halfway decent. She knew she must have looked a sight the last time Des saw her, so she wanted to be somewhat presentable when he returned. She was glad she'd made sure that her lip gloss was packed in her overnight bag.

"Hey, handsome," Yarni said, extending her arms for Des to hug her. "I wish I wasn't laid up in this hospital bed," she whis- pered in his ear. "I'd rather be alone with you working on our second bundle of joy."

"One thing at a time, beautiful," Des said, smiling. "You keep it interesting." He pulled away and looked into her eyes be- fore kissing her on the cheek.

"I have to," she said, returning a smile.

"You heard what the doctor said: No sex for six weeks. And by all means we're listening to the doctor."

"I know, baby. I was just playing anyway. My whole body is aching. Where are the damn painkillers?" She tried to slide in a joke.

"You want me to get the nurse?" Des hated seeing his wife in pain. It took everything he had to sit through the birth.

"I already told them."

"Where's Baby Girl?" he asked.

"At the nursery. They should be bringing her in soon."

"Baby, did I tell you how much I love you? Thank you for giving me such a beautiful baby girl."

"Oooh, you're welcome."

Des took a deep breath and then sat down in the chair next to Yarni's bed. "Look, baby, I need to talk to you."

"Okay," Yarni said, shifting her booty from side to side, trying to get in a comfortable position without hurting herself. The last thing she wanted to do was bust one of those stitches the doctor had sewn on the bikini-line cut he made, when he did her cesarean section. "About what?" She looked up at him, knowing by his tone that something heavy was on his mind.

"When I was holding the baby this morning, I looked down at her, and she literally changed my life. Having held our child makes me want to make sure that she has all the things that we didn't have."

"I feel the same way, too," Yarni shared, touched by Des's sincerity.

"Then, you'll understand that I have to leave to go handle some business."

"When?"

He paused for a minute before he answered. "In a few hours."

Yarni started. "What do you mean 'in a few hours'?" She squinted her eyes from the pain she felt after her sudden movement.

"It's something that has to be handled right away."

"So you're leaving me by myself with our baby? I don't know how to take care of a baby," Yarni said, raising her voice in fear.

"Bambi, your mom, and my mom are here to help you out."

"Your momma? You promised you'd never leave me."

"I'm leaving only for a few days; and between my mom, your mom, and Bambi, you're going to be okay."

"What if you don't come back? How am I going to explain this to our daughter? How? Tell me how!" she shrieked, trying her best to lift herself off the bed. The pain was too much to bear, and she finally collapsed back on the mattress in exhaustion and frustration.

"I'm coming back," he said as he looked into her eyes to try to reassure her.

"But what if something happens to you?" she asked with a tinge of fear in her voice.

Des felt his heart unraveling. The last thing he wanted to do was cause Yarni any more pain, especially on what was the happiest day of their life.

"Nothing's going to happen to me." He took a deep breath before leaning over to kiss her on the forehead. "I promise."

"You never know." She looked away and started to cry. "You just never know."

He hugged her and wiped her tears before forcing her to look into his eyes. "Everything is going to be okay," he said firmly, holding her gently by the shoulders.

"You can't guarantee it," she said, sniffling.

He sighed deeply, having second thoughts about leaving her and the baby, but he knew he had to. "Baby, listen to me." He dabbed more tears from her cheeks. "Listen to me," he repeated in a more tender voice. "We have a child and have been together for how many years? Baby girl, we're connected forever. I'm willing to do anything that I have to do to make sure that our daughter has all the finer things that life has to offer her."

Yarni knew in her heart what Des wanted for his child, but

she also knew that he was going to go handle his business no matter what she had to say. She didn't want to argue at the hospital, and, quite honestly, she didn't have the strength. Now she understood why they called it labor—she had worked her butt off bringing their baby into the world—and she didn't regret a minute of it. So she just sucked it up and said, "Do whatever you have to do. We'll be here when you get finished. Go handle your business." Then she added, "Just be safe."

Des knew her words were only halfheartedly spoken. "You sure?" he asked.

She nodded, and then they both heard a knock at the door.

The nurse peeked her head in the door and said, "Your brother, Rico, is outside. He said he's the baby's godfather. Should I let him in?"

"Definitely," Des instructed the nurse.

Yarni dried any trace of her tears away and tried to get herself together as Rico entered the room bearing gifts.

"There's nowhere for me to set these," Rico said, amazed at all of the flowers and balloons that Yarni had already received.

"Hey, Rico," Yarni said. "You trying to spoil your goddaughter like that already?" she asked, looking at the armload of presents.

"This ain't nothing," Rico said as he walked over and gave Yarni a kiss on the forehead. "This is just all I could carry in. The rest is in the car." Now that opportunity had knocked, Rico opened the door wide and walked through it. "Yo, Des, man. Come help me bring in all the rest of the stuff."

Knowing that Rico wanted to use that time to school him on the situation that needed to be handled, Des agreed. "No problem," Des said to Rico before turning to Yarni's side. "You'll be all right for a minute?"

"Considering that pretty soon here I'm going to have to be all right for more than a minute, I guess I can handle it," Yarni said sarcastically.

Des kissed her on the cheek and said, "I love you." Then he followed Rico out of the hospital room.

As Des walked through the long corridors of the hospital, he realized that although his wife and daughter had very private quarters, the rest of the place looked like the scene from *The Godfather* when Don Corleone's daughter got married and everyone who was anyone showed up to pay their respects to the don and to ask for favors. Even the maternity floor had players and ballers standing in the hallways making deals on their cell phones, which they weren't supposed to be using, as they waited for their ride-or-die bitches to give birth to the next generation of thugs. If the Feds wanted a who's-who list of all the high-profile drug purveyors in Virginia, as well as some on an international level, the hospital was the place to be. In the lobby he saw mothers wearing two- and three-carat diamond earrings and tennis bracelets, waiting to hear if their drug-dealing sons would survive knife wounds, gunshots, or old-fashioned beatings. Girlfriends were there with teddy bears and flowers, hoping to be the first thing their men saw when they came out of surgery, and a few devoted junkies skulked around praying their favorite dealer wouldn't die.

Des and Rico had walked outside to find a place to talk without all the intruding ears, when Des saw his nephew, Nasir, coming toward the entrance. "So you decided to show up, I see," Des chided Nasir, the teenage son of Des's deceased older brother, Les. Des loved Nasir like a son.

"Wouldna missed it for all the dope in Afghanistan, Uncle Des," Nasir said, smiling.

"Go check on your aunt Yarni and your new cousin, Desi," Des shot back. "Your uncle Rico and I got something we need to discuss in the car."

"Sure, Uncle Des. Peace, Uncle Rico."

"Wa 'Alaykum As-Salām, young Nasir," Rico returned the greeting.

As they walked, they slowed their pace. "I'm sorry to 've had to bother you on such an auspicious occasion," Rico expressed, "but I'm in trouble, and I need your professional help and expertise."

"Tell me what you need me to do," Des said. "Or, shall I say, *who* you need me to do?"

"You know me too well, brotha," Rico said, sighing. "Too well."

"The feeling is mutual," Des responded.

"Enough of the small talk, though," Rico said. "Let's get down to business. His name is Jarbo Classettes." Rico pulled out a picture and handed it to Des.

"I've heard of him," Des acknowledged. "Don't he work for you?"

"He did . . . well, he thinks he still does—"

"But?" Des cut in.

"But I don't like the company he's been keeping these days."

"Such as?" Des inquired.

"Such as the police."

"I see," Des said. "And what brought this unsavory relationship about?"

"He got tore off with twenty keys of soft white and decided he'd rather be an informer than an inmate. I got an inside tip that says he's supposed to meet with the grand jury the first session of next month to give a deposition." Rico looked at Des for his reaction.

"So I got eighteen days to eliminate this . . . problem," Des calculated. "Where is he staying?"

"Saratoga Springs, New York," Rico answered, "with a stripper named Twinkle."

CHAPTER 3

The Two-Step Viper

Des arrived in Saratoga Springs, New York, twelve hours after his conversation with Rico. Following almost nineteen hours with Yarni while she was in labor, until finally the doctor decided to do a cesarean. He was dog-tired, but he decided to go ahead and make the drive without resting. He didn't fly because he didn't want his name in the airline system, so he had hopped into his seven series BMW without so much as yawning. But after a couple of hours on the highway, he struggled to keep his eyes open. He even had to pull over to the side of the road to get a cup of coffee, which wasn't something Des typically drank.

Whether he had the coffee to thank or not, Des didn't fall asleep. He made it, without incident, to his destination. As he was about to pull into the parking lot of the hotel he chose to stay in, he saw a black-on-black Aston Martin complete with oversized rims speeding by. The driver had the music turned up as he passed Des, heading down Broadway, the main drag in town.

With the exception of the month of August, when the horse races were going on, Saratoga Springs was a real down-low kind of town. During the other eleven months, the town was populated by wealthy people with a lot of old money. Since it was February, that Aston Martin cruising down the strip was out of the ordinary. Des's gut told him that the car's owner came from new money, and he strongly believed the car was very likely one of the dots to connect him to his mark, Jarbo. On a hunch, Des followed the Aston Martin. Ten miles later they arrived at a luxurious resort. He laid back, parked, and watched as a female driver exited the car in front of valet parking. She wore a nearly see-through shirt and a small skirt that showed off her long legs. She definitely looked as if she could have been the stripper accompanying Jarbo up here, Des thought.

"How long will you be?" the valet asked her, trying desperately to keep his eyes focused on her face instead of her double-d chest size. It was amazing what a little wind making its way through a chiffon top could do to a girl's nipples.

"Ummm, I'm not sure," she said, almost as if she were talking to herself. "Maybe I'll go back out shopping while he goes to the sauna, or maybe I'll have a massage." She turned to the valet. "I'm not certain. Keep it close, an outside spot." She winked, then waited while the valet grabbed the bags out of her car and handed them to her after she surrendered her keys to him.

"Nice car. How does it ride?" Des asked as he walked around the Aston Martin.

"It's actually my boyfriend's," she replied, watching Des admire the car. "But I think he really got it for me." She threw her long hair over her shoulder. "He has plenty of other cars—the Maybach, a Maserati. I drive this one all the time, and, as they say, possession is nine-tenths of the law." She smiled, but Des acted as if he wasn't paying her any attention. He stayed focused on the car. "But yeah, I like it." She nodded. "I like it a lot."

"Really?" Des said, pretending to be impressed. "A Maybach, huh? What color Maybach could possibly compete with the color of your eyes?" he asked, laying it on thick, figuring she was the type who would run her mouth after receiving a compliment.

"Oh, thank you. It's burgundy," she announced proudly.

"The burgundy joint may give you a run for your money. I don't know," he teased. "How long has he had this?" He pointed to the Aston Martin.

"Ummm . . ." She rolled her eyes upward as if trying hard to find the answer in her airhead. "He had it like nine or ten months, but I've been driving it like eight months. Like I said, possession is nine-tenths of the law."

"He must really love you to let you drive such an expensive car, huh?" Des assured her, making her feel special.

"You think?" She smiled, loving what her ears were hearing. "He does tell me that I'm the twinkle of his eye. That's what he calls me, you know—Twinkle."

After she unknowingly confirmed the details that Des needed, Des knew what he had to do. He checked into the hotel under an alias so that he could get a better read on his mark.

Later that night, Des followed Jarbo and Twinkle to the bar, where he copped a seat nearby so he could keep tabs on them.

Jarbo's cell phone rang. "Hold on, baby," he said to Twinkle as he took the call.

Des, who was casually sitting with his back toward Jarbo and Twinkle, listened to Jarbo carry on his business transaction over the cell phone. For the next couple of days, Des watched Jarbo as he made his moves and, in the process, Des even saw him meet with a police officer. Jarbo was so carefree in the little town that he never noticed Des watching him.

After a week of studying Jarbo's routine, Des put his plan into motion. He first packed up his things so that he could check out of his hotel room quickly when he was done. He then went to the hotel gift shop and purchased a bottle of hotel springwater before heading to the sauna. Upon entering the room, he picked up the business section of the newspaper someone had left behind, took a seat on the wooden bench, and read the newspaper. Des patiently waited for Jarbo to make his daily trip to the sauna with his bottle of hotel-issued springwater in hand, the same thing he did every day at 1:00 P.M. sharp, right after having lunch with Twinkle at the hotel's five-star buffet.

Jarbo picked up the part of the paper that Des wasn't reading and made himself comfortable on the wooden bench about two feet away from Des. Once the heat came up, they both put down their papers, and Jarbo began talking Des's head off.

"We don't see too many brothers around these parts much. Where are you from?" Jarbo asked, without looking up at Des. Jarbo twisted the cap off his water bottle and took a long, thirsty sip. It was as if he had been contemplating whether or not to make the comment.

"I peeped that." Des nodded as he sat and appreciated the relaxing effects of the sauna. "I'm from North Carolina."

"You here on vacation?" Jarbo asked.

Des followed suit, twisting the cap off his own water bottle and putting it to his lips. "Well, my wife has a convention for her job not too far from here, so she suggested we stay here to get some quality time in." Des turned the tables. "And you? You here on vacation?"

"No, not at all," Jarbo said, laughing. "I've been here for about a month. Just laying low from the hustle and bustle of the city." He placed his water down between himself and Des.

Des shook his head and replied, "Must be nice. What do you do for a living that you can take off a whole month?"

"I own a few lucrative businesses." This time Jarbo turned the tables. "And you?"

"I'm a repetologist," Des said proudly.

"Really?" Jarbo sounded interested. "Damn, man, I ain't never met no brother who was into reptiles before." The heat was starting to relax him. Jarbo put a towel over his head to help clear his sinuses. Des smiled and leaned back on the bench.

"I never met a brother who owned a bunch of lucrative businesses." Des quickly took his water bottle and placed it down next to Jarbo's. He immediately picked Jarbo's up. Just as he had it in hand, Jarbo spoke. "What are you doing?"

Des was caught red-handed.

"Huh?" Des said, with a hint of nervousness.

"What are you doing now? What are you studying?" Jarbo's words were muffled, coming from underneath the towel.

"Studying?" Des echoed, almost losing his cool.

"Yes, for work. What is your latest study?"

"Before I came here I was studying this incredible venomous snake out of Africa," Des said. "The two-step viper."

"Oh yeah?" Jarbo said as he sat up, removed his head cover, and took a sip from his water bottle.

"Yeah," Des said.

"Sounds interesting." Jarbo took another gulp of water.

"Yeah, well, I guess it's not your everyday work thing." Des shrugged his shoulders as if he could take it or leave it.

"So, what about those Pistons?" Jarbo said, switching the subject. He could sense that Des didn't really feel like talking about his job.

Before Des could even respond to Jarbo's last question, the three drops of the two-step viper poison Jarbo had just drunk took effect, sending him into cardiac arrest. Within thirty seconds he fell over in the sauna and was dead. Des picked up the water bottle, stood, and walked out.

He checked out of his hotel room and headed back down I-95 to go be with his daughter and wife. When he stopped to get gas in Maryland, he called Yarni to let her know he was on his way. As he heard their daughter cry in the background, he became even more anxious to see her. Looking at the line of cars the gas station clerk was dealing with, he decided he wanted to get back to his family as soon as possible, so he paid at the pump with his credit card and continued his conversation with his wife. He talked to her on and off the entire drive home, even asking her to put the phone up to the baby's ear so that Desi could hear her daddy tell her how much he loved her.

Once Des read the WELCOME TO VIRGINIA sign, he was overcome with emotion. It was a feeling that had been foreign to him for quite some time. He had been in the game for as long as he could remember. Hell, even a jail sentence doesn't truly remove you from it. Sometimes in the game lives were lost; sometimes they had to be taken. But it wasn't until that moment that Des confronted the act he had just committed.

He was less than an hour away from his family, a family he

was bound and determined to do right by. He had always considered Yarni his wife, even before it was on paper. Even then she was his wife in his heart. But something was different now that it was by God's will and not man's flesh. And now there was another life involved, that of little Desi. Des did something he had never done before, probably because he had never before had to acknowledge that he was responsible for the precious lives of others. He made a covenant with himself that things were going to change . . . and for the better.

$$\$\$\$$$

As Des pulled into the gated community where he lived with his wife, he waited for the gate to open, but for some reason it stalled. Before he knew it, police swarmed him and the car. They had him surrounded, with their guns drawn.

"Step out of the car," he heard an officer yell through a bullhorn.

Des was shocked and confused. He knew that he had planned Jarbo's murder down to the last minor detail and had been very meticulous about it. He had taken the water bottle with the poison in it and thrown it over the bridge, and had wiped the other water bottle off. He destroyed and burned all of the evidence, down to the newspaper he shared with Jarbo. There was absolutely nothing that could have led the police back to him.

"Out of the car with both hands up, now," the voice shouted through the bullhorn again, angrier and louder this time. Des had no choice but to step out of the car with both of his hands raised.

Knowing good and well that they had Des cornered, Detective Columbo did the honors. He limped over toward Des's car, swaying his huge butt. He slapped the cuffs on Des's wrists.

With a big smile, he looked in Des's eyes and said, "Desmond Lamont Taylor, you are under arrest. You have the right to remain silent . . ."

Desmond glared back into Detective Columbo's eyes, and replied, "Anything you say can and will be held against you. You have the right to an attorney . . ."

Des smiled as Detective Columbo finished reciting the rest of his Miranda rights on his own, and then asked, "For what?" Des refused to believe that he had left a trail that connected him to Jarbo.

"For murder," Columbo replied. "The murder of Mike Richards."

"Who?"

"Mr. Richards. Don't play stupid. He was your attorney."

"Don't be ridiculous. Why the fuck would I waste my time with that clown?" Des exclaimed.

After Des had gotten out of jail, he wasn't salty at all against his old attorney. He knew that Richards would have his day at some point, but Des wouldn't be the one to give it to him.

Detective Columbo put Des in the backseat of a police cruiser and then climbed in after him. "Desmond, I haven't seen you in over a decade, and when I do, let's just say it's a good day." Columbo, a huge smile on his face, folded his arms and rested them on his protruding belly. "I tell you. You give me a big prize."

"Columbo, have you had a case stick yet?" Des asked. "It's a wonder that you still got a job on the force." Des normally would never indulge in any conversation with a police officer, but Detective Columbo was different. He was the kind of police officer who gave the men in blue a bad name. Detective Columbo was worse than a hemorrhoid. He was always up a man's ass and full of shit. It got his dick hard to lock up a black man who was making more money than he was—legally or illegally.

"Scum like you make me work harder to keep the streets clean" was Detective Columbo's comeback.

"You're a waste of good taxpayers' money, Columbo," Des said, fighting down the urge to spit in the man's face.

"Too bad I can't work on this one," Columbo said, pretending to be dejected. "Well, you won't have to worry about the good taxpayers of Virginia's good money going to waste. The state of Maryland will be here to pick you up soon."

Des looked at Columbo, dumbfounded. "Maryland?" He asked.

"Just keep playing stupid," Columbo grunted. "That'll make a good defense."

The Take Over

After his court hearing, just as Yarni had promised, Des was released from jail. Once out on bail, he decided to take things slowly and spend a couple of weeks enjoying his little baby girl and catching up on missed time with Yarni. But it wasn't long before it was back to business as usual.

Des was in his study, ending a call on his cell phone, when he heard the doorbell ring. He looked through the peephole before opening the door to find his nephew standing there.

"How you get past my gate?"

Nasir ignored the question. "Unc, I need to talk to you," he said, coming through the door in an uproar. Perspiration was on his forehead, and worry, rage, and frustration were all over his face.

Des was concerned. "What seems to be the problem, nephew?" He started leading Nasir toward the study but stopped short with his nephew's words.

"I need some guns," Nasir said, pacing the hallway.

"Guns? What for?" Des was surprised that whatever the problem was, it was already out of hand.

"This nigga gots to go." Nasir continued pacing the floor.

"Come on in here," Des said, ushering Nasir to his study. He closed the double doors behind them before asking, "What nigga? And why does he have to go?"

"The motherfucker I been getting my work from," Nasir said, fuming. "He trippin'."

"About what?"

"He a hating-ass nigga, that's all." Nasir balled his fist as he explained, "I move three onions a week for this nigga, Monte, all in eight balls. And the only reason I ain't movin' more is because the chump put me on a limit."

"Calm down and take a seat," Des said, pointing at the couch to the left of his desk. "What happened? What exactly did he do?"

Nasir sat down while Des took the seat at his desk. "Look, Unc," Nasir started, "I ain't got time to get into all that with you. The nigga disrespected me, and either you gon' loan me yo' tools or you ain't."

"Hold tight, youngin." Des put his hand up. "I'm not gonna send you running into a brick wall." Des tried to reason with his nephew. "What's this . . . about him disrespecting your name?"

"He ain't nobody for real. I'm slinging the majority of the work fo' him. I'm moving shit faster than a nigga on a laxative diet, and the motherfucker still charging me top dollar. That's some bullshit."

"Besides a disagreement in prices and inventory, why you so mad?" Des said with a smile.

"Like I was saying, I move more shit than any of dem other

niggas copping from him combined," he stressed by pointing to his chest. "My money ain't never short. But when I tell this nigga that I need better numbers and mo' product, he tells me to suck his dick. Ain't no motherfucker gon' disrespect me like that. I'ma give him something to suck on, that iron dick."

"Aaahhh, now we getting somewhere," Des agreed, finally understanding his nephew's frustrations. "Peace this, though. Let me tell you something an old head told me a long time ago about murder." Des walked over to the couch and sat down next to his nephew. "Murder is not a crime you commit on someone else's time. You don't want to be in prison for the rest of your life and have to tell your family or anyone that'll listen that you're there because someone made you mad. You have to learn to master your emotions if you want to make it in this world."

"I never looked at it like that," Nasir admitted, calming down a little as he gave some thought to what his uncle was saying. "But how do I get 'im to play fair?"

"Don't play with him," Des said with a no-nonsense attitude.

"But that nigga got the best dope in town," Nasir explained. "I can put a one on it and more than double my money."

"Then go out of town and find some better shit and put him out of business. Make him your competition, and he can do one of two things: Ride with it or collide with it."

"I ain't got time to shut down shop to go out of town on a scavenger hunt. That's too much trouble."

"Now we have a new problem, huh?"

"I guess I'll just have to put up with this clown until I get what I need."

Des listened to his nephew go on, but in his head, he already knew what he had to do. He wasn't going to let anybody carry his nephew, who was the closest thing he had to a son.

Des stood up and took a deep breath. "I can make things happen for you," he said. "But you ain't playing for marbles anymore." Des looked down at Nasir. "You playing for keeps."

"You ain't said shit," Nasir said, standing up and giving Des a pound. "On the real, a nigga like me is done playing period. It's time to bring it to these fuckin' cockroaches. Oh, it's on," Nasir said with a devilish smirk as he paced excitedly and pounded his fist in his hand.

"Look, you gotta understand that this is serious," Des said, stopping Nasir in his tracks by grabbing him by one shoulder. "Your involvement could cost you yo' life, my life, yo' freedom, and it can put you on the proverbial path of no return. This ain't no muthafuckin' movie. This shit is real. Once you take it there with them clowns, there ain't no turning back."

"No risk, no rewards—that's what you always told me, right?"

"That's right," Des agreed, proud to know that his nephew had been listening.

"I know the dangers of the trade, and I ain't under no delusions," Nasir assured him. "Look, Unc, I want to eat. Please give me my place at the table," Nasir pleaded. "I can't lose at this. I mean, Unc, let's look at it like this. If I'm taking instructions from one of the masters of the game, how can I lose? You been a playa at this shit long before I was even born."

Des didn't really want to see his nephew do what so many had failed to do before him: try to tame an animal that was untameable. The drug game was a wild beast that was obedient to no one.

But Des could see the hunger in his nephew's eyes and could hear it in his voice. He knew that Nasir was going to keep trying his hand whether Des helped him or not.

"Listen, Nasir, I know with yo' father getting killed when you were lil' and with me being in the penitentiary that you found your way the best way you could."

Nasir looked at Des before he could finish and hopped on the defense. "Uncle Des, I been doing a'ight for myself."

"And I ain't knocking that," Des said quickly.

"But like I said, it's firsthand from a nigga like you," Nasir said. "You're a legend in this city."

Des held up his hand as if to tell Nasir that he needed to say no more. Des walked over to his desk and sat down in his dark burgundy high-back leather chair. Both the chair and the high-glossed, solid cherry desk with the matching credenza were compliments of one of his associates, crafted and shipped all the way from Hong Kong. He opened the top drawer of his desk and pulled out two Zinos cigars and handed one to his nephew. He then pulled out his white-gold engraved lighter, placed his cigar in his mouth, and put the orange-blue flame to the tip. He got up, walked over to Nasir, and lit his, too. He then took a seat in his leather chaise.

"Sit down," he instructed Nasir. "Listen to what I'm saying and listen good." Des pulled on his cigar, crossed one leg over the other knee, and then spoke. "See no evil and hear no evil. Never fold or faint, and 'no, I can't' is always the wrong answer."

As Des shot straight from the hip the vital rules of survival, Nasir sat like an obedient student listening to his instructor.

"It's a lot of things you gotta watch out for—the wolves, women, fake friends, and snitches, but remember, the police are our common enemy. And for no reason whatsoever do we ever cooperate with our common enemy. I don't give a fuck if they are torturing you for information, lie like a dog. Lie your way into something, lie your way out of something, lie on your gun, your money, your dick—but never, *ever* cooperate."

Nasir focused his undivided attention on Des, sitting forward in his seat to make sure he didn't miss a word that was being spoken.

"Your word must always be your bond," Des continued, taking another puff on his cigar and waving it in the air. A cloud of smoke hovered over his head like a crown. "Always pay your debts off the front end of your money, not the back end. Never become a victim of your hustle."

Nasir nodded, almost unable to contain his excitement: He was entering the majors.

Des continued. "If you sell drugs, don't use them. If you pimp hos, don't trick."

"I feel that, Unc." Nasir nodded as his uncle dropped jewels, trying to hide his excitement at finally being made privy to something he had wanted his entire life.

"And never let a woman come between you and your man or before your business."

Nasir wanted to comment right there, but he didn't because he wanted his uncle to continue to bestow his blessings. "The best-fought war is a war that you don't have to fight, but if it has to go down . . . whoever shoots first usually wins."

Nasir laughed, the cigar dangling from his mouth, but Des gave him a cold stare that took the smirk right off the younger man's face. "Be quick to forgive, but slow to forget. And when in doubt, kill them all and let God sort them out." Des pulled on his cigar before continuing.

"It's never personal. If it turns out that you were wrong, take comfort in the knowledge that it's better to be live-ass wrong than dead-ass right."

Nasir laughed to himself at how Des was laying down the law and thought about how he would one day pass this on to his own son. He was glad that his uncle had given him such powerful pieces, and he was prepared to live or die by them.

Des got up from the chaise and walked over to the liquor cabinet. He retrieved two glasses from it and said, "These have been universal rules of the game, generation after generation, decade after decade. The rules never change—only the players. So make sure through it all you stay true to this . . . and to the game."

"I will," Nasir said, nodding with sincerity.

Des poured them both a shot of cognac. He handed Nasir his drink then raised his glass to toast. "Welcome to the major leagues, nephew."

They clinked their glasses, and they both drank the potent brown liquor. Des promised Nasir that he would make a formal introduction to his new supplier within the next couple of days. He gave his nephew a fatherly hug and walked him to the door.

A few minutes after Nasir left, the doorbell rang again. Nasir was back, and this time he wasn't alone.

"What the . . ." Des said to himself as he opened the door. He looked at the short brick-house-built girl standing before him with black hair. Her eyebrows were the same color as her hair, and they stood out on her chocolate complexion.

"Unc," Nasir said, one arm thrown around the girl standing next to him, "this is my girl, Lava."

"Hi, Unc," Lava said, reaching out and giving him a warm hug. For such a strong name, she had a soft, squeaky voice. "Nasir talks about you so much, I feel like I already know you."

"How you doing?" Des greeted the girl in a sour tone.

"She gotta use the bathroom," Nasir cut in.

Des shot Nasir a puzzled look then nodded to the girl and said, "Go ahead."

Nasir showed Lava to the restroom, cut on the light for her, and then returned to Des.

"You had her sitting in the car all that time?" Des asked him.

"Yup." Nasir nodded with authority, like he was the man.

Des shook his head and warned his nephew, "POP—paper over pussy."

"Unc, no disrespect, but it ain't like that. She's my Bonnie, my gangsta boo, my thug misses."

Des turned his nose up.

"She's my Yarni." Excitement lit up Nasir's whole face as he continued to describe what Lava meant to him. "She's the most thorough chick any nigga could love. And she got heart," Nasir stressed in the most sincere tone. "And guess what, Unc?"

"I'm scared to guess," Des said to his nephew.

"She's mine, and she loves the fuck out of me," Nasir said proudly.

Des had never heard his nephew talk about a woman like that—ever. He knew that at an early age his nephew had gotten plenty of pussy and had never been sheltered when it came to women, so he was baffled by this girl.

"Yeah, it sounds like you fell victim to the pussy."

"It ain't the pussy, Unc," Nasir assured Des. "For real." He paused. "I done had better pussy than that. Besides, I make the pussy good. It's her loyalty and her will to love me and me alone that stands out."

"How can you be sure, man?" Des questioned. "Bitches change with the wind."

"I know hos come and go, but Lava is staying. She passes test after test. Matter of fact, she welcomes that shit."

Des could see that there wasn't any need to argue with Nasir concerning this girl. She had him convinced that she was the Virgin Mary. Des just hoped Lava was the real thing. If not, she could pose a distraction or major flaw for Nasir.

"I need to ask you something," Des said, looking around to make sure Lava was still in the restroom.

"What?" Nasir asked, walking closer to his uncle.

"What you 'bout to get into is real dangerous. It can cost you your life if anyone around you folds. Do you really trust her?"

Nasir answered without hesitation, "Without a doubt."

"With your life?" Des gazed at his nephew.

"No question. Shit, I'll die for her, as she'd die for me."

"So, if she ain't who you think she is, then you'll take the hit."

"However I got to."

"Even if it means death?" Des questioned.

"Don't you trust Yarni?" Nasir answered with a question of his own.

"A'ight," Des said, giving Nasir a five before slapping him on the back. "I'ma take your word."

Just then, they heard the bathroom door open and then Lava appeared. Des studied her from head to toe. She wore her jet-black hair in a ponytail. She had on jeans with a T-shirt and the same brand-new Air Jordans that Nasir was wearing.

"How's the baby?" Nasir said, changing the conversation so that Lava wouldn't be able to tell by the awkward silence that they had been talking about her.

"The baby is good." Des smiled.

"Is she sleep, Unc? Lava would love to see her," Nasir said.

Des pushed the intercom button and spoke. "Baby girl," he addressed Yarni just as he had been doing for the past decade and a half, "is Desi sleep? Nasir and his girl want to see her."

Yarni sat up in the king-size bed where she had been going over some case files and pushed the intercom button to respond to Des.

"As long as they're quiet," Yarni said, "they can come up to see her."

Des led them up the huge, wide spiral staircase to the nursery. Yarni met them in the hall.

"Lava, this is my wife, Yarni," Des introduced. "Baby, this is Lava, Nasir's girlfriend."

"Hi, how are you?" Yarni said. She initially went to extend her hand, but then hesitated. There was something about Lava that made Yarni want to give her a hug. Lava had her own arms extended to embrace Yarni back.

"I don't know why," Yarni said after hugging Lava, "but I feel like you are already a part of the family."

Nasir looked over at Des and winked before his face broke into a huge grin. Des shrugged and smiled back.

"I feel the same way," Lava said. "I feel like I know both you and your husband, as much as Nasir talks about you."

Yarni smiled. "Your hair is so pretty. You know how many women wish they could pay to have that beautiful silky hair?"

She smiled at the compliment.

Yarni proceeded to lead them to the nursery. "Follow me."

"I saw her at the hospital when you gave birth," Lava said, "but I know she's gotten really big since then."

"I didn't know you came to the hospital," Yarni replied.

"Yes, but I didn't come in to see you. There was so many people there," Lava said. "I didn't want to bother you."

"Awwww, I wish you would have." Yarni smiled as she opened the door to the nursery.

Both women entered the room, followed by Des and Nasir.

"I would love to hold her," Lava said, "but I know if I were a new mother, I wouldn't want anyone holding my baby." Lava had read Yarni's mind.

Yarni chuckled, "That's exactly how I feel, but here . . ." Yarni lifted Desi out of the crib. "You can hold her."

The men just stood back and watched Yarni and Lava interact like they had been friends for years.

Lava cooed over Desi, and she and Yarni made more small talk while Lava gently rocked the baby.

After they all finished admiring the baby, Yarni and Des walked Nasir and Lava to the front door.

"Lava, you are invited back here anytime," Yarni offered as they stood in the open doorway.

"Thank you," Lava said, hugging Yarni again.

"All right then, Unc," Nasir said, giving Des a hug. "All right, Yarni." Nasir then hugged Yarni, and soon he and Lava were on their way down the walkway.

Nasir and Lava weren't even in their car good when Yarni said to Des, "You know what?"

"No, I don't. What?" Des wrapped his arms around her.

"They remind me a little bit of us fifteen years ago." Des didn't respond. He just watched Nasir and Lava drive off. "Lava's a good girl," Yarni added. "And Nasir aspires to be a big-time hustler like you were. He wants to follow in your footsteps." Only Lady Fate would know where those footsteps would carry young Nasir.

Whose Baby Is It?

"**M**ake sure you lift the baby's neck and wash up under there," Des's mother, Joyce, nagged as she stood over Yarni. "You know when babies be spitting up, that milk will get all up in their little fat rolls up under the neck and get to stinkin' if you don't, so you got to wash up under there good. Grandma don't want her baby stinkin'." She began to coo at Desi, "No, she doesn't. You tell your mama to wash that baby's neck. Tell your mama she gotta clean you real good up under that little baby fat. Yes, she does."

"I know." Yarni cringed, knowing damn well that Joyce was using her cooing at Desi as an opportunity to tell her how to take care of the baby. Two can play this game, Yarni thought as she followed Joyce's lead. "Yes, Mommy does know," she cooed. "You tell Granny that Mommy knows how to wash that baby up, yes she does. Mommy doesn't want her baby stinkin' any more than Granny does. Isn't that right, Mommy's baby?"

Joyce rolled her eyes, quickly catching on to Yarni's sarcasm. She watched for a second as Yarni undressed the baby and double-checked the temperature of the water before placing her in the tub. "I don't know why y'all young kids use those bath-tubs," she started up again, tapping the blue Fisher-Price bathtub with the yellow sponge lining. She stood over Yarni's shoulder. "Shoot, when I was raising my kids and they were that little, we used to sponge bathe them right in the kitchen sink."

Since her back was turned to Joyce, Yarni rolled her eyes and made a face before she spoke. "That was like thirty years ago, be-fore they even had invented these baby tubs." She snickered under her breath at the shot she took at Joyce's age.

"Yeah, that's what I did with *my* Des," Joyce said, ignoring Yarni's comment. Yarni didn't respond. When Desi's bath was done, Joyce watched Yarni like a hawk when she lifted Desi out of the tub and onto the towel that she had placed in her lap. "Did you get her ears good before you finished up?"

"Yeah, I did." Yarni nodded.

"Because a lot of new young mothers forget about the ears, and they're important. All kinds of little crud will form in the baby's ears if you don't get in there with those Q-tips."

"I know," Yarni said. Her patience began to wear thin, but she tried to keep her composure.

Ever since the baby came home from the hospital, Joyce had hounded Yarni about Baby Desi. At first it was just phone calls all day, checking on Desi or offering some unsolicited advice. Then Joyce started stopping by to drop off whatever it was she had purchased for Desi while she had been out shopping that day, but now she was just doing drive-bys like a crazy, deranged, jealous girlfriend.

Yarni hated that Joyce treated her like she wasn't Desi's

mother as if she had just been babysitting for a spell. It was making Yarni feel like a surrogate mother, like all she had done was go through nine months of pregnancy only to hand her baby over to her mother-in-law.

Joyce did everything for Desi, but don't get it twisted, Lord knows with all the drama in Yarni's life, she did appreciate it. But the fact that Joyce had practically moved in and taken over was really starting to get to her. Joyce was always riding her and being critical about every little thing she did when it came to Desi. But it was hard for Yarni to set Joyce straight, because, after all, she was Des's mother, and their past wasn't always peaches and cream. For the first few years of Des and Yarni's relationship, Joyce hated Yarni and the ground she walked on. It wasn't until the past couple years that she had embraced Yarni as more than just her son's wife—as a woman—and Yarni wanted to keep it that way. She found herself biting her tongue so much, she was surprised it hadn't fallen out of her mouth.

Yarni wrapped Desi up in the towel and carried her from the bathroom over to her changing table. She then proceeded to dry her off and put a Pamper on her. Packs of Pampers in every size imaginable covered one of the nursery's walls. Des had been bringing home Pampers since he found out Yarni was pregnant. Where he got them from, she never asked, but it would be a while before Yarni would have to purchase any, and she was glad.

Joyce was on Yarni's heels, continuing to watch every move Yarni made when it came to her grandbaby. "I don't know why you don't use the cloth diapers like I suggested to you in the beginning of your pregnancy," Joyce said, shaking her head in disagreement. "I used cloth diapers with my kids."

"Like I told you before," Yarni said, never looking up at Joyce, "it's a new day and a new time." She gave a tight smile.

"Well, that's what Des had. That boy wore cloth diapers. Natural cotton. No telling what they use to make them Pampers."

"Joyce, listen," Yarni said, sighing, "both Des and I are always on the run, and neither one of us has time to fool around with washing cloth diapers. Plus nobody in America uses those things anymore. This is a new day. You need to get with the program." She couldn't resist getting another dig in.

"All you have to do is dump the number two out into the toilet, then let the diaper soak a little bit and—"

"We're on the go too much for that," Yarni interrupted, barely holding on to her anger.

"Well, I think it's something you should consider. At least use them when you know you're going to be at home for at least a couple of changes. With all these diaper rashes going on from the chemicals and deodorants in the Pampers and things, the cloth diapers would be good for her little bottom, wouldn't they, sweetie?" she cooed at the baby.

"It's simply not an option, plus we have a room filled with enough Pampers to last her until she's graduated high school," Yarni joked.

"Me and my sisters all used cloth diapers," Joyce said, having to get in the final word.

Yarni decided to ignore her mother-in-law. Instead, she focused more on getting her daughter in a clean sleeper. Once Yarni was done dressing Desi, Joyce swooped in like a hawk and picked up the baby and paced the floor with her.

"I'm going to go fix her a bottle," Yarni said, leaving Grandma and her grandbaby alone. She headed downstairs to the kitchen to warm up the baby's formula.

Once in the kitchen, Yarni grabbed one of the bottles she had prepared that morning and placed it in the microwave. As she stood waiting, Joyce entered the kitchen and startled her.

"I know good and well that you ain't warming up that baby's bottle in no microwave," Joyce admonished.

"And why not?" Yarni asked, getting even more irritated with Joyce for telling her how to take care of *her* baby.

"Because radiation isn't good to put in the baby's body, and, besides that, the heat isn't distributed evenly, so you might burn her tongue. Don't you read the articles?" Joyce said, stomping across the room. "Now just move out the way and let me show you how to do this."

With Desi on her shoulder, Joyce used her wide hips to move Yarni aside, almost knocking her down. She stopped the microwave, went to the cabinet where Yarni kept the pots and pans, and pulled out a little saucepan. She filled it halfway up with water and then placed it on the stove.

"YaYa gonna take care of her baby," she said to Desi as she cut on the burner, removed the bottle from the microwave, and then set it down in the pan. "These young kids don't know nothing about raising a baby. But don't worry, *my* Desi, your YaYa is here."

YaYa this, Grandma's baby that. Yarni was sick of it all. She rolled her eyes and walked out of the kitchen, finding it almost unbearable to stay in the same room with Joyce. Although the house was over ten thousand square feet, it just didn't seem like it was big enough for the both of them. Yarni took a deep breath and thought about how much Des loved his mother, how much he wanted them to get along, and how far they had come even to be able to be under the same roof, period. She would just have to learn how to live with Joyce and her constant interference.

Joyce was indeed a piece of work and would give anybody hell: man, woman, or child. For many years Joyce made it her business to give Yarni a hard way to go. Since Yarni was so much younger than Des and was the first girl Des ever truly loved, Joyce suspected that Yarni would break her son's heart. But over the years, time and time again, Yarni had proved her undying love for Des. It didn't happen overnight, but Joyce finally accepted Yarni. Having Joyce as an ally was better than being at war with her, so for those reasons, Yarni decided that she wouldn't give Joyce a piece of her mind and kick her bossy butt out. Instead, Yarni did herself a favor. She left the house to get some fresh air, air that she didn't have to share with her mother-in-law.

$$\$\$\$$$

Yarni headed to the office to pick up the résumés of attorneys who wanted to work with her pro bono on the Samuel Johnson case. Most people didn't realize that if you committed a crime heinous enough, you could get a team of lawyers for free who just wanted the publicity. And Johnson's was just the type of case the local attorneys salivated over. Their names would be in the paper for months. People thought O.J. had the dream team because he was so rich, but the dream team would have been there no matter what, dreaming of all the money they'd make on future clients—not to mention the book deals.

While at the office, Yarni called Des. Johnson's case wasn't the only one on her mind.

"Hey, baby," Yarni said after he answered the phone. "I just got a message from Mark to remind you that we have to meet with him next week to discuss your case."

"Yeah, I know," Des told Yarni. "He called me, too." Des switched the subject. "So, you at the office, huh?"

"Yes. Your mother ran me out the house."

"How?" Des inquired.

"Because nothing I ever do is good enough. She's riding me like a drunk behind the wheel of a car . . . all over the road."

Des laughed. He was happy that Yarni was able to make light of the situation, but he knew that it wasn't easy. "Baby girl, she's only trying to help."

"But baby, she's so overbearing," Yarni whined.

"I know," Des agreed. "If it makes you feel any better, she does me the same way with the baby, too."

"But you don't get it as hard as I get it," Yarni said, now sitting in her chair and flipping through the stack of résumés.

Des could hear the uneasiness in his wife's voice. "Look, since Mom Dukes wants to take care of the babysitting needs, how about we let her? Let's do dinner, get a hotel room, and make love while Grandma is at home loving her grandbaby. You had your six-week checkup yesterday, right?"

"Yeah. The doctor says everything looks good. An evening alone with you sounds like a plan to me," Yarni said, sighing. "A night away from *YaYa* is just what I need."

"So, I'll come by there in about thirty minutes to scoop you up?"

"I'll be waiting with bells and horns."

As soon as Yarni hung up the phone, it rang. She picked it up, thinking that it might be Des calling her back for something. "Law offices," she said.

"Yes, is Mrs. Taylor in, please?" the deep voice asked.

"Who's calling?"

"Marvin Sledge, of Sledge and Associates."

Yarni recognized the name from the stack of messages on her desk. "This is Yarnise Taylor. How may I help you?" she said.

"You're a hard lady to catch up with," the caller said.

"Please forgive me, Mr. Sledge. I usually return all calls within twenty-four hours," she said, rummaging through the résumés on her desk in an attempt to find his. "However, I just had a baby, and I'm technically still on maternity leave."

"Yes, I heard. What did you have?"

"A little girl."

"Well then, congrats are in order."

"Thank you," Yarni said as she placed her fingers on his résumé. It was the only one that had a photo accompanying it. Marvin Sledge was definitely easy on the specs.

Switching the subject, Marvin continued, "I am interested in assisting you with the Samuel Johnson case. I heard you were looking for a second chair."

"That's correct."

"I think that's a great idea. And I feel I would make a great co-counsel."

"Oh, and why is that, Mr. Sledge?" Always up to see if a man could suck his own dick until he burst, Yarni leaned back to get comfortable, not knowing just how long he might be able to verbally gratify himself.

"You've never heard how I devour the courtroom?" he asked, almost in shock.

"No," she lied. She had indeed heard of him. Lawyers knew lawyers and especially black lawyers. There was a small fan club of female attorneys who kept the chatter going on about Marvin Sledge.

"Well, basically, I know my stuff, and I know it well," he started. "In the courtroom, pardon my comparison, if I took a dump in the middle of the floor, my shit wouldn't stink . . . and that just about sums it up."

Yarni moved the phone away from her mouth so he couldn't hear her laugh. *Hmm, a minute man,* she thought. *Didn't take him long at all to get his off.*

"I hope I haven't come on too strong, but you asked, and usually my work should speak for itself; but on the rare occasions I have to defend it, I suppose I can seem a bit sure of myself. But like I said, I know my stuff, and I know it well."

"As do I, Mr. Sledge. As do I." She put him in check because the cockiness was coming through the phone, but after looking at the photo on his résumé, she knew she shouldn't have been surprised.

They continued to talk, and Yarni knew Marvin was full of bullshit, but she liked it because he was slick with it. She found his charisma and confidence in himself appealing, and she knew that he had the kind of game that would enable him to sell ice to an Eskimo. He had the ability to push the verdict he wanted over on a jury. She needed that on her team.

"Well, Mr. Sledge, I've enjoyed speaking with you, but, in all fairness, I have a couple more candidates I need to interview before I make any final decisions," Yarni said.

"Understandable," he agreed. "So I should look to hear back from you by—"

"Soon," Yarni cut him off.

"Well then, I must say it has been my pleasure, and I look forward to working with you," Marvin threw in.

Yarni shook her head at his level of confidence as she saw Des enter her office and sit down in the leather chair in front of her desk. "Yes, Mr. Sledge, just as soon as I conduct these last interviews I'll be making a decision, and I'll give you a call back then," Yarni said before she hung up the phone. She smiled. Her mind was definitely already made up. "You ready, baby?" She quickly called Joyce to check on the baby as she pitched the other résumés in the trash. She walked from behind the desk and into Des's arms.

CHAPTER 6

Get Money

Yarni and Des barely noticed the food on the plates in front of them as they sat across from each other in the quiet restaurant, gazing into each other's eyes. He had never seen his wife look more beautiful, and it took everything in him not to take her right there on the floor of the private room he had booked for their intimate night out together.

She had been to see the doctor the day before for her six-week checkup, and he knew with all she had gone through bringing their daughter into the world, he had to take his time and make it like their first time, but better.

After leaving the restaurant, and leaving behind barely eaten food, they headed toward the next private setting that awaited them for the night. Just as they reached suite 1064, Yarni's cell phone rang. She answered it, and it was her sister, Bambi.

"Oooh, I am so happy!" Yarni screamed in excitement when

she heard Bambi's news. Yarni covered the phone and told Des, "They dropped the charges against Lynx."

Des smiled. "That's great."

"B, how about I plan a little dinner at my house for him?" Yarni suggested.

"How are you going to be the event planner? That's my job," Bambi reminded her sister.

"I know, but we got the same blood. I'm sure I can pull it off. So let's do it next week, once Lynx is settled and y'all have caught up."

"I'll think about it," Bambi teased. "Where's my niece?"

"At home with her YaYa."

"Where are you?"

"At the Jefferson." Yarni kicked off her shoes and lay across the bed next to Des.

"Getting your freak on, huh?"

"Trying to, but you holding me up. Cock-blocking just like a lil' sister would," Yarni added.

"Well, let's definitely do breakfast, or lunch, or maybe even dinner, depending how he put it on you."

"You mean how I put it on him," Yarni said, giving Des a sexy smile.

"A'ight, kill it," Des told Yarni, no longer trying to control his excitement at being with his wife again. "You can jabber with your sister on your own time, not during our quality time. No cell phones allowed."

"Well, call me in the morning or whenever," Bambi said. "Go handle your B-I."

As Yarni was finishing the call with her sister, Des's cell phone rang. "You need to turn your phone off while you making demands on me," she said.

Des looked at the caller ID on his phone. "Baby, let me get this. It's Sister Khadija giving me the nightly update."

Sister Khadija was Des's personal assistant. Her husband, Ahmeen, had been Des's cellie, and she kept things in order for Des. She was organized and extremely loyal to Ahmeen, who was doing life in the penitentiary, and she was also loyal to Des. Des looked out for a bunch of guys in the penitentiary, men who didn't have any business being incarcerated in the first place and weren't leaving there unless someone broke them out or pulled a legislative Houdini. Des knew that he had been spared from the system by the grace of God, but some of the brothers he met were doomed, and one of the things he vowed after doing a dime in the joint was that he wouldn't forsake them.

From the first day his lungs inhaled the sweet taste of freedom, he had kept true to his word. That was part of how Sister Khadija came into play. She kept up with the inmates' kids' birthdays and made sure Des sent birthday cards, paid for parties, or supplied whatever a specific situation called for. She reminded Des what needed to be taken care of. She kept up with the new addresses when his comrades were moved to other prisons as well as got money orders to ensure his friends' inmate accounts were plentiful. That was the lightweight part of her job.

The heavyweight part was making sure that Des's boy, Slim, kept his girls in check. She made sure that the cars were serviced and that there were rides and wake-up calls for the girls who smuggled his drugs into the penitentiary, an endeavor that generated a net profit of over $150,000 a month. Then there was Des's ghetto philanthropy work and the money he blew on attorneys to work on his loyal comrades' dead-end, sometimes hopeless cases. Thanks to Des, some little white boy was able to go to private school because Des was pouring money into the hands of his appeal-fighting father. Keeping up with the attorneys and their caseloads was all Sister Khadija, too.

Yarni had no problem with Sister Khadija, mainly because she was the ultimate Muslim woman. She kept her head wrapped and was always so pleasant and so submissive to her husband. There were days that Yarni felt she could learn a few things from her.

Des answered and listened as Sister Khadija filled him in on the work that was supposed to be done at the shop. "Brother Des, I forgot to tell you that the phone company is coming tomorrow to transfer the lines over to digital."

"I'll be there first thing in the morning," Des informed her, then hung up.

"You gonna cut our date off early?" Yarni whined.

"Sister Khadija just called and said that they were going to be digging up around the office, and I need to be there."

"I understand but—"

Des cut her off with a passionate kiss. "We'll deal with that tomorrow," he said. "Right now is about you and me."

Yarni smiled. She placed a gentle kiss on his lips and whispered, "I'll be right back."

Yarni grabbed the overnight bag that she always kept at her office and hurried into the bathroom. She returned a few minutes later wearing a short, red see-through nightie and red high heels.

Des felt his breath catch, and his heart stopped for a minute. It was like he had stepped back in time and was reliving the first night he and Yarni made love. She posed and turned around for him. Like fine wine, she had definitely gotten better with time.

In spite of just having had Desi six weeks ago, she was almost back down to her prepregnancy weight, but the little bit of extra that remained definitely looked good on her.

He grabbed her hand and pulled her so she was standing between his legs.

"You know how much I love you, right?" he whispered.

She nodded before placing gentle kisses on his hairy chest. Des lay back, ready to enjoy the ride. He closed his eyes as Yarni straddled him, and he ran his hands up her thighs. Des moaned at the thickness and softness of them. He then allowed his hands to cup her butt, drawing her closer to him.

She started fondling his nipples, and Des took in a ragged breath. She knew that drove him crazy, and he felt himself about to go over the edge. It had been entirely too long since he had been wrapped up in her womanhood. He made his way to her clit, a spot he'd played with many times before, but that night it felt like the first time. She smiled at him, seeing what he was thinking in his eyes. It did feel like their first time, but it was so much better. She was no longer an inexperienced little girl. She was a grown woman, and she knew how to please her man.

She slid down his body until she met his erection. Slowly she took him into her mouth and loved him until he thought he couldn't take any more. Just as he was about to explode, she kicked things up a notch by sitting on top of him and riding him, surrounding him with her warmth, until he thought he would pass out.

He flipped her over onto her back and held her close as he buried himself deep inside her, finding their perfect rhythm before finally letting go.

"You okay?" he asked a short while later, as he was still trying to catch his breath.

Yarni nodded before giving him a shy smile.

"I was planning on us taking things slow since this was your first time since the baby, but I see you had other ideas."

"You got that right," Yarni said. "Six weeks is a long time. I don't know about you, but tonight I plan to make up for lost time."

She went to the bathroom and returned with a small bowl of warm water and a washcloth. Gently she cleaned him, all the while placing soft kisses across his chest and sucking on his nipples. Once she finished the sponge bath, she reached over to put the bowl on the nightstand; before she could turn around, she felt him planting himself inside her from behind. Never one to back down from a challenge, Yarni tightened herself around him, and before the night was over, he was calling her name.

The next morning, Des dropped Yarni back off at the law firm so she could pick up her car. "Thank you for an amazing night," she said. She opened the door to get out, but he grabbed her and pulled her back inside, kissing her until she was breathless.

"Thank you for an amazing life," he said. "I'll see you when you get home."

"No problem, baby," she said, and she tried not to think that one day it could all be snatched away from them.

The Monster-in-Law

Yarni headed for her car, ready to go home to see her daughter. It was the longest she had ever been apart from her, and she was missing her terribly. She decided to hold off for a few minutes longer, when she realized she had to go back into the office to get Marvin Sledge's résumé so she could check his references before she secured his position on the team. She knew there was a lot of ground that needed to be covered, and she was certain that Marvin Sledge would have the know-how, the drive, and the ups on how to put in the footwork to get on top of the Samuel Johnson case.

As she walked in the door, her paralegal handed her a stack of messages, including one from Des's attorney, Mark Harowitz. He wanted to meet with her and Des at 3:00 P.M. Yarni looked at her watch. It was only nine o'clock. It was still early, but she knew she had a busy day ahead of her and the time would fly.

She needed to go home to see the baby, shower, and change clothes. She hadn't had a chance to shower at the hotel since she and Des had been running late. Then she had a noon conference call at the office before meeting her sister for lunch. It was doable, if she left immediately.

"Layla, confirm this appointment," Yarni said, handing the other woman the message from Harowitz as she rushed out the door. "Oh," she said, swinging around, remembering how efficient her paralegal was. "I'll call Des to let him know." Then she ran out the door.

She called Des on her way home. "Hey, boo."

"Hey, baby," Des said, happy to hear from her. "What's going on?"

"Harowitz called, and your discovery came back. He wants to discuss it with us.."

"Cool," Des said into the phone, a bit preoccupied. "What year is that?" he asked someone at his shop.

Yarni carefully spoke, "Boo, I don't have to go to the meeting, if you don't want me to."

"Why wouldn't I want you to go? I don't have anything to hide from you."

"I know, baby, but I respect client/attorney privacy." In her most sincere tone, she said, "Just so you know, I would not be offended at all if you wanted to hear the evidence alone."

Des was silent for a minute, and Yarni knew him well enough to know that he thought he was talking to Yarni the lawyer. His silence indicated that he felt there may be doubt in her mind about his innocence. "Look, baby, I ain't got shit to hide from you. Whatever evidence they got is bogus."

"I know it's BS, baby," she said, assuring him that she believed in his innocence, and realizing that Des knew her all too well, "but you know whatever they got stacked against you, I'm going to have your back, baby."

"No doubt, so come by here and scoop me when you're on your way to Harowitz's office."

"Okay. See you later, baby. I love you."

"I love you, too."

Yarni hung up the phone and thought about what outfit she was going to change into after she showered. Once she arrived at the house, Joyce greeted her.

"What are you doing here?" her mother-in-law asked.

Yarni bit down the urge to say something she would regret. "I came home to take a quick shower and change before I head back to the office. I have a busy day today," Yarni replied. "Where's Desi?" She looked around, surprised Joyce wasn't holding the baby.

"She's in her nursery. I just put her down for a nap, so you shouldn't disturb her."

Yarni ignored her mother-in-law and went directly to the nursery. She immediately noticed that things had been changed around. All of the Pampers were gone.

"Joyce, did you move all the Pampers to the garage or into the attic?" she asked while picking up Desi.

Joyce casually answered, "No, I donated them to a good cause."

"What cause? And why would you do that?"

"A charity," she said, kissing little Desi. "My granddaughter doesn't need to wear those Pampers. I told you she needs to wear cloth diapers, just like her daddy did."

"Didn't I tell you"—Yarni took a deep breath—"neither Des nor I have the time to deal with those diapers."

"That's why I got a diaper service," Joyce said calmly. "They come twice a week to pick up the diapers and bring you clean ones. I'll pay for it myself. It's way cheaper than those Pampers anyway."

"But we already had the Pampers. They were paid for already."

"Well, I wanted to do it for my baby, and it ain't costing you a thing, plus it's much better for her."

Yarni took another deep breath. "Look, you don't do something like that without asking us. This isn't your baby. I'd appreciate it if you'd stop making decisions as if Desi was your daughter."

Joyce dropped her head, looking like she was about to cry.

Joyce's wounded feelings did not evoke any pity from Yarni, nor did they make Yarni bite her tongue this time. Enough was enough. "I don't appreciate you coming in here doing whatever you want to do. This isn't your baby," she said brazenly. "The last time I checked, this was my and Des's baby."

Joyce quickly transformed from a cub to a lion. "I just want to help," Joyce shot back. "Since neither one of y'all know how to take care of a baby, never had one before, I thought I was doing y'all a favor."

Yarni ignored her comment. "Look, Joyce, by all means we do appreciate you, but either you are going to respect what we ask you to do or we can hold interviews for a nanny." Yarni stared her mother-in-law in the eyes, refusing to back down.

In the midst of the argument, Desi dumped a load. Once the smell hit her, Yarni turned her nose up at the baby.

Joyce immediately took control. She looked at her watch. "I thought you were in a hurry. From the smells of it, you don't have time to change her. You need to get into the shower." Joyce took the baby out of Yarni's hands, and if Yarni wasn't grateful for Joyce at any other time, she was then. She watched as Joyce talked to Desi, making fun of her stinking up the place. She smiled as she listened to Joyce and shook her head. What was she going to do with her mother-in-law? She couldn't live with her and damn sure couldn't live without her.

CHAPTER 8

The Toy Store

Jaguars, Bentleys, and Lamborghinis were just a few of the many luxurious, over-the-top automobiles that filled the five-acre lot of Des's dealership, hot like the females at a G-Unit video shoot. "Des's Grown-Man Toy Store" was the place to come if a person was making money, legal or illegal, and he wanted to make a statement by driving one of the hottest vehicles ever manufactured. A person could spend two hundred thousand on a new whip and then, easily, another hundred thou just tricking it out to one's own specifications. If Des didn't already have the vehicle on the premises, then he would special order it and have it flown in within less than seventy-two hours.

"Hey, Paulie. This is Des in Richmond." He paced the floor with the phone receiver to his ear.

"How could I not recognize your voice?" Paulie smiled on the other end of the phone. "You're just one of my favorite customers."

"I'm glad you still feel that way because I thought I was going to have to begin looking for somewhere else to shop for my Ferraris. My man, I ordered those three flavors over a week ago." Des gazed out a window that overlooked his fleet of cars.

"I apologize, Des. I've just been a little backed up," Paulie confessed. "I had to fire my regular shipping man, and the new one just doesn't quite get the hang of things yet. I got your order right here, ready to go out. Three Ferraris: red, black, and platinum silver. They'll be on your lot in seventy-two hours."

"I can't ask for any more than that," Des agreed. "Tell the wife and kids that I said hello." Des hung up the phone without waiting for a reply.

It was 12:15 p.m., and the sun was at full blast when Nasir pulled into his uncle's place of business. It had been two months since Des had turned Nasir on to the heroin connect, and things were certainly looking up. He'd bought a new car, compliments of the toy store, and money was pouring in like Kool-Aid on a hot summer day in the projects. Lava was driving the Range Rover while Nasir rode shotgun returning calls.

"Pull around the side, boo," he instructed Lava, motioning with his hand. "We don't need anyone spotting the whip and running into Uncle Des's shop looking for work."

Des heard the water in the puddle on the side of the building make a splash, followed by tires on the pavement outside the side door to his office. His first instinct was to grab his gun—well, Sister Khadija's gun. She kept her registered gun around the shop for Des to use in case something hopped off. Once he checked the surveillance camera, he saw the Range and knew it was his nephew. He released the locks and went to greet Nasir at the door. He saw Lava sitting behind the wheel and said, "If I was hiring for a getaway-car driver, you would definitely have the job."

"Keep me in mind when you need one." She smiled, but Des knew she was dead serious.

Des chuckled at Lava, and asked Nasir, "She coming in?"

"Naw, she good."

They went back through the showroom, past a pair of shiny white Lamborghinis and a customized black Maserati, to Des's office in the back. A large mahogany desk occupied one half of the room. In the other half, a large French mirror hung on the wall over a light tan plush leather sofa. Two oversize leather chairs framed the sofa, and a gorgeous teak coffee table stood between the two in front of the sofa. Yarni, with her exquisite taste, had decorated the room so that it was luxurious yet comfortable. An original Romare Bearden woodcut hung over the desk.

Des and Nasir sat down.

"Look, nephew, I ain't trying to chastise you, but you know how I feel about mixing women with business. I don't think she should be with you as much as she is."

"Unc, trust me. Lava is just as good as any nigga I got on my team."

"What she do?"

"She watch my back."

"Oh, really?"

"That's right. Just yesterday I went to serve somebody, and I took too long to come out of the house. I decided to take a shit and left my phone on the table, and when I finally walked out the house, she was on the side of it, Desert Eagle cocked, 'bout to come in there blazing." Nasir's phone rang, and he put it on vibrate and placed it on the coffee table as he spoke to his uncle.

"That's all fine and dandy, but she should be at home or out with her friends or finding a hobby or something."

"She don't have no friends. I'm her best friend, and I'm her hobby. Besides, I need her."

"Nephew, we ain't never been in the business of needing women. Why do you feel you 'need' her?"

"Because business is good. A lot of people trying to get down. Niggas is getting fat bellies and pockets because they eating good—real good. My prices are cheaper than any other nigga in this state." Des noticed his nephew was gloating and proud of his trade.

"Okay, but why you need yo' girl with you?"

"Because she'll die for me."

"Don't be certain of that, Nasir."

"Have I ever lied to you, Uncle Des?"

Des could see his nephew really believed the words he spoke, so he didn't go back and forth with him about Lava. He knew better.

"Unc, I came here for two things," Nasir said, leaning forward in his seat, excitement evident in his voice.

"What?"

"Advice and a new whip." Nasir's phone vibrated again, and again, he hit the button to silence it.

"A'ight, I can handle both of them. Give me the automobile info first."

"I want the Lexus drop, pearl white with the cream leather seats."

"I ain't feeling that fo' you."

"It ain't for me. It's for Lava."

Des glanced out the window at Lava, who was putting on lip gloss, using the rearview mirror. "Is that what she wants?"

"No, that's what I want her to have. Let her tell it, she don't want no car."

Des was surprised. "She don't want a whip? I never ran across a woman who didn't want a car."

"That's because you never met a chick like Lava before. She'd rather ride and drive my shit than have her own. She feels like since we together all the time, ain't no need in wasting money." Nasir's phone vibrated again, and once again he silenced it.

Des smiled. "A woman after my own heart."

"I want to bless her with something fly."

"What about a red one? I got a red one."

Nasir shook his head. "Nope, it gotta be pearl white."

"Why pearl white?"

"To match the pearl white handle on her Desert Eagle."

Des nodded his approval. "I'll put some calls in and have an estimated delivery date for you tonight." Knowing his nephew was in love, he said, "Now don't tell me you want advice on marriage."

"Unc, I'm already married, so I don't need that."

Des couldn't fuss. He knew how he was about Yarni when they first met, although he had been a little bit older than Nasir was.

"I need you to tell me how to handle this motherfucker Felix."

"Felix?" Des hadn't seen Felix once since the monumental day when he had been sentenced to sixty years in prison for a murder that Felix had committed, and he was surprised that Rico had Nasir dealing with his nephew. "What seems to be the problem with Felix?"

Nasir stared his uncle in the face. "Straight up? I know he's suppose to be family, but I don't trust him. He's greasy."

"Why? What makes you say that?" Des asked, half surprised at what his nephew was saying.

"My gut says it. The first few times Rico hit me off himself, but then he met me one day telling me he's going to let his nephew hit me off." The hot box vibrated again.

"What's wrong with that?"

Nasir looked at the number. "Look, I gotta meet the dude tomorrow night. I want you to come and see what type of vibe you get from him. I got somebody waiting on me." Nasir's phone continued to blow up. "Duty calls, but I'ma hit you tomorrow when I'm ready to go handle that B-I."

"Business good, huh?" Des smiled at his nephew.

"Real good," he said as he headed for the door. Des watched as Nasir let himself out.

Living with bin Laden

Des looked at his watch. It was almost time for Yarni to pick him up for their meeting with Harowitz. He was slightly anxious about seeing his attorney, wondering what kind of evidence they could possibly have on him.

Yarni arrived just as he was finishing up a call to check on the Lexus for Nasir.

"Hey, baby," she said, greeting him with a kiss. "You ready?"

"Yup," he said, grabbing his cell phone.

They rode to the attorney's office in silence, lost in their own thoughts.

As they were riding up in the elevator, Yarni turned to him. "Boo, I'm serious. If you don't want me to sit in on the meeting, it's okay."

Des looked at her and shook his head. "Like I said, I have nothing to hide. Don't you trust me?" he asked.

Yarni nodded, and the elevator doors opened. They looked at

each other and both took a deep breath before walking through the double glass doors. A receptionist told them that Harowitz was expecting them. Yarni's hand was wrapped around Des's arm as they walked into the spacious corner office, then closed the door behind them.

A Persian rug covered the floor. Large glass windows showed the cloudy skyline. Harowitz was bent over an open file on his cluttered desk when they walked in and didn't seem to hear them. When Yarni cleared her throat, he looked up, startled. His eyes were red and tired-looking behind his thick glasses. His burgundy silk bow tie was untied. He stood up, walked around his desk, and shook Des's and Yarni's hands.

"Please have a seat," he said, inviting them to sit in the comfortable chairs on the other side of the desk. As he sat down in his chair, he took off his glasses, rubbed his eyes, and said, "Desmond, I have to be honest with you. The evidence is not looking good for you right now."

Des didn't respond, but Yarni cut straight to the chase. "What's in the discovery?"

"Well, for starters, you have this." He handed Yarni a letter that Des had written to Richards two weeks after being convicted.

"They can't be serious," she said, shaking her head. "This is typical of what any man who has been railroaded by his attorney for a crime he didn't commit would send." She looked at Harowitz and asked, "You've never gotten one of these before?"

"I have." He nodded. "You know I have, but it gets even more complicated."

"What is it?" Yarni asked while Des sat in total silence, taking in the entire conversation between his lawyer and his wife.

"There was an appointment with Des in Richards's appointment book for the same day he was murdered, and Des never showed up."

"That's because I never made an appointment with him. Why would I?" Des broke his silence.

"We know this, but the kicker is that Richards got called away on an emergency, and you got gas a few miles from the scene of the crime."

Des could tell by the tone of Harowitz's voice that he was doomed. "Look, this shit may not look good, but I didn't kill that motherfucker. That's real talk."

"We know, baby." Yarni put her hand on Des's shoulder to console him. "We're going to beat this," she said, shooting a look at Harowitz.

"We're going to do everything in our power to make sure you walk," Harowitz said.

Des leaned forward and asked, "Look, you do know this is some bullshit, right?"

"Yes," Harowitz agreed.

Des stood and looked back and forth between Yarni and Harowitz. "If we can't get this resolved, I'm bouncing. I'll live in Afghanistan with bin Laden before I go back to the penitentiary for something that I didn't do. I'll do a hundred years for something I did do, but for some shit I didn't do . . . it's not happening."

Des headed for the door before turning back to Harowitz. "You need to work this shit out. Do what you're known for doing—find a loophole, or find the motherfucker who did it. For all that gotdamn money I'm paying you, you need to put on your suit and play Matlock."

Yarni followed her husband as Des opened up the door to let himself out.

"Oh, and we ain't cutting no deals, pleading out, or any of that shit, so don't even think about it."

"I'll be in touch, Mark. Thanks for everything," Yarni said hurriedly as she and Des exited the office.

In the elevator, Des didn't utter a word; Yarni knew he was steaming mad, and rightfully so. As soon as they stepped out of the elevator, her cell phone rang. It was Harowitz. He gave her the rest of the info on the discovery.

When they approached the car, Des stood by the door waiting to hear the chirp of the alarm, but Yarni didn't unlock the doors. Instead, she walked around to the driver's side where Des was. "Listen, baby, we need to talk."

"We can talk in the car," he said drily.

"No, we can't," she firmly said.

"Why is that?" Des asked.

"Because I don't know if it's tapped. It's apparent someone is trying to set you up."

"No shit."

"No, baby, I'm serious."

He looked at her as she took a deep breath and continued.

"Listen," she began, "I need you to tell me everything. From start to finish. Someone is out to get you. I don't know who, what, or why, but you and I gon' get to the bottom of this. I promise."

Des didn't have much to say, so Yarni tried her damnedest to lighten the load. "You know I don't make promises to break them. We can and will beat this case, but I need you to tell me everything that happened from the time you left me and Desi in the hospital."

Des looked at Yarni. "Baby, I told you I didn't do it. I wasn't thinking about that clown."

"I know you weren't, but in order for me to get you off, I need to know everything." She went on. "Baby, I need you to bend one of your rules."

He looked at Yarni. "What might that be?"

"Never confess to anything."

He laughed and shook his head. "I take the fifth."

"Seriously, you've got to tell me everything. You gotta trust me. I'd die before I'd ever betray you."

"What did Harowitz say?"

"He said that . . ." She took another deep breath. "You ain't gon' believe this shit."

"Try me."

"He said that they have a witness who said a black man wearing a mask shot Richards in the head. The witness saw the man take off the mask and identified that man as you."

"What will they come up with next? They gonna pin the Kennedy assassination on me, too?" Des looked into a passing car that was driving by slowly in the parking lot.

"The witness described you to a sketch artist."

"These motherfuckers are really trying to railroad me." If Des's words were not convincing enough, his expression could have persuaded the jury.

"You got that right, but baby," Yarni said, leaning in, "you know wifey ain't gon' let that happen."

"If I can't clear this up, you know what I have to do, right?"

"I know, baby, but that ain't gon' be necessary. We gon' have to spend a lot of money and pull from all our resources, that's all; and I'm going to start off by hiring a private investigator. We're going to find out what else Richards was into besides selling his clients out. Who would want him dead, and who would want you off the streets?"

"That's why you my baby." Des sighed and kissed his wife on the forehead. "Now, can you unlock the door so I can get in the car?"

In One Ear and
Out the Other

es sat across from Sister Khadija's desk as she updated him about all the goings-on with the business. Although her mouth was going a million miles a minute, what she was saying was going in one ear and out the other. Des's mind was focused on his case and on the Cadi rolling up on his car lot. The driver looked familiar and was someone whom Des knew from the inside. One of his salesmen walked outside to try to make a sale, but he returned quickly.

"The dude says he looking for you, boss," the salesman said, tilting his head toward the man getting out of the passenger side of the Cadillac.

"Who is it?" Des asked, knowing that the person looked familiar, but not able to place him.

"He say he yo' brother-in-law."

Then it clicked. Yarni had mentioned that Bambi's husband, Lynx, was coming by to get a car.

Des smiled and hopped up. He always openly embraced a thorough brother who had just been released from the belly of the beast, and it especially ran deep in the family.

Des walked out onto the lot as Lynx stood at the side of the Cadi. He wore a rose-gold chain around his neck and a two-carat diamond in his ear. He was a good six feet tall and looked like he had spent plenty of time in the prison gym. Lynx had known of Des before he did his bid, but he had never done business with him or talked to him. But now they were related, so it was mandatory.

Des gave him a brotherly hug. "What's good, my man?"

"Just glad to be home."

"Don't I know that feeling," Des assured his brother-in-law. "How much you do?"

"Two and a half."

"B was holding you down, huh?"

"Fo' sho," Lynx answered. "Her and Yarni got some party they planned for me."

"Yeah, we got ourselves two special sisters. The party's at our house."

"I 'preciate you letting them have it at your house. I know how that can be."

"Don't mention it. You family." Des switched topics. "So, what you trying to do?"

"I need some wheels, and they say you the man to see."

"They told you right. What you thinking 'bout?"

"I need something hot; and my wife paying."

Des smiled. "I got you, my brother. You see anything you like?"

While Lynx looked around the lot, the driver of the Cadi got out of the car and asked, "How much you want for that white Porsche?"

"We can work something out," Des said, before redirecting his attention to Lynx. Des was surprised that Lynx was rolling with Cook'em-up.

"Cook'em-up, this is my brother-in-law Des. Des, this is my man Cook'em-up."

"I know who he is," Des interjected.

Lynx was surprised. "Word?"

"Yeah. Didn't you do a little bit at Greensville?" Des asked Cook'em-up.

Cook'em-up's smirk left his face, and he nodded. "Yeah."

Des searched his eyes. "You was cellie with Pompay for a minute, right?"

Cook'em-up silently nodded.

"Yeah, I thought that was you."

Lynx knew both guys' bios all too well. Des was a stand-up dude, and Cook'em-up was a stone-cold killer; if their two worlds ever collided, it wasn't anything to take lightly. Judging by the tension, it was apparent that somewhere and somehow the two paths had crossed before. Sensing the propensity for fire, Lynx tried to ease the tension. He focused on why he was there: the cars.

"So what's the deal, man? I need some hot shit."

"You in safe hands. I got you," Des assured his brother-in-law. "What you like? Benz, Beamer, Ferrari, Lex? If we ain't got it, we can get it."

"Ummm, I've been gone for a minute, so I'm not sho what I'm feeling. My whip game may be a lil' slack."

"It never takes long to get your car game back."

Lynx looked around the lot. "An S Class could work, but I ain't really feeling that one." He pointed to a champagne-colored one with customized piped seats.

Des gave him a crazy look. "I wouldn't put you in that anyway. A stripper just traded that in." Des put his hand up on his chin. "I got something real special for you." Des nodded as if a lightbulb had just gone off in his head. "A welcome-home, redlight special for my brother-in-law. I just bought a CLS Mercedes from a dealer. It was their demo—got only ten thousand miles on it. Brand-spanking-new. Son of a bitch ain't never even been registered."

Des had just given Lynx a hell of a welcome-home present, and Lynx was feeling it. "Good-lookin'," he said as he extended his hand out to shake Des's.

Just then they redirected their attention to a Yellow Cab that rolled up in front of the car lot. A teenage kid jumped out of it with his rose-gold forty-two-inch cable swinging from side to side, and he made his way over to the champagne-colored souped-up S Class. They all watched as he tried to keep up his baggy pants and carry the Gucci overnight bag in his hand.

"How much you want for this joint?" the youngin asked, adjusting his pants.

Des shook his head. "It was just traded, so we haven't done anything to it."

"You ain't got no quarter to eights?"

"Yeah, I got a couple of seven forty-fives." Des nodded.

The kid started walking, then another car caught his attention. "What about that?" He pointed to a late-model convertible six series BMW.

"It got a few miles, so I can do that for fifty-nine, fully loaded."

"A'ight put the bow on that bitch, and I'm going to get my momma or baby momma to come back up here to put it in her name." He tossed the Gucci bag to Des. "That's sixty. Wash it and fill it up for me."

"Wait a minute, partner." Des put his hand up to stop the young fella. "Slow up, my man."

"What? We need to make this transazzion go down, 'cause a nigga straight tired of pushing these Jordans."

"Peace, I feel that, but you got to slow down, shawdy."

Sister Khadija came to the door wrapped in her garb, holding the phone, and called out, "Des, Tommy's on the phone from Miami and says he got a Bentley Continental GT in—an '05. He says it's pretty as a honey-roasted turkey on Thanksgiving. Are you interested?"

"Ask him to hold tight for a few minutes—got a couple customers." Then he added, "Write up the paperwork for the new CLS that we got coming in for him," he said, pointing to Lynx, "and give him some tags and whatever he wants to drive until we get it here."

Sister Khadija nodded and obediently did what she was told.

Lynx and Cook'em-up walked inside the building while Des broke the game down to the youngster.

"Look, baby boy, you trying to send me and you to the penitentiary."

"What da fuck you mean? I don't know you, and you don't know me."

Des gave him a look. "You right, but listen here, you can give me nine thousand a week as far as I'm concerned, but you coming in here paying cash like that, that's not going to work for me or you. I know you don't know how it goes down, so I'm going to put you up on it."

Des was trying to give Lil' Man some jewels, but Lil' Man's thoughts were on one thing and one thing only . . . that BMW. And anything else was in one ear and out the other as far as he was concerned.

"You give me the whole fifty-nine, I gotta report every dollar of that to the IRS. That's a red flag for you and your momma. You become a walking investigation straight up."

"So what I'm supposed to do? Ride around in a Pinto?"

"My man, it's always two ways to skin a cat."

"Good, because a Pinto ain't a good look for my image."

In a matter of time, Des had Lil' Man off heels and on wheels. Five sales in one day wasn't bad at all.

CHAPTER 11

The Queen
Protects the King

Des went to scoop Nasir so that they could go see Felix. When Des arrived at Nasir and Lava's deluxe condo, Lava let him in and informed him that Nasir was almost ready. She offered him something to drink, but he declined. Lava shrugged and headed to another room, and Des decided to follow her. Des thought she and Nasir must have had an argument because she seemed a little distant.

He looked around the condo and was pretty impressed with what the young couple had pulled together. The living room was decked out in a *Scarface* theme—soft, red leather furniture and *Scarface* mini-blinds featuring the classic Tony Montana picture. Built in the wall diagonally across from the *Scarface* reflection was a huge wall-size aquarium, which housed two piranhas— Nasir told him once that they had named them Bobby and Whitney. Off the living room was an enormous game room, which had a professional-size pool table in the middle of the floor, a large dart board with a police officer's face as the target on one wall, and a flat-screen plasma television on another.

"Who did the decorating?" Des asked, continuing to look around the room.

"We both did." Lava plopped down on the couch and grabbed the remote. "We pretty much do everything together," she added.

Des rolled a few of the balls on the pool table with his hands, growing uncomfortable with the silence. "Real nice art," he said, nodding toward the collection of fictional and real-life people showcased on the walls. Every photograph had been carefully selected and professionally matted and framed. There were posters of films, television shows, and their stars: *The Sopranos, Goodfellas, The Godfather,* as well Tony Montana, Biggie, Tupac, and Suge Knight. Des was surprised they had some political figures mixed in, including Fidel Castro, Malcolm X, and Martin Luther King Jr. They had somehow managed to get hold of federal mug shots, with the inmate numbers underneath, for Baby-face Nelson, Cool C., Wayne Perry, and Kenneth "Supreme" McGriff. In the middle of all the photos was a huge portrait of Lava and Nasir dressed up like Bonnie and Clyde, holding street sweepers.

Des caught sight of a chessboard in the corner of the room. "Does Nasir play chess?" he asked, not recalling his nephew having an interest in the game.

"All the time," Lava said, never taking her eyes off the six o'clock news to look at Des. "We both do."

Finally Des could take the awkward silence no longer. "Lover's quarrel?" he asked. He could see that something was clearly bothering Lava by the way she had her arms folded across her chest.

"No, Uncle Des," she said, sounding annoyed as she sucked her teeth.

Nasir walked in the room and headed over to Des to give him a hug and a pound. "She's just mad because she can't roll with the big boys. She gets an attitude anytime my immediate plans don't include her."

"Uncle Des, it ain't that," Lava interjected, and hopped up off the sofa.

"I don't care if he goes out with you, Uncle Des. We love and trust you. It's just those other niggas . . . I don't trust them. None of them, especially Felix. That nigga ain't nothing but trouble."

Des smiled as he listened to Lava. "I agree that you shouldn't trust those other niggas. In the game, you always have to stay on your guard around everyone, male or female," Des commented. Although he was starting to like Lava more and more, and believed that she was Nasir's ride-or-die chick, he still didn't like Nasir having her so deeply involved in his business.

"Uncle Des, he forgets sometimes that I'm a woman, and the fact that I have women's intuition. Sometimes I sense things . . . and I just know things," Lava shared. She stopped and thought about what Des had just said. "Wait a minute. Are you trying to say Nasir shouldn't trust me?"

"Should he?"

Nasir shook his head. "Unc, we've already had this conversation," he said.

"Oh what, y'all talking about me behind my back?" Lava asked, rolling her eyes at Nasir.

"Baby, it ain't even like that . . ." Nasir said.

Lava ignored him and turned to confront Des. "You trying to say I don't have my man's back?" she asked.

Des looked directly into Lava's eyes before he answered. "Do you?"

"You damn right I do. Just like Yarni has yours. Don't you ever question my loyalty to Nasir. *Ever.* I love this man with all my heart, and I will die for him. Like I said, it's just these niggas I don't trust."

Des saw the sincerity shining in her eyes, and he knew she had spoken with her heart.

"She's more suspicious of me being with some niggas handling business than me being at a strip club with a room full of naked bitches," Nasir said, shrugging his shoulders in amazement.

Des gazed at Lava, waiting to hear her side. She wasn't embarrassed at all. "That's right. I ain't worried about no sweaty bitches on him. All they can give him is some stank pussy, and he ain't tripping on that. It's the niggas that I'm worried about. They so shysty."

"Right." Des tried not to smirk. Lava was slowly winning him over by the second.

"She thinks that anytime I don't include her in the business I must feel that she can't cut it. Let her have her way, and it ain't nothing streetwise that she can't do."

"Clyde had Bonnie, didn't he?" she said, as she made her way to the kitchen. "And she never let him down, did she?"

"No, baby, she didn't," Nasir said, looking at his Rolex. "It's time to make moves." He grabbed the Louis Vuitton overnight bag filled with money, and he and Des headed for the door.

But before they could exit the house good, Lava called out, "Boo, wait a minute. Hold up." Nasir stopped in his tracks and turned to look at her.

"Sorry, baby. I forgot to give you a kiss, huh?" He moved to kiss her.

"Nope. It ain't even that. You forget this?" She handed him his gun.

Nasir took the gun from her, looking a bit embarrassed. "Thanks," he said sheepishly.

"Now you can give me a kiss." She puckered up and shared a wet one with her man.

"Good looking," Des commended Lava before giving Nasir a hard look.

"Ain't nothing. I'm just playing my position. That's what the queen is supposed to do. Protect her king."

"You know the queen is the most powerful piece in chess, right?" Des said, as he shut the door behind him. Lava just smiled.

The Brain on Drugs

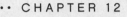asir and Des met Felix at his upscale condo located in Virginia Beach. Although it was an expensive spot on the Atlantic Ocean in a gated community, the furnishings were very simple, which surprised Des.

A half-naked girl wearing spandex short-shorts with the cheeks of her butt hanging out and a halter top with her nipples barely covered answered the door. She showed Des and Nasir into a room with a sofa, two chairs, and big-screen television and handed them the remote before leaving. Another girl wearing a micro-miniskirt had been sitting on the sofa, but she got up and left when they came in. Nasir and Des were there for about ten minutes when a third girl, a cigarette hanging from her mouth, walked in to retrieve a plastic bag that was sitting on the floor beside the sofa.

Pretty soon Felix, wearing a plush robe that looked like he had copped it from Hugh Hefner's closet, entered the room.

"Nas," he said slowly, his Spanish accent making it sound like the name had five syllables, knowing full well that Nasir hated to be referred to that way.

Nasir and Des both stood to greet Felix.

"How you doing?" he said to Des, avoiding eye contact as he wiped his runny nose with a handkerchief.

"I'm peace." Des nodded, studying the man in front of him.

"How's business?" Felix redirected his attention to Nasir.

"Business is good on my end," Nasir answered. "And yours?"

"Business is good for me, as long as it's good for you, my man." Felix smiled as his eyes scanned the faces of both men.

The small talk went on for a few more minutes, and Des continued his study of Felix's body language. Felix continued to avoid looking Des directly in the eyes. As Des watched the transaction between his and Rico's nephews, he began to think about something that had never crossed his mind before: Although Rico had tried to express his gratitude to Des by giving him a million dollars in cash the night he and Yarni were married, there was really nothing Rico could ever give him to repay the ten years of Des's life that had been stolen while he was in prison.

Make no mistake about it, a million dollars was a nice piece of change to get one's hands on, but at the end of the day, ten years of life were worth much more than that. That would equal a hundred thousand a year. Des would have made that in a slow month while he was on the street. The more he thought about it, the angrier Des got that he had accepted such a loss for such an unappreciative motherfucker like Felix, who had never offered Des even a simple thanks.

"Is this the same stuff that you had the last time?" Nasir asked.

"Same shipment, same shit," Felix responded.

Felix had raw dope that could take twelve ounces of cut to every ounce of pure dope. He charged twelve hundred an ounce, which was a natural steal. Nasir could turn ten ounces into fifty o's that could still hold a cut on the street, and sell them for eighteen hundred, the best price in the state and on most of the East Coast. The profit was enormous, and the turnover rate was rapid, eliminating any competition, especially from Monte, who Nasir used to cop from.

Nasir was there to buy seven thousand grams. He had just over three hundred thousand dollars in his overnight bag, more than enough to make the purchase. The swap went smoothly, and he and Des were out of there in less than thirty minutes.

Once they were back in the car, Nasir asked, "So, Unc, what you think about this motherfucker?" He turned around in the passenger seat so he was facing Des as he drove.

"The chump got a dope habit, and an expensive one at that. That dope dick keeps money and drugs keep da hos around," Des said, never taking his eyes off the road. "Like flies on shit."

As they rode back to Richmond, Des shared some of his war stories and lessons with Nasir, and, as always, Nasir absorbed every word.

"Always let an arrogant man think he's smarter than you, and he will provide you the opportunity to sit back and watch him play himself."

CHAPTER 13

Filet Mignon

Yarni went into the nursery to check on Desi and was relieved to find her baby girl sleeping peacefully. Leaning into the crib, she rubbed Desi's belly and kissed her on the forehead, then walked back into her bedroom and climbed into bed. She had just taken a long, hot soak in the Jacuzzi and had slipped into her black La Perla nightgown. The satin gown brushed up against her skin like a soft, much-needed hug. Although it was almost eleven o'clock at night and she had court the next morning, Yarni couldn't go to sleep. Between going over her case file and checking on Desi, she was running out of things to do with herself, so she propped herself up on her heavenly down feather pillows, leaned back, picked up the remote that lay on the bed, and flipped the channels on the television.

She was watching the end of *Chappelle's Show* when her cell phone rang.

She looked down at the number displayed on the caller ID and smiled. "Hey, baby," she whispered into the phone.

"Hey, boo. I got caught up, but I'm on my way home," Des informed his wife. She could hear traffic in the background and figured that he must be driving, making his way home to his family. She smiled and felt her heart quicken at the thought of seeing him.

"Okay, baby," she said, "can't wait 'til you get here."

"The battery on my phone is dying, and the charger is in the other car, so I can't talk, but I'll be home in a minute."

"I hear you. That's cool," she assured him. "I love you."

"Love you, too."

After they hung up, Yarni tried to watch television, but she found herself watching the clock. One o'clock turned into two o'clock, and two o'clock soon became three o'clock; still there was no Des. Yarni knew that she couldn't stay up all night playing the role of watchman. She had to get some rest for court, so she considered taking a Tylenol PM to knock herself out, but she knew that would make her feel groggy the next morning, and she had to be on her A game in court. She once again checked on Desi, and after changing the baby's diaper and giving her a bottle, she took a Percocet which would put her out like a light. She just prayed that if Desi woke up, her father would have made it home to tend to his daughter. She'd be feeling a bit sluggish and groggy the next morning, but it would be worth it to escape her misery for the moment.

The next day the preliminary hearing for the Samuel Johnson case went much better than Yarni expected. Although she was a little sluggish from the Percocet, she didn't let that keep her from doing the best possible job on Samuel's case.

After court, Marvin Sledge was so excited that he made plans to take Yarni out to celebrate. She agreed until Des called at the last minute wanting her to go out with him and Desi. The decision wasn't hard to make. It was Des—her man, her husband, her child's father, the love of her life—over the womanizer Marvin Sledge any day.

Yarni and Des settled into their seats at the plush five-star restaurant, and Yarni felt the stress of the day melt away.

"Yes, I will have the filet mignon, medium well," Yarni told the waitress when she came to take their orders. "Please make sure that it isn't wrapped in the bacon."

"Of course, ma'am," the waitress said before turning to Des. "And what would you like, sir?"

Des looked at the menu thoughtfully before snapping it closed. "I'll have the crab cake dinner with a fully loaded baked potato. On second thought, forget the crab cakes. I'll take a filet mignon as well, and I don't want bacon on mine either."

"You still want the potato?" the waitress asked.

Des nodded, and the woman collected the menus and prepared to leave.

"Can I get you something to drink in the meanwhile?"

Des looked at Yarni, and she shook her head. "Just water," he said.

While they waited for their food, they sat and talked, mainly about the baby. Des could see clearly that Yarni was a bit aggravated. He couldn't put his finger on why.

"You okay?" he asked, grabbing her hand.

She nodded. "Just a little tired," she said, suddenly feeling the stress of the day returning.

"How'd everything go in court?"

"It went well, better than I expected, actually." She gave him a tired smile.

"You want to leave?" he asked, looking concerned. "You look really tired."

She shook her head as she gave him a dry laugh. "I am tired. I have a newborn at home, and I'm fighting one of the biggest cases of my career. I have a lot going on." She smiled at him wickedly. "If that's not enough, my husband was missing in action last night after he told me he was on his way home, so I'm not getting enough sex."

He laughed as he squeezed her hand before kissing it. "I'm sorry, baby. Something came up that I had to deal with."

"I figured as much," she said.

They both grew quiet, both staring at Desi, who had fallen asleep in her high chair.

"I can't believe how beautiful she is," Des said, gazing at his daughter. He turned to his wife. "You know, I don't think I've told you, but you're doing a great job with her. I know this has to be hard on you. . . . I know it's a big adjustment, but baby, know I'm here for you, and my mom is, too. You have people who want to help you with Desi. Promise me you'll lean on us if you need to."

Before Yarni could answer, their food arrived. She squeezed Des's hand in appreciation. Then looked down at her plate, preparing to dig in.

Her steak was wrapped in bacon. Yarni turned her attention to the waitress and stared at the woman in disbelief, frowning as she said in a firm tone, "Didn't I . . . precisely tell you . . . that . . . I," she stressed each and every word to the rhythm of her animated neck, "did not want my steak wrapped in bacon?"

"I will get it fixed for you, ma'am." The waitress reached for Yarni's plate.

"How long is that going to take?"

"Probably about twenty minutes, since you had it medium well."

Des jumped in, seeing the fire in his wife's eyes, "Can't you pull someone else's steak that's almost done?"

"Yes, that shouldn't be a problem," the waitress replied, knowing good and well that she was under the gun.

"This don't make no motherfucking sense," Yarni snapped on Des.

"You're absolutely right, baby," he said, trying to lighten the mood. "I don't want you stressing, baby. We're supposed to be here celebrating. Do you want my steak?"

She ignored his question. "I can't celebrate when they're trying to force pork down my throat."

"You're right about that," Des said, cutting into his steak. He tried to feed her a piece, but she shook her head.

"I'll wait for mine," she said. "You go ahead."

He shrugged and started to eat.

"Excuse me," another patron said, stopping at their table, "she's so adorable." The woman went to touch Desi, but thought twice about it after Yarni glared at her.

"Thanks." Des smiled at the couple, but Yarni didn't open her mouth.

The server appeared with a hot plate in her hand, with Yarni's food on it. "Wow, that was quick." Yarni gave a slight smile, but she had peeped the game.

"I pulled one like you suggested," she said to Des.

"Well, look,"—Yarni looked hard at the woman's name tag—"Tonya, I'm going to ask you something: Isn't this the same steak, and you just pulled the bacon off it?"

"No, ma'am," the server said. "We—I would never do anything like that."

"Listen, let me explain something to you."

The waitress looked at Yarni as she went on.

"I don't eat pork at all. The last time I was at somebody's home for a Thanksgiving dinner, I ate greens with pork in them, and I turned purple. My whole body was swollen up from an allergic reaction. That was my aunt's house, but this is a multimillion-dollar franchise, and *now* I have my law degree and I know the power of a lawsuit."

Yarni knew she had the server's attention. "Let me ask you again." She asked the question as if she was in court, "Did they take the bacon off my steak, or did they give me a new one?"

"Ummm, ummm, I don't know, let me check." Tonya picked up the plate from in front of Yarni and ran back to the kitchen.

"You do just that," Yarni said to the server's back.

After the waitress was gone, Des spoke, "Baby, here, you can have the rest of mine." He felt really bad about the whole situation.

"I don't want yours, boo. I'm good."

The server reappeared. "They're cooking you a new one."

"So, they had just taken the bacon off it, huh?"

"Well, yes, since you never said you were allergic."

"Why the *fuuuck* does it make a difference if I'm allergic? What happened to the customer having it her way?" There was no winning with Yarni. "As a matter of fact, get me the damn manager—*now.*"

The manager didn't have to be directed to the table because she could see the smoke coming from Yarni's head.

"Ma'am, I'm terribly sorry for this whole mix-up. I'm going to take this steak off your bill."

"I know you are. You weren't expecting me to pay for it, were you?"

"No, ma'am. I wasn't." The manager stayed professional.

"You should be paying for our whole dinner simply because of the great inconvenience. My husband is not able to enjoy his meal because he's been sidetracked with my drama," Yarni said, getting louder by the second. Other patrons were starting to look at them.

"The meal is on the house, and please let me get you a drink. What would you like?" the manager asked, trying her best to appease Yarni.

"I just want my shit cooked right. Who can drink on an empty stomach? And not to mention we have our baby with us!" She pointed to Desi.

"Your food will be out very shortly," the manager said, trying to do her very best to make Yarni happy, but Yarni was making it very hard for her.

"Thank you," Yarni said in a tone that indicated: I'm done with you now.

"Yes, ma'am." The manager walked away.

"Baby, let me apologize for being out so late and caught up in the Nasir stuff."

Yarni interrupted. "I have to go the ladies' room." She grabbed her Yves Saint Laurent bag and headed to the restroom.

Des knew a great deal of her anger and disappointment in him was being taken out on the restaurant, but he had to come up with something to get back in Yarni's good graces; she was like a Mack truck when she was on a rampage and would roll over everything in sight.

He had to figure something out—and quick. He reached for his cell phone and called Sister Khadijah.

"Hey," Des said, after getting Khadijah on the phone, "what are you doing?"

"Talking to Ahmeen on the other line. What can I do for you?"

"I need you to pull some strings to get the best seats in the house to the old-school concert that's coming up."

"Consider it done. The promoter is Disco, a client of ours, so he'll make it happen."

"Cool. I'm going to take Yarni. She needs a break. She has a lot going on right now."

"I thought you didn't like crowds," Khadijah reminded him.

"Anything for my wifey."

"It must be nice. I wish my man was here to do things like this. I know Yarni is going to love it!"

Back in the ladies' room, Yarni looked in the mirror and threw some water on her face, lotioned her hands, then went into her decorative pill bottle and pulled out a Xanax. She exited the bathroom and went to the water fountain to take the pill before heading back to the table.

As she returned, the waitress was bringing her food.

"It all looks good. I'm famished," she said. She seemed like a different person. She went from being Des's lion to his cub. One minute she was a bull in the china shop, the next minute she was as cool as the other side of the pillow. He wrote off her mood swings as the stress of having a high-powered career, being a new mommy, and, of course, living the life of a hustler's wife.

CHAPTER 14

Old School Rules

A few nights later, Des walked into the bedroom and frowned when he saw Yarni sitting on the bed, surrounded by papers.

"Are you planning on working all night?" he asked.

Yarni tried to hide her annoyance. "What do you think?" she snapped. "You know I have to be on point with this Samuel Johnson case."

"You're right, baby," Des said, kissing her on the forehead before he turned to walk out the room. "I know you have a lot of work to do. That's too bad, though, because I just happen to have tickets for the Doug E. Fresh concert tonight. Since you're so busy, I guess I can just tell my mother she doesn't have to watch the baby—"

Yarni leaped off the bed, scattering papers everywhere, and flew into Des's arms, smothering him with kisses. She screamed, her work forgotten. "What time does the concert start?" Des opened his mouth to speak, but she cut him off. "Never mind. I'll be ready in twenty minutes."

Yarni flew to her closet and pulled out a strapless denim dress and the matching shoes.

"You sure you want to go?" Des asked, trying to keep a straight face. "I know you have a lot of work to do," he teased.

Yarni stuck out her tongue at him. "You make me sick," she said before breaking into a smile. "Thanks, baby. I love you."

"I love you, too," he said, leaving the room so she could get ready. He knew he had gotten some brownie points indeed. Des hadn't seen Yarni with that kind of energy in a long time.

During the concert, she sang every Doug E. Fresh and Slick Rick song word for word. When they left the show, Des smiled, knowing that he was officially out of the doghouse. It would be smooth sailing for the rest of the night.

"Thanks, boo." Yarni reached over to put a big, wet kiss on his cheek. "I really needed that to get me out of my zone. Thank you, baby."

"How thankful are you?" He raised an eyebrow but kept his eyes on the road.

"Real thankful." She gave him a naughty smile while rubbing his leg.

"You gonna show me?" He smiled.

"I always do," she purred, as she reached to unbuckle his belt and undo his zipper.

"I didn't say now, but that's definitely what's up." He chuckled before she cupped him, then he drew in a deep breath. "All right, you really know how to make your man feel grateful to be married to such a beautiful and thoughtful woman."

"How grateful are you?" she asked, as she unbuckled her seat belt and leaned down to lick his stiffening penis. Their car swerved out of its lane. She looked up at him and ordered, "Pull over and show me."

He checked his rearview mirror to get back into his lane, and, as he gazed into it, he noticed that the same black Ford Taurus had been trailing him since they left the Arthur Ashe Center. Des wasn't sure if it was 5-0, stick-up boys, or just a coincidence, but he didn't believe in the latter. He signaled as if to change lanes, and the Taurus did the same thing. When he slid to a new lane, so did the Taurus.

He reached down to confirm his blue steel .357 was on the left side of his seat. Yarni was too busy enjoying herself and giving him pleasure to notice.

Des slowed and moved to the side of the road, almost coming to a stop; the Taurus kept going. Yarni thought they were about to get busy and was disappointed when he explained, "We're gonna finish this when we get home." She thought he was joking and proceeded to bless his wood with another warm lick, but Des pushed her back firmly into her seat and zipped his pants.

Although he wanted to have sex with his wife right then and there, he knew something wasn't right, and he didn't want to get caught with his pants down—literally. He drove for about two miles before he came to an Exxon gas station. He passed the gas station's first entrance and, without signaling, pulled into the second entrance, causing the car behind him to slam on its brakes. As soon as Des pulled up to the gas pump, a green Ford Explorer drove into the gas station parking lot. A clean-cut black guy pulled close to the pay phone, rolled down his window, and appeared to dial.

While Des pumped the gas, he got a good look at the driver

of the Explorer and was now sure who was following him. He walked into the station's convenience store, giving himself enough time to think of a plan. Once he got back in the car, he handed Yarni a cold bottle of water and instructed her to "Buckle your seat belt."

She heard the seriousness in his voice and did exactly as she was told without question.

"Make sure it's tight," he said with a smile, trying to mask the seriousness of his tone.

"What?" she said, looking confused.

"We've been followed since we left the concert, but don't worry. If these motherfuckers want to play cat and mouse with me, then I'm going to raise the playing level." He took a sip of his water and adjusted his mirror. "Let the games begin."

Des put the car in drive, popped in his *Me Against the World* CD, and pulled off. While Tupac was continuously predicting his own untimely death, Des proceeded home, taking a long detour. Des wasn't the average street guy, nor was he a creature of habit. He made it his business to learn and practice different routes, under various conditions, and to study ways to get in and out of places. He knew most of the cities that he visited like the back of his hand, so he was able to navigate through his hometown of Richmond much like a professional gambler travels the tables of Atlantic City.

After about thirty minutes, he was sure he had shaken the green Ford Explorer as well as the maroon Impala that had also been tailing him, so finally he started making his way home. Once he got to Sunrise Springs, the neighborhood just before his gated community, he noticed that the first black Ford Taurus was on his ass again, but Des was on his home turf, so he knew he was good.

Des and Yarni lived in Hanover County, in the suburbs. So there were no streetlights spaced every eighteen feet apart, glaring down on everything in their radius like in the city. There was simply pitch-black darkness, except for the nights when the stars were shining, and lucky for Des they weren't out that night. Except for the sound of crickets, silence filled the air. Fortunately for Des, the motor on his $200,000 German-manufactured automobile was quiet, and the crickets concealed what little sound it did emit, allowing Des to kill his headlights and disappear into thin air.

For more than two years, he had been preparing himself, unknowingly, for this very day. For kicks as he cruised home, he would kill his lights and do the last block in total darkness, forcing himself to learn the course. Once he'd mastered the first block, he'd add another block, then another until finally he could make his way through the whole neighborhood in total darkness. After a while, Des grew bored with navigating through his own neighborhood in the darkness; in time, he conquered the three communities before his, never knowing just when what he'd started out doing for fun would come in handy.

Once their garage door opened, Des said to Yarni, who had been silent since the gas station, "They gotta do better than that." He laughed, silently congratulating himself on outsmarting the men following him.

Yarni was not amused. "Des, this shit is serious." Before he could even cut the car off, she was out the passenger side heading toward the door to the house. "You could've been dirty. They could've torn you off. We have a *baby* now. You can't be putting yourself in jeopardy like that. I'm not raising Desi alone, Des. This shit was cute when we were younger, but you're a grown man now. You need to start acting like it."

Yarni stormed into the house with Des hot on her heels as she made her way up the stairs. "Look, baby, chill the fuck out," he said. Des still had a triumphant grin on his face.

"Oh, you think it's funny, huh? I betcha it don't be funny when you in the penitentiary and I'm in the visiting room with your baby girl."

"Would've, could've ain't never got nobody no time," he muttered.

"Oh yeah?" she asked, as she slammed the bathroom door in his face.

Yarni tried to get herself together before going to check on the baby. How could a night that started off so wonderfully end so horribly? She still couldn't believe that they were being followed. Her heart slammed into her rib cage. She placed a hand on her chest, trying to calm herself down. But she couldn't do it. Knowing she needed to get some sleep, she took a Percocet from the bottle she kept hidden in the bathroom and washed it down with water.

After going to check on the baby, she felt much better. The pill made her worries about Des disappear. She knew sleep would be coming soon, but before it overtook her, she decided to finish what she'd started in the car. She found Des in bed flipping through the television channels. She surprised him by silently taking the remote from him, turning off the television, straddling him, and sexing him like he'd never been sexed before.

CHAPTER 15

Welcome Home

WELCOME HOME banners were strung over Yarni· and Des's great room for Lynx's coming-home party.

Although Yarni had tried initially to plan the party herself, the Samuel Johnson case was keeping her busy, so she finally left the plans to her sister, who was one of the most successful event planners in Richmond.

Bambi had outdone herself. The main focal point of the room was a huge portrait of Lynx, posing in front of his new car, courtesy of Des's dealership. Waiters dressed in tuxedoes blanketed the place, serving everyone Dom Perignon as well as crab cakes and chilled shrimp. There were stations set up all around the room where guests could get their fill of appetizers or drinks before the main course was served. Only family was invited to the party, and Bambi wanted nothing but the best for her husband. Music courtesy of a local deejay was blaring in case anyone wanted to take advantage of the small hardwood dance floor with WELCOME HOME, LYNX stenciled in the middle, which Bambi had had constructed in the center of the room just for the party.

The men of the family sat around in the great room for a few minutes before Des gathered them up and invited them to his sanctuary. When they entered the G-room, Des turned on the basketball game, but no one was really watching it because they were shooting the shit.

The G-room belonged solely to Des. It was the only room in the house—the only thing in the world—that Des wouldn't share with Yarni. She had no idea what lay behind those doors. He could have had some other family shacked up in there, and Yarni would have never known it. It was his own sacred place, and no women were allowed past the threshold. There were no exceptions to the rule.

The door required a combination to get in, and Des was the only one who possessed the digital sequence for entry. The place was set up like a loft apartment—if Des didn't want to leave the room, he didn't have to. There was a full-size refrigerator and a bar fully stocked with the best liquor money could buy. The room had been painted a dark brown, and everything a man could want was in there. There were *Playboy* and *Black Gold* magazines, car books, a huge flat-screen television, a collection of DVDs—including every black movie ever made—and a PlayStation 2 and Xbox with every sports game imaginable. There was also a pool table and dartboard at the far end of the room. Several leather Ferrari couches and recliners were scattered throughout the room so Des and his guests could kick back and chill while smoking Cuban cigars. There was also a secret escape door in case things ever got complicated or out of control. Des had planned the room well, and although he had a strict no-women policy, he didn't open his space up to all men—only those in the game.

Lynx walked into the room. "This is some nice ma'fucking furniture."

"My nigga, that's Ferrari furniture," Nasir said, as he calmly handed Lynx a cigar. "Have a smoke."

Lynx smiled, glad to see a brother was shining. "Damn, ma'-fucker, you selling Ferraris and rockin' the furniture in your house to boot. Bro, you are doing big thangs. Can I get a job?"

"I ain't the man you need to see." Des looked Lynx in the eye as he handed him a drink. "Patron and cranberry."

"Patron? What the fuck is Patron?" Lynx had heard a few rappers make reference to the liquor but had never tasted or seen the stuff.

"Tequila." Des grinned.

"I've been gone that long?"

"Pretty much. Time don't stop for no one," Yarni's uncle Stanka said.

Lynx looked around the room. "Look, man, I'm serious about needing a job. I'm trying to eat and feed my family, too. Break bread, my nigga."

"I ain't the nigga to see," Des reiterated.

"If you ain't, you one hell of an illusionist," Lynx joked.

"I'll ask around and see what I can do." He glanced over at Nasir, who had settled into one of the recliners.

Nasir was all ears and had caught the whole conversation, although no one would have been able to tell from the way he was into text messaging Lava, who was downstairs with the other women. "What kind of work you looking for?" Nasir asked, his eyes glued to his T-Mobile Sidekick.

"I can move anything that needs to be moved."

Nasir nodded, and he took a puff of the cigar. There was a knock on the door asking for entry. Des checked his close-circuit monitor and saw Lloyd, Yarni and Bambi's father, standing there. Des buzzed him in.

"O.G.!" Excitedly, Nasir stood and embraced Lloyd. "What you know good?"

"Nothing, man," Lloyd said, taking a seat on one of the sofas. "I just came to hang out with my family, see what's up with you cats."

Des handed him a glass of Patron, which he readily accepted. Lloyd took a sip and lifted his glass, nodding. "This is some good shit."

Des nodded in return. Each man in the room had a drink in his hand. "I'd like to propose a toast," Des said, after getting everyone's attention. "To my man, Lynx. We're glad you're back home, and we're looking forward to spending more time in the G-room."

"Why do you call it that?" Lynx asked.

" 'Cause I'm a gangsta, baby. You ain't know? And this is the gangsta's room," Des said, before lifting his drink in the air. "Cheers, man."

$ $ $

Yarni went upstairs to get the new photos of the baby to share with the family. As she was searching for them, a noise behind her startled her, and she swung around.

"You scared me," she said to her sister, her heart almost skipping a beat.

"Sorry, sis, but I didn't want to give this to you in front of everyone. I've been so busy today, I didn't have a chance to do it earlier." Bambi handed her a piece of paper. "Here's the info."

"Thanks, sis." Yarni took the paper from her. "What do I owe you?"

"Chile, please. I gave my DMV girl fifty dollars and kept moving after assuring her I'd have some more work for her."

"Damn, I really missed out having a sister when I was growing up, huh?" Yarni said wistfully as she hugged her sister. She hadn't found out that Bambi even existed until a few years ago. The sisters had been trying to make up for lost time ever since.

"Shit. Me, too."

Yarni turned around again to look for the pictures. Once she located them, she looked at Bambi and smiled. "You okay?" she asked, looking at her sister, who was watching her strangely.

"I'm fine. Are you okay?"

Yarni smoothed down her hair and gave her sister a weak smile. "Yeah, I'm fine. Why do you ask?" she said nervously, hoping it wasn't evident that she had taken a pill seconds before Bambi walked in.

Bambi shrugged. "No reason. I know you've got a lot going on lately. I just want to make sure you know I'm here for you."

Yarni looked relieved. She gave her sister another hug. "I know that, but thanks for saying it. Come on. Let's go feed these folks. Even with all the appetizers, you know they're probably hungry by now."

The food was set up like a scene from the movie *Soul Food.* Bambi's mother, Tricia, was a gourmet chef who owned seven restaurants. She had come in that morning to prepare all the food as a favor to Bambi and Yarni, and was planning to fly back out that evening.

Yarni had tried to convince Bambi to serve filet mignon and

several other high-class dishes, but Bambi wouldn't hear of it. She insisted soul food was Lynx's favorite, and she had everything imaginable on the table—fried chicken, ham, collard greens, macaroni and cheese, black-eyed peas, corn bread, and more. Yarni knew there would be plenty of leftovers. Even if everyone had seconds or thirds, there was enough food to feed her entire gated community.

Lynx's brother Cleezy had arrived, showing off his wife, Mercy, in her new fuchsia dress, so now the party was complete. Yarni had never met Mercy before, but she had seen the movies based on the screenplays that Mercy had written so she felt like she knew her. Yarni gave her a big hug and introduced her to Lava, who had suddenly gotten shy, but Mercy put her right at ease and said that Lava ought to be in her next movie with that beautiful hair and skin of hers.

It was a perfect party, Yarni thought, a nice break from the stress of working on Sam's case and worrying about Des's case. The pill was starting to kick in, and nothing was going to ruin her night.

Before they started eating, Lynx stood to make a toast.

"Everyone got glasses? Here's to family and friends and good times and to not a single ma'fucker in here ever going back to the ma'fuckin' penitentiary," Lynx said, and clinked glasses with Des.

Des said, "I'll drink to dat," and took a huge gulp, causing everyone to laugh.

The lights went out for a moment, then came right back on. Des went to make sure that the alarm and the other electronic household devices hadn't been disarmed. He had taken only a few steps when someone banged on the door three times. It took him a second to recognize the noise since the music was still blaring. He went to the door and looked out the peephole as someone banged again. He hurried back to the dining room.

"Yo, it's the police," Des said loud enough for everyone to hear him. "Flush anything that ain't right and take the kids upstairs."

Tricia grabbed Desi while Lava grabbed Nya, Bambi, and Lynx's daughter, and they hurried to the nursery.

When the house was kosher, Des sent Yarni to open up the door. She heard the police officers trying to get through the steel door, and when she opened it, she took them by surprise. "What happened to using the doorbell? Is it broke?" she asked with an attitude.

"We have a search warrant for these premises," said a tall female officer, who was standing beside Detective Columbo.

"For what, and where is your search warrant?"

The officer behind Detective Columbo handed him the papers, and he presented them to Yarni as he pushed his way in through the door and the other cops stormed past him.

"Everybody on the ground; everybody on the motherfucking ground," Detective Columbo yelled, as more officers swarmed in with their guns drawn.

"Let's round these gangsters up, boys," the detective said.

"Just follow orders and nobody gets hurt," another officer said, as he watched over the fellas as they lay on the floor.

"Isn't life good?" Detective Columbo said, walking into the dining room, where everyone was congregated. "You got the infamous Lynx and the Mrs." He smiled at Bambi. "So nice to see you again. And little brother, Conrad, what are you going by these days? C-Note or Cleezy?"

He made eye contact with Mercy. "How was your flight in? By the way, I saw that last movie. I liked the first one better." She rolled her eyes at him.

"And the up-and-coming young Nasir Taylor. No, we haven't had the chance to meet. However, I know your whole family, and I know we'll be getting acquainted soon."

"Suck a dick, cocksucka," Nasir responded.

"Don't let that pig get you to entertain that swine he talking. That shit-eatin' muthafucka ain't shit and ain't gon' ever be shit," Des told his nephew.

Detective Columbo chuckled and said to Nasir, "You, too, will know me before it's all over." Then he turned his attention to Bambi and Yarni's father, Lloyd "Slot Machine" Pitman. Acting like a groupie who had just met his favorite rock star, he clutched his heart. "Sir, you inspire me so much. Why, you are the very reason I became a police officer."

Yarni read over the warrant and headed over to Detective Columbo. "Can I talk to you for a second?" She didn't wait for an answer as she walked into the hall. Detective Columbo followed a few seconds behind.

"You're here to look for evidence for a murder case, not to arrest anybody," Yarni reminded the overweight cop.

"If anybody gets out of line, they will be taken to jail or shot."

"Listen," she said, leaning toward him, "I know like you know, you don't want that. The department and the mayor don't want that. The mayor is up for reelection, and the police chief doesn't want a lawsuit, so we're all going to act like we've got good sense. I know you have a job to do, just like I have one." Yarni tried to maintain her cool.

"Well," Detective Columbo sneered, "hand over the evidence, then."

"There is none because my husband is an innocent man."

"Oh, I don't believe that," Detective Columbo said, pulling out his handcuffs and smiling.

"Look, no one here is going to do anything stupid, so there's really no need for any handcuffs."

"Bull-motherfucking-shit. I got known assassins and gangsters here. I've got to make sure my officers are safe at all times." He gave her a fake smile. "Now let me do my goddamn job before I give you an obstruction of justice charge."

"You do your job, but you better inform your boys not to go into my office, the third door on the right upstairs. It's off-limits because of attorney-client privilege."

He laughed.

"I'm an attorney. Do *not* go into my office. I have privileged information in there, so don't mess with anything in that room. I mean it. Nothing—not my computer or my files. Not a damn thing."

"I'll think about it."

"If you violate any privileged information, I'll have a judge on the phone so fast to quash your search warrant, your head will spin." She turned to walk away and swung back around, getting angrier by the second. "Don't fuck with me."

"Your idle threats don't scare me," he said with a chuckle.

"Laugh now, cry later. From what I hear, you spend a lot of time crying over spilled milk," Yarni said, referring to his past failed attempt to incarcerate her. Then she turned and walked back into the dining room with the others.

Everyone tried to get back to the celebration while the police searched the house, but no one was in the mood. They sat at the table, picking at their food, making small talk, until finally Detective Columbo and his boys came back downstairs, empty-handed. Another waste of the city's money.

CHAPTER 16

Fighting Back

Yarni and Marvin were in her office, getting their game plan together for the Samuel Johnson case. When they finally took a break, Yarni was surprised at how late it was. It was well past eight o'clock. She called Des but was unable to get in touch with him. She called to check on the baby, and Joyce told her Desi was already asleep.

She plopped back into her office chair, exhausted. As though reading her mind, Marvin went to his briefcase and pulled out two glasses and a bottle of vintage Bordeaux. She definitely could use a drink, but she quickly decided against it. The case was turning out to be more challenging than she'd originally thought. Samuel didn't have an alibi, and to top it off there was a witness who stated that he'd seen Samuel pull the trigger.

"Since we didn't get to celebrate how well the preliminary hearing went, I thought I'd bring this," Marvin said, flashing a smile.

"Oh, that's nice," she said tiredly.

"Yes, a 1949 Chateau Gruaud-Larose. This has been in my family for years, but you're the only person with whom I've ever wanted to share it."

"You didn't have to do that for me," Yarni said, blushing in spite of herself.

"It's for a great cause, so I hope you won't let me drink alone."

Yarni had taken a Percocet earlier that day. Desi had been crying, and because Yarni had felt a slight migraine coming on and she knew it was going to be a long day at the office, she'd needed something to help her relax. She knew good and well that she should decline because the wine wouldn't mix well with the pill; however, she also knew Marvin was still a little disappointed that she hadn't gone to dinner with him. Against her better judgment, she appeased her colleague and accepted a glass.

"To our first battle together and many great things for us to come," he toasted. They clinked glasses, and, as Yarni took a sip of her drink, he stared at her for a few moments and smiled.

"Cheers," she said, to break the uncomfortable silence, then took another sip of the drink. She stood and walked back over to the mahogany coffee table where they'd been working, sat on the leather sofa, and started to focus again on the papers scattered all over the table.

He walked over and sat beside her and stared at her again. She wasn't sure if the pills were making her paranoid, but it felt as though he was undressing her with his eyes.

"Let's get a game plan going. I want to make sure that the trial goes our way. If there's one thing I'm good at, it's cross-examination. What do you know about this witness?" she said, fighting the urge to shudder and trying to get things back on track.

His eyes scanned her body like a bar code as he took a sip from his glass. "What else are you good at?" he asked, looking her dead in the eyes.

"I think we're getting off the subject matter, Mr. Sledge," she said, trying to keep their conversation professional.

"I agree."

"Listen, if we are going to win this case, we've got to get this strategy down to a T." Yarni picked up some papers and pretended to read through them.

He removed them from her hands and moved closer, stealing a peep down her shirt. "Oh, you like to go down, huh?" He looked at her with a smirk on his face.

Yarni couldn't believe the stupid shit he was saying. She tried to ignore the comment but found herself getting annoyed. "Look, you know Miles is the prosecutor, and from what I gather, he turns cases like this into witch hunts."

"Look, I got this here. Don't worry." He moved in even closer to her, and ran his finger across her knee. "I can eat Miles and that dumb assistant of his for lunch. You're playing in my playground, so don't worry your pretty head about that." He moved his finger up her thigh, getting close to where it didn't belong.

Yarni pushed his hand away, abruptly rose from the sofa and moved to look out the window, trying to ignore his vulgar behavior. "That's all fine and well, but we still have to be prepared."

"You know my reputation. I'm the best at this. That's why you got me on this team." He walked over to her and leaned in to whisper, "You want to win," then he blew in her ear.

Yarni pulled away, took a step back, put her hand up, and firmly said, "Don't do that." She wanted to say more but being so relaxed under the influence of the pills and the wine, she just dropped it. They were interrupted by a knock at the door. It was a courier bringing a file for which Marvin had been waiting. He tipped the guy and quickly sent him on his way, then focused his attention back on Yarni.

"I apologize. I know I was a bit out of line, maybe just a little beside myself. I promise it won't happen again."

"A little?" Her first instinct was to kick his butt out right then and there, but instead she cleared her throat. "Look, are you ready to get down to business?"

"Yes, let's," he said as he held up the file. "This is going to be our ace in the hole. Here's the info that I was waiting for. We're going to win because of this alone." He gave off a cocky chuckle.

"Great! What is it?"

"Don't worry about it. I'll present it at trial. You know I like to win." He sat beside Yarni and placed it in front of her. Before she could reach for it he said, "For the record, everything I set out to conquer, I do. You know Marvin always gets what he wants." He placed his hand on her leg again.

"Marvin, listen," she said, the expression on her face matching the coldness in her voice. "I'm a married woman, and I love my husband."

"Yes, but the bigger question is, Does your husband love you? We've been here what"—he shrugged—"a good three hours. You're working late, and he hasn't called to check on his wife, even though you've called to check on him. Where is he? At home with your newborn baby? Oh no, he isn't, because you just spoke with your mother-in-law to see how the baby's doing."

"That's none of your business," Yarni tried to say sternly, but she choked on the words. Lately Des hadn't been around, and hearing Marvin question Des's love for her forced her to face the truth.

"You know I can have *any* woman I want—shoot, women throw themselves at me all day long. But guess what?" he said. "I choose you."

"As I said, I'm happily married." She looked into his eyes so that there would be no misunderstanding about what she was saying. "I am here to work and discuss business, not talk about my personal life."

"I've never understood women like you," he said, shaking his head and chuckling.

Yarni stood. "I think the wine and the long hours are really getting to you."

Marvin got up and cornered her between the sofa and the coffee table. "I've never understood women like you," he repeated, his voice taking on a steely edge. "You don't want a good black man, you want an ex-con hooligan masquerading as a businessman."

"This work session is over. I'm leaving," she said, attempting to walk around him.

Marvin wasn't having it, though. "No, you're not." He pushed her down on the sofa, almost tipping the coffee table over. "You don't leave until I say so," he yelled.

He delivered a backhand to Yarni's face that knocked off her earring and left a handprint on her cheek. She was stunned. She had never been hit by a man before, so she definitely wasn't prepared for the next punch that landed on her left eye. Yarni held her eye and bent over in shock. Marvin took advantage of her position to try to push her onto her back and get on top of her, but she managed to kick him hard. The kick accomplished one thing: It pissed him off, and he revved back and released another violent blow to her already bruised face. Before she knew, he was on top of her.

"No, no, stop, Marvin!" she screamed, trying her best to fight him off.

"Stop really means go," he whispered, ignoring her blows and kissing her on her neck.

At what point did shit go haywire and take such a drastic turn? She couldn't believe that this supposedly well-respected lawyer was attacking her in her own office. She had defended murderers, extortionists, and drug dealers who had treated her with more respect. Briefly, Yarni considered lying there and surrendering. Marvin was so much stronger than she was. But then the hustler's wife in her came out. She had picked up a thing or two from Des over the years, and one of them was not to take shit from anyone. She and Marvin were not two consenting adults, and he was not going to make her do anything she didn't want to do. This was no time to play the blame game. The plan was simple: She was going to defend herself or die trying.

She took a deep breath and tried with all her might to push him off her. However, Marvin weighed over two hundred pounds and had her pinned down tight. She couldn't stop him or move him, but she didn't lose hope. Yarni kept hitting him on the back, but it didn't seem to affect him as he tore at her clothing. She reached up and started pulling on his chain and scratching him on the neck, but he kept at it. She was about to be taken. He was getting closer to winning, but right before the victory, she latched her teeth onto his earlobe and bit down as hard as she could. With one swift twist, she tore off a small chuck of his ear.

Stunned, he sat up and screamed, "Bitch!" He responded with another vicious slap in the face. "Keep it up, bitch," he said, punching her again. "Comply now and complain later. The more you fight, the harder you make it on yourself."

Yarni stopped fighting, which he took as a sign of surrender. She was exhausted, and the Percocet was slowing her reaction time.

"That's right, fucking relax. Relax," he said in a whisper as he hovered over her, preparing to finish what he had started. "Relax."

She lay there for a second, pretending she was going to give in, but all the while picturing Des's and her baby girl's faces. That image brought about strength she didn't know she had. She spread her legs and bent her knees to give Marvin access.

"Yeah, that's what I'm talking about," Marvin said, standing up slightly and looking down to undo his pants.

In that brief second, Yarni took off one of her Manolo Blahnik pumps, pulled back, and swung, using the shoe like a four-inch spear and striking Marvin in his head. "Get da fuck off me, motherfucker!" she screamed, breathing hard from the exertion. She gathered her strength and continued attacking him.

The continuous streams of blows rattled him, and they kept coming. He fell sideways and threw up his hands, trying to protect his head. That was the break she needed; finally she was able to push him off her. She got up and tried to run, but he grabbed her by the ankle, trying to drag her back to him, but he lost his grip.

"Where you going, bitch?" he screamed, blood running down his face. He stood and chased her around the room. When he caught her, he hit her a few times, almost knocking her out cold.

Seeing Yarni's blood made him hesitate slightly, and Yarni took advantage of it by hitting him with the CD player that she grabbed from a bookshelf near her desk. Yarni then pulled out the chrome-plated duce-duce revolver Des insisted she keep in her desk. "Get da fuck out before I kill you, motherfucker," she said, cocking the small pistol as tears rolled down her face.

Marvin looked at her, and it finally dawned on him that she meant business.

He held his head to keep the blood from gushing out as he grabbed his files and briefcase. He dropped his head and walked out, defeated, like a predatory wolf caught in a snare.

Yarni was so frightened and upset, she didn't think to call security or the police. Still crying, she reached for the phone to call Des. He picked up on the first ring.

Thank God, she thought.

"Baby, let me call you right back. I'm in the middle of something," he said, trying to rush her off the phone.

"But—"

"I'ma hit you back, Momma."

"I need you, though."

"After this I'll be on my way home. I'll meet you there. Love you." He hung up before she could say another word.

$$ \$\$\$ $$

Later that night, when Des arrived home, he made his way quietly up the stairs and entered the bedroom. He smiled as he looked at his wife under the covers sound sleep. He took off his clothes, threw them on the chair, and got in the bed with Yarni, snuggling up against her back. It had been a long day, and he was glad finally to be home where he belonged. He kissed Yarni's back, sensing she was awake, but she didn't budge. He tried to cuddle up against her a bit more, but there was no response. He could tell something was wrong, but he figured she was just angry that he'd come in so late. He knew that she had to be pissed off because he had been burning the midnight oil a little bit too frequently lately.

"Don't be like that, baby," he said. He wrapped his arms around her and placed another kiss on her neck. He frowned when she pulled away from him.

Her voice was cold like a dagger and twice as sharp. "You can go back to where you came from. I don't need you now."

"I know you ain't trippin' because of the phone call," he said, sitting up, trying to look at her face.

"It's deeper than a motherfucking phone call," she said, refusing to look at him.

Des was confused by her reaction, but then again she had been running hot and cold lately. "I know you ain't jealous, baby."

"I ain't worried about no bitches," she said, sniffling.

Her tears touched him as they always did. "Then, what is it? Is it that I'm back in the streets? Is it the late nights?" Des tried to get her to look at him, but she refused.

"For ten motherfucking years, while other bitches was sliding up and down poles, chasing behind niggas with the biggest knot in they pockets and God knows what else, *I* was on the highway en route to the penitentiary visiting yo' black ass. I thought what we had was solid." She shook her head and took a deep breath. "I take your carefree and reckless ways without question. I pick up the slack with our daughter when you're out running the streets. The *one* night I need you, I mean when I *really* need you . . ." she sighed.

Puzzled, he reached to turn on the light. "Baby, tell me. What are you talking about?" He saw the blanket rise and fall from her heavy sobs. He tried to hold her once again, but she wouldn't let him.

"You're never there when I need you anymore." Slowly, she tried to turn to face him, but her body ached all over, and she grimaced from the pain. "I know you love me, but I feel . . ." She sniffled again before continuing. "I feel like you're married to the streets."

"What? That's bullshit. Why would you even say that?" he said. "You're everything to me. You're the frame to my picture."

Yarni finally turned toward him. Des was shocked by his wife's battered appearance. "Yeah, well take a look at this picture," she said angrily. "Do you like what you see?"

"Who did this?" he whispered. He couldn't believe what his eyes had revealed to him. Both anger and guilt consumed him at the same time. He reached out to touch her face gently, but she moved away from him. "What happened?" He shook his head. "Better yet, who the fuck did this shit to you?" He jumped out of the bed and reached for his pants.

"It's not important now," Yarni said sadly.

"It's not important? Baby, I raise my hand to Allah, I'm going to kill the motherfucker who did this!" Des exploded. He went to his secret hiding place in their walk-in closet and returned with his gun, then checked to make sure it was loaded.

"That's how I wanted you to react six hours ago when I called you, but you was too busy handling what you thought you needed to handle. Don't worry about it now." Yarni turned so her back was once again to Des.

Des was inundated with guilt. He put the gun on the chair and walked around the bed so he was facing her. He touched her face gently. Tears filled his eyes. "I'm so sorry, baby. I'm sorry I wasn't there for you." He took a deep breath, trying to control the rage growing within him. "But I'm here now, and you got my undivided attention. I want to know who did this to you," he said as calmly as he could.

She closed her swollen eyes. "I had six hours to think this over, and it really doesn't matter who did this to me since I was partly to blame," she said quietly.

"What you mean, you were partly to blame? I don't give a damn if it was all your fault. Yarni, just tell me who did this shit." His voice grew louder as his anger soared.

"See, that's what I am talking about right there. You never listen to me anymore. You want to kill niggas and ask questions later. Why don't you try listening and paying attention to what's going on around you for once?"

"What are you talking about?" Despite his rage, Des looked at his wife, confusion all over his face.

"If you'd been paying attention to me, you would have noticed that I've been popping pills as if I've lost my mind."

"What pills?"

"It doesn't matter. I dumped them all out."

He was baffled and asked her again, "What pills?"

She took a heart-wrenching deep breath. "When I had Desi, the doctor gave me Percocet for my pain after the cesarean." He nodded in understanding and she continued. "I never really took them because they made me feel drowsy and put me to sleep. But I still kept them in the cabinet just in case. Once I had to go back to work and you started keeping late nights, things just got crazy." Des stared at her in amazement, finally starting to comprehend what she was saying to him. "I knew I had to be on point at work, but I couldn't get to sleep. It started out with me taking a Percocet to help me fall asleep."

"What?" he said, shocked for the second time that night. He considered himself an expert on human behavior, spending many years studying people in the streets and in the penitentiary. He was ashamed that he hadn't noticed that the person closest to him was abusing pills and calling out for his help.

"I'm sorry." The tears trickled down her face as she looked up at him.

He took her in his arms, and she tensed up from the pain, so he loosened his grip a little but refused to let go. "Baby, don't worry. We're going to work through this. You're going to be okay, I promise."

As he held her, he tried to analyze the situation. He thought about Yarni's mood swings, her snapping at him—in hindsight the signs had all been there.

Tears formed in Des's eyes once again as he pulled Yarni in closer. On the streets, if he misread an action or situation, the consequences could be fatal, costing him his life—or his freedom—but if he lost his wife, what was the point to living anyway?

Des swore on everything he loved, if it cost every dollar he made for the rest of his life, he was going to find out who had done this to his wife. And when he did, may God have mercy on that person's soul, because *Des* sure wasn't going to have any.

CHAPTER 17

Slipping

"Uncle Des, I'm 'bout to go to the gentlemen's club for that appointment I told you about, and I got a bad feeling. You feel like rolling with me? Lava's sick with a stomach virus," Nasir explained to Des.

"I can't make it either. I need to spend some time with Yarni. We've got a little situation I need to deal with." Des hated to have to turn Nasir down, but his wife would have to come before anything and anybody from now on. "Yarni is sick herself," Des told Nasir.

"She okay?" his nephew asked with concern.

"Yeah, she'll be okay," Des responded. "Listen, if you got a bad feeling, then don't go."

"Naw, I'm good," Nasir assured his uncle, who could hear Lava getting sick in the background. "I gotta go. Lava's throwing up." He ended the call and rushed to Lava's side. "Here, baby."

He gave her a paper towel to wipe her mouth. Then he helped her get back into bed.

"Baby, don't go. Wait until tomorrow so I can go with you," Lava said weakly.

"It's a seventy-five-thousand-dollar sale, and I ain't trying to let that slip through my hands," Nasir said, brushing her hair off her forehead.

"Boo, it'll be there tomorrow."

"But I gave the nigga my word. I'ma be in and outta there, I promise." Nasir pulled the covers over Lava. "Now get some rest. I'll be back before you know it." He grabbed his keys. "I'll call you when I get in the car," he said to Lava as he was about to exit the condo.

"Wait, I'm going with you," Lava said, trying to throw the covers off.

Nasir stormed back over to the bed. "No, you're not. You need to stay in bed and rest. Baby, why you trippin'? I'll be fine. You need me to bring you anything back?" he asked.

Lava shook her head and leaned back against the fluffy pillows of their king-size bed.

After making sure she was comfortable, Nasir headed to the door again.

"Didn't you forget something?" she asked, struggling to sit up.

Nasir patted himself. "Nah, I'm cool. I got my piece."

"I meant my kiss," she said, puckering her lips.

Nasir grinned sheepishly. "Sorry," he said, hurrying back over to the bed and pecking her on the forehead. "Get some rest. I'll see you in a few. . . ."

Lava nodded and lay back down. "I love you," she said softly.

"I love you, too, baby," he said looking at her before he left their home.

$$\$ \$ \$$$

Redd's Gentlemen's Club wasn't packed, but there was still a nice-size group in there. Almost naked women strutted around the club on the hunt for a big spender. Maybe it was the bubbly or the bling, but either way the money was definitely in the place. Some dudes stood by the stage throwing money like it was blowing from a fan while the women onstage tried to fulfill their every sexual fantasy.

There was a break in a song, and a new girl took the stage just as Nasir entered the club. As soon as he came through the door, it seemed like all eyes were on him. He was now known throughout town as a major player in the game, and the girls hoped he was there to trick some money off, so they ran over to him, practically swarming him. A Naomi Campbell look-alike, right down to her long weave, locked eyes with him. She would have to get in line with about six other strippers trying to lock him down for the night. Nasir waved them off and headed off to get a private VIP room in which to handle his business. The girls all hoped that one of them would be his choice for the night.

Bam-Bam walked up to Nasir before he could make it to one of the private rooms. "What brings you to these parts, partna?" He gave Nasir a brotherly hug.

"What else? Bitches," Nasir lied. He turned to walk away, not wanting to be bothered with Bam-Bam. He had outgrown his connect a long time ago and was not about to walk down memory lane.

"I feel that. Why don't you let me hit you off with Twinkle?"

Bam-Bam said, motioning to a big-booty girl wearing a hot pink G-string.

"Naw, man, I'm good."

"You sho?" Bam-Bam asked. His attitude toward Nasir had changed. He was more humble since the tables had turned and Nasir was the new man in charge. Now Bam-Bam was buying from Nasir.

"I'ma holla before I leave," Nasir said, dismissing him.

"No doubt. We still meeting tomorrow, right?" Bam-Bam asked eagerly.

"Yeah, just call me," Nasir said, waving him off like he was an annoying mosquito.

Bam-Bam extended his hand to give Nasir a pound. Nasir shook his head and laughed before returning the gesture. It was so funny how much things could change with time.

The private VIP room was small. One wall featured a two-way glass so that the people inside could see out but no one could see in. The three other walls had been painted black, and the furniture in the room was hot pink, black, and white snakeskin. There was a black coffee table with a few glasses and an empty ice bucket for champagne. Nasir placed his bag on the table, leaned back, and called Lava to check on her and let her know what was up.

"I just called dude, and he say he out in the parking lot, so I'm cool," he said. Even though Lava wasn't saying much, just knowing she was on the other end of the phone made him feel better.

He was startled when the door opened and in walked a big-booty stripper. Nasir looked her up and down and said, "Wrong room," before returning to his conversation.

"No, it's compliments of the lady sitting at the bar," the woman said, standing so her butt was in Nasir's face.

"No thanks, baby. I'm cool," he said, trying to figure out what lady she was talking about. He shrugged and focused again on his conversation with Lava.

"But she already paid me," the stripper said, refusing to take no for an answer. She proceeded to try to remove her top, but Nasir stopped her.

"Here you go." He reached in his pocket and peeled off a fifty-dollar bill.

"Thank you." She stuffed the money in her garter and smiled. "You a'ight wit' me," she said, adjusting the top of her outfit before she left the room.

"Baby, why you ain't let her give you no lap dance?" Lava asked.

"Because I don't want no sweaty bitch all on me. Why would I want her when I got someone like you at home?"

"That's what's up," she said, smiling on the other end of the call.

They kicked it for a minute, then the door opened again. It was the Naomi Campbell look-alike.

"Thanks, baby," Nasir said, figuring she was the one who sent the stripper. It happened all the time in strip clubs. Nice-looking women would send in strippers before they approached men they were interested in.

"For what?" the woman asked curiously.

"Sending me the dance."

"But you didn't enjoy it?" she teased, batting her eyelashes.

"I'm just not really into strippers like that. I'm just here to meet my man."

"So can we hook up later?"

"Naw. I don't think so. I got a girl at home," he said. "Ain't that right, boo?" he said into his Bluetooth headset. "Thanks anyway." He returned to his conversation, imagining Lava was probably on the other side of the phone listening with a smile on her face.

"Too bad your girl ain't got a man at home," the woman said.

"What?" Nasir said, looking at her in confusion.

Instead of responding, the woman went into her bag, and, with the dexterity and swiftness of David Copperfield performing at the MGM, she pulled out a small banger with a silencer screwed on the end of it and fired eight times. Nasir sat there in shock. He had been taken down by a bitch and had never seen it coming.

"Oh shit. Baby, she got me," he said as his chest started burning.

"What?" Lava said, not following the conversation.

"I've been hit," Nasir said, gasping for breath.

"Nasir?" Lava said. "Nasir!" she screamed when he didn't respond.

The mysterious lady left the room as smoothly as she entered and headed to the unisex bathroom. She tossed her wig in the trash, changed her contact lenses and blouse, and mixed into the crowd as Nasir lay on the sofa slumped over, bleeding.

"Nasir!" Lava screamed through the phone. "Hold on," she reached for the house phone and called 911. "Please send an ambulance to Redd's Gentlemen's Club on Jahnke Road. Baby, are you there?" she said into her cell phone, but Nasir didn't answer.

"Nasir, baby," she cried out. "Baby, please, please answer me!" There was no response, but she could still hear the music in the background.

"Ma'am, are you at the club?" the 911 operator said.

"No, no, I'm not!" she screamed. "I was on the phone with my boyfriend, and someone shot him."

"Do you know who shot him?"

"No, but I need you to stop asking me all these fucking questions and get an ambulance over to that club."

"Ma'am, help is on the way. Are you still on the phone with him?"

"Yes, but he's not responding," she said before yelling into her cell phone again. "Nasir, baby, please, please, hold on, baby." The phone went dead.

"Nooooo, noooo!" Lava screamed.

"Ma'am, what's happening? Talk to me."

"Please, please just get someone over there." Lava hung up and slipped some jeans and a shirt on over her pajama tank top, grabbed her keys, and was out the door.

$$\$\$\$$$

Lava sat patiently glued to Nasir's bedside, silently praying, begging God not to take the only man she had ever loved away from her. *Lord, please spare him.*

"Lava," Nasir said, his voice barely a whisper. At first, she didn't hear it. Then there it was again. "Lava."

Her eyes opened. Indeed God was responding to her prayer, "I'm here, baby," Lava said, grabbing his hand. "I'm right here." She looked up for a brief second, thanking God.

Nasir's breathing was imperceptible, almost nonexistent. But he knew he had to stay alive a little longer. He opened his eyes, and a smile became visible on his face. "Love . . . you . . ."

"I love you, too, Nasir," Lava responded, tears running down her face. She was happy that he was at least talking and that he knew she was there for him. "God only knows how much I love you. I knew you would never leave me." Lava waited a few moments for Nasir to speak again. Besides the humming from all of the machines that were connected to him, the room was as quiet as a monastery. "Nasir," she called out to him.

There was no answer.

"Baby, please, stay with me," Lava begged. "I know I sound so selfish right now, but I can't live without you. Please, please, don't leave me. I love you so much."

Still no answer.

Then she heard him speak again. His voice even softer than before. "Where's Des?"

"He's on his way here," Lava answered, wiping away her tears. "He told me to tell you that 'erything will be all right. He said just stay with us, baby, and he'll take care of it all. Uncle Des is gonna make it all right again, baby. He's on his way."

Des was with Yarni when he got the call from Lava that Nasir had been shot. Hearing the news felt like someone had punched a hole in Des's chest and pulled his heart out with his bare hands. If Des had been there for Nasir when he'd been growing up, maybe he could have guided him toward another lifestyle before the streets infiltrated his veins. If only he'd never given Nasir his blessing to expand . . .

"It was a bitch." Nasir's voice was now barely audible. "Professional . . . hit." He labored. "I shoulda . . . peeped it."

"Who did this to you, baby?" Lava asked. "Tell me who did this to you."

He tried to put his hands up to shut her up; she understood and was now quiet. He closed his eyes and opened them quickly. "I love you."

"I love you, too." She wasn't strong enough to control her

tears, not even for Nasir. She could feel his pain in the depths of her stomach.

He took two ragged breaths before he began again, "A lotta niggas . . ."—his voice caught—"schemin'." There was a pause, then he continued. "Always . . . schemin'." Nasir took another twisted breath. "Most . . . frontin' some . . . real." He then closed his eyes.

"Nasir!" Lava screamed. "Naaaasir!"

Nasir managed to open his eyes one last time. "Trust . . . your . . . instincts . . ."

Eulogy

Des sat in the limo outside the funeral home, shaking his head in disbelief as he waited for the family to go inside for his nephew's funeral. Nasir's death still felt unreal to him. Yarni sat beside him, holding his hand.

Nasir's mother, Emma, was screaming and hollering, "*Noooo oooo!* Why my baby, Lord? I don't understand. Take me, Jesus." She got out of the limo and ran around outside, screaming and yelling and putting on a show like her only son was everything to her. She had kicked him out of the house when he was sixteen after her boyfriend, whom she had met when he was in jail, was released and came to live with her. Ever since then, Nasir had practically been on his own, forced to become a man and deal with grown-up situations before his time.

Joyce sat in the limo, rolling her eyes in disbelief as a few family members put Emma back in the car. "Now, you know she should be ashamed of herself," Joyce said loud enough for Emma to hear her. "She needs to sit her ass down. She ain't do nothing for that boy when he was alive, and now she wants to act a fool 'cause he's dead."

"He was my son," Emma snapped.

"Well, you should've been a mother while he was here; he don't need you now," Joyce returned fire.

For once, Yarni agreed with Joyce.

"Don't start with me, Joyce," Emma said, pointing at her ex-mother-in-law.

Joyce, who as usual was mean as a snake, pointed right back at her. "Don't you start with me, Emma. I don't care if we are at the funeral. I can act a fool, too."

"Ladies, ladies," Des pleaded.

"It's sad that she picks now to feel guilty," Joyce said, as always having to get in the last word.

"How you holding up?" Yarni asked Lava as the funeral director came over to the car to let them know it was time to go in.

She nodded to indicate she was doing fine, although tears rolled from under her black Chanel sunglasses. Yarni felt so bad for the girl. She didn't want ever to imagine being in her place.

The funeral home was packed inside and out. People were crammed in the chapel like groupies at a rap concert as the family walked in to take their last view of Nasir, resting in front of the chapel. Des had to look at him a couple of times to make sure he wasn't breathing. He kept expecting his nephew to get up any second and greet him with a smile and a pound.

When Lava saw Nasir lying there, her cries roared out. She reached to touch his hand and to kiss him, then she laid her head on his chest and sobbed, "I love you so much." It took three people to pry her away from Nasir.

As Lava was seated, Emma approached the casket and began crying out, "Lord Jesus, why my baby? Take me, Lord. Take me." She threw herself across the casket, wailing and screaming, before trying to climb inside, almost knocking it over. When the ushers finally were able to pull her away, her black hat was cocked at an outrageous angle and looked like it would fall off at any second, but it never did.

Joyce shook her head in disgust, and Des touched his mother's leg, silently warning her not to make a scene.

After the choir sang and the bio had been read, the preacher got up and took his place at the podium to give the eulogy.

Although he was grieving, Des couldn't help but notice how sharply dressed the preacher was. He had on what looked like an expensive custom-made suit and more bling than the whole left side of the funeral home.

The preacher began, "In the death of Nasir, we have lost a son, a brother, a friend, a lover, and an example of how to be genuine in life. Nasir did not invent anything about himself; he was the real thing. He was direct, brilliant, sometimes cranky, but generous and loyal. Nasir showed us that we must speak, live, and defend our individual truths with who we are, not just with what we do. He was an example to those of us struggling to truly breathe freely in our own skins and leave this often dark and harsh world a bit better than we found it."

Des looked at the man in disbelief and laughed inwardly in spite of himself. This dude didn't even know his nephew—Emma had insisted they get him to speak at the funeral because he was so well known in the community—but he was talking like they were the best of friends.

"In all his years, at one time or another, he encouraged, enraged, or served all of us. In some way he nurtured and defended our existence by keeping it real through thick and thin. He taught us that faithfulness and loyalty would open doors for us in this life that no amount of money could." The preacher raised his voice, "Hallelujah . . . I praise God for him." The minister used his handkerchief to wipe the sweat from his pudgy face before taking a sip of water. "Nasir played fair all the way across the board. He understood what life is all about. It's all about love. He showed his love by opening up doors for himself to change his world. And once he went through those doors, he didn't close them behind him. He put himself in the doorjamb, using his life to keep the doors open so others might walk through—so you and I might walk through." The minister took a deep breath and looked out over the crowd, as though gathering his thoughts. "In order for us to breathe life and change into a world that desperately needs it, we must make a difference. The Bible says in Isaiah 41:10: 'So do not fear, for I am with you; do not be dismayed for I am your God. I will strengthen you and help you; I will uphold you with my righteous right hand.' May you find strength in knowing that Nasir has gone on to a better place and that his living has not been in vain."

"Oh, Lord . . . nooo, my son. God knows I loved him!" Emma screamed, and Lava began to sob again. Des felt himself welling up, although he was not moved by the preacher's words. He believed Nasir's death was his fault. If he had only done things differently . . . If he had gone with Nasir that night . . . If he had never given his blessings over Nasir's enterprise . . .

The preacher continued. "When I was called to do this eulogy, I wrote something out, but you know what, Church? I see a lot of folks in here, and my spirit is telling me to shoot from the hip." He walked from behind the podium, and Des watched in amazement as the congregation began egging him on.

"Yes." Someone on the left side of the church stood up. "Preach, Pastor, preach."

"Ummm-humm . . ." some other folks cosigned.

"Pastor, preach," another shouted.

Des couldn't believe people were buying into what this man was selling. *Bullshit,* he thought. *This ain't nothing but bullshit.*

"See, I knew Nasir. I knew him and watched him grow up."

That nigga lying like shit. He ain't never met Nasir before. Emma just paid him to do the eulogy, Des thought.

"A few years ago, I saw him driving a beautiful Infiniti Q-Forty-five, and boy, was that baby pretty—nice shiny rims, big tires, and clean as the Board of Health." He held his handkerchief up to his face.

Everybody knew he had that car, Des thought. *This nigga probably asked somebody when he was walking in the church what kind of car Nasir drove.* "He had to have that automobile at the car wash every day, as clean as it was. Y'all who knew him," he said, pointing, and the crowd loosened up a bit. "Y'all know what I'm talking about. Then one day, somebody hit the car, and it was banged up pretty bad." A few of the people who were sitting stood on their feet to let the pastor know they liked what they heard. "So he searched and he searched for someone who could fix the car for him. He was asked, Why don't you get another car? Why save that one? and I quote him: 'Because the motor is good in that car.'

"You see, Church, it's not about the outside, it's not about the flesh. Your body can be shot up and banged up like that car was. But you see, it's the inside—the heart, the soul—that matters."

"Ummm-hmmmm." The cosigners nodded.

Des sat there studying the preacher's body language as he

kept it coming. He looked around the crowd, stunned that people were eating it up. He caught Slim's eye, and Slim raised his eyebrow, silently conveying, *Do you see this game this nigga playing?*

Des nodded and squeezed Yarni's hand.

"You see, Nasir's heart was right. We can't worry about his body, we can only focus on his heart, and his engine was in great condition."

The volume of sobs throughout the chapel only got louder.

This nigga should know about games, Des thought. *He's running one of the biggest ones I've ever seen.* He was so impressed with how the preacher was winning the crowd over, he stood to applaud the man's performance. Yarni looked at Des, happy that he had gotten something out of the message. *Maybe he'll go to church with me on Sunday,* she thought.

"Let us not indulge in too much grief. Our souls are incapable of death. And Nasir, like a caged bird that has been released, is free to fly away to purer air. Since we trust that God has him in a better place, let our outward actions be in accord with it and let us keep our hearts pure and our minds calm and stay on point at all cost."

The entire church heard his words, but his sermon didn't stop the people from grieving.

"God is with Nasir as well as with us. Nasir as a son, a brother, a friend, and soldier is irreplaceable; as a living symbol of love and loyalty, he will live on. He believed in the power of staying true to himself, to build us up, conjure love, make us laugh, and turn men to giants. He will be remembered. He will be missed. He will not be forgotten.

"Church, I know this isn't your average funeral. I know Nasir would not want his life to be in vain. The kind of man he was, he would want us to let his life be a sacrifice for someone else. He would want us to use his leaving us as a way to get our lives in order. He would want you to try God, if you don't already know him. See, Church, I may be a preacher, but I know it ain't about me. It's about Nasir. But God just placed this on my spirit, and I have to do what my master says. I'm looking around this church, and I see folks here from all walks of life." He paused for effect.

"With that being said, I think, in the name of Nasir, some souls here can be saved, so I want to open up the doors of the church. Now, I know this is a funeral home and not a church, but church is any place you rejoice, and my master told me to tell you my testimony. See, I've been through it all. I was a stone-cold junkie who had done everything and gone everywhere all in the name of 'Beam me up, Scottie.' "

Des looked at the preacher and continued to peep his game. The man had everyone in the audience caught up in what he was saying. The funeral home was on fire as people thought they were witnessing a man of God. Des knew better. He knew this man was talking a good game, but half the stuff he said hadn't been true. It had just sounded good, and people were buying it, no questions asked.

"Then after running the streets of Richmond, I went to Jamaica and tried to smoke up everything in sight. Then I went over to Peru and tried to find the purest drugs I could. Then I came home, chased down some Tussionex with a Heineken, and that didn't fix any of my problems. It only sent me to jail. I realized I had tried everything, but I had never tried God."

The sinners and the saints were on their feet waving their hands and saying "Amen." Des soaked up every ounce of the preacher's game.

"So I want to open up the doors and invite anyone here who's lost, confused, brokenhearted, or don't know which way to turn. I have a place for you. My church is Faith and Love Ministry, located on Mockfield Lane, and you can come as you are."

Des watched in disbelief as several people walked up to the front to give their life to Christ. A few even went up and started throwing money on the pulpit. Major players in the game were throwing hundreds of dollars at the minister's feet and congratulating him on an awesome sermon.

As Des sat there watching the rest of the service, an idea began forming. He realized that in spite of his nephew's death, life went on, and he smiled as he realized he had just stumbled on the perfect hustle.

The preacher paused as he wiped sweat off his brow. "People," he said, "we can't let him die in vain." He stomped his foot after every word, demanding the crowd's attention. He looked around the room to make sure all eyes were on him. "I said we can't let him die in vain. We must take the lessons of his life and the pain of his death and use them as motivators to be successful in our present and future." He danced back and forth in front of the podium, flinging sweat onto the members of the congregation. "Because . . . true soldiers, *true* soldiers don't die. They live on through us. Though Nasir has ceased to be numbered with us, he's entered upon a heritage of a more divine life. Since he's gone, he knows no pain, he feels no pain, nor does he have to suffer in the game called life any longer."

CHAPTER 19

Repast

At the repast, Des was outside trying to get his mind clear when Slim joined him. Slim put fire to a freshly rolled blunt. "Man, you good?"

"I'm fucked up fo' real, but I'm holding on."

"Damn, I wish he would've called me." He passed the blunt to Des, who hadn't smoked weed in years.

Des took a pull on it as he watched Emma slide off and hand an envelope to the preacher who had given the eulogy. The preacher kissed Emma on the cheek and held her hand a little too long before watching her sashay off. As soon as he thought no one was looking, he counted out the money down to the last dollar. He smiled and whispered a soft "Amen."

"Look at that nigga," Des said as he passed the blunt back to Slim. They watched as the preacher looked both ways before he crossed the street and got into his Bentley.

Slim shook his head and exhaled smoke from the hydro through his nose into the air.

"Did you hear that shit that motherfucker was feeding those people?"

"Yeah, I peeped it, but did you check out how they was falling for that shit?"

"You know what, my nigga, while listening to that lame game, I started thinking, maybe we should trade our triple beams in for a Bible."

"That shit might not be a bad idea." Slim laughed a bit.

"It's legal money and tax-free, I think." Des looked up at Slim with a smirk while Slim laughed.

"Let me in on the joke," Rico said, walking up from behind.

"Ain't nothing." Slim offered Rico some of the blunt, but he declined. Slim put it out by the rubbing the tip on the wall of the building. "I'ma go back in there and get me some of that good food," he said, giving Des and Rico some privacy.

"I'll be right behind you," Des called out to Slim.

As Yarni chatted with Rico's wife and daughter, she wished she had a pill to help her escape the grief and pain of Nasir's death, but she knew that Des would never stand for it. Ever since she had told him about the pills, he had been watching her closely, which only made her crave them more. She looked over at Des and realized he was deep in conversation with Rico, which gave her a good chance to slip away. Even if she couldn't get a Percocet, she figured she'd be able to find something in the medicine cabinet to help take the edge off. Just as she was about to walk off, Des looked at her.

She walked over to him. "Baby, you need anything?" she asked.

"Naw, I'm good. Where you going?" he asked suspiciously.

"Nowhere," she said defensively. "I saw you looking at me, and I just wanted to check on you."

"I'm good. Thanks." He kissed her on the cheek. "I love you."

"I love you, too," she said. *So much for that idea,* she thought.

Des turned back to his conversation.

"Brother, I don't know what to say," Rico said, giving him a hug. "You know Nasir was like a nephew to me, too."

"There's nothing to say."

"If it's any consolation, that cocksucker Bam-Bam's family will be carrying flowers and picking out caskets, too."

"Appreciate it, man," Des said softly.

"If you or the family need anything, I'm here."

Des wanted to speak more with Rico, but he got distracted when he spotted Lava sitting alone outside, just staring into space. She looked as though she had lost her best friend. "Hold on, man. Let me go holla at shawdy."

He went over and sat beside Lava. At first he'd had his doubts about her, but she had proven her genuine love and loyalty to Nasir, so that made her family. "How you holding up?" he asked.

"It still really hasn't sunk in with me yet. I can't believe he's gone. He was my best friend and damn near my only friend."

Des took a deep breath and put his arm around her. "We're all going to miss him."

Her head was still down. "I know. He didn't deserve that shit, Uncle Des."

"I know he didn't." He paused. "I just found out that the nigga who did it is dead."

"Who?"

"That motherfucker Bam-Bam."

Lava was quiet. Des was expecting her to respond, but she

didn't. They both were silent for a while. "Do you trust your instincts, Uncle Des?"

"Yeah, I do, and I seem to come up late only when I don't follow them."

"What if I told you something that nobody else would believe?"

"What you getting at, Lava?"

She changed the subject. "Did that lady who works for you tell you I called?"

"Khadijah? No, she didn't. When did you call?"

"I don't trust her either," she said, totaling ignoring Des's question.

"What did she do?"

"Nothing to me. I just don't trust her."

Des could see that the stress was getting to Lava, so he tried to pacify her the best way he could. "I know you're kinda out of it right now, and your mind is all over the place, and rightfully so, but you're going to be okay."

"Will I?" she asked, her eyes filling with tears.

He hoped she wasn't on the verge of a nervous breakdown.

"Look, Uncle Des, this is hard for me to say because I'm between a rock and a hard place. I know I'm new to the family, and why would you accept my word over those you've known for years."

Des gazed at her and could see that Lava's emotions were running amuck. "Why would you feel like that?"

"I want to be blunt with you, but it's so hard."

"No time for riddles. Just say what's on your mind," Des said, starting to get impatient.

Lava took a deep breath. "My position right now is hard."

"Just calm down and tell me what you want me to know." Des reached out and touched her hand.

"Uncle Des," she said, drawing another deep breath from the bottom of her stomach, "Nasir was my everything, my life, my love. He protected me like a big brother but loved me as only a man can love his wife."

He nodded, with a wry smile on his face, and Lava asked, "What's funny?"

"He felt the same way about you."

She smiled. "Being close to you and Yarni means a lot to me because you were the people closest to him."

"Lava, as long as you don't do anything to disrespect Nasir's name, you will always be a part of this family."

"I will never do that," she said, and it was clear she meant every word. She took a deep breath. "Straight up, I don't trust Felix."

Maybe she had already suffered a nervous breakdown, Des thought, although he didn't care, he still asked to make conversation. "What did Felix do to you?"

"I think he had Nasir killed."

"What would make you think that?"

"I don't have any cold facts. It's just my intuition, and the last thing Nasir said to me was to trust my instincts and . . . that Felix, he's a rat."

CHAPTER 20

Hurricane Katrina

Hurricane Katrina coverage dominated the airways. Yarni cried as she witnessed people being treated as less than human, packed on bridges and inside the Superdome with no way to get out of the city. Some were separated from loved ones and didn't know if their family members were dead or alive.

"Why do reporters keep calling them refugees, like they're immigrants?" Yarni asked, folding her arms in disgust.

"Because that's the way they feel about us. This is a white man's country," Des said, staring at the television screen, watching a man pick up a loaf of bread floating in the putrid waters that had flooded the city's streets. The news kept showing footage of African Americans going in and out of stores and taking supplies—calling them uncivilized thieves and looters. Des got up and kissed her from behind. "This shit is ridiculous. When the white man goes in the store and steals, he's simply providing for his family, but when the black man goes in and does the same thing, he's looting. What kinda shit is that?"

"What's even more appalling is them saying they can't get people out of the houses, but that's bullshit," Yarni said. "They don't *want* to get people out!"

"No shit." Des nodded his head in agreement. "If it was Beverly Hills or Miami, they would be flying in with gold-plated helicopters, plucking folks off the roofs and giving them gift baskets filled with fruit or champagne. There's several ways they could've rescued those people."

"How you figure?" Yarni asked, never taking her eyes off the television.

"Look, baby," Des started, "they should have flown in with the police helicopters and used the search beam to see if people were in the house. Then, all they would have to do is shoot the house with a paint gun, and the rescuers on land could go to those houses and rescue the stranded people. Quick and simple. I don't know why they doing that door-to-door shit."

Half listening to Des after watching a family cry because they had nowhere to go, Yarni asked, "Can we take in a family?" Her heart went out to all of New Orleans's displaced residents.

"Hell no!" Des was quick to say. "I mean, I feel sorry for all those folks, but we don't know those people. We could be letting a potentially dangerous person around our baby. There was crackheads before Katrina; they still crackheads after Katrina. There were child molesters, rapists, and serial killers before Katrina; they still child molesters, rapists, and serial killers after Katrina." Des shook his head. "Uh-uh, I ain't even trying to put you and Desi at risk like that."

"Well, what about our rental properties? Can't we put a family in one of those?" Yarni asked hopefully.

"What are we going to do, evict the people already there?" Des responded reasonably.

Yarni sighed. "Well, we can just donate some money?" she said, more a question than a statement.

Des laughed as he kissed her. "Slow down, Mother Teresa." But he thought about what she said. Getting donations wasn't a bad idea. There was plenty of money to be made off this type of stuff. One man's bad luck could be another man's good fortune.

Yarni smiled before she turned back to the television. "Come look. Now they're leaving people on the bridge."

Des sat beside his wife and watched the Katrina Special Reports for the rest of the evening. He considered an idea that had been going around in his mind for a while, and for some reason he couldn't get Lava's words about trusting her instincts out of his head. His thoughts were interrupted when his boy Slim called.

"Man, I'm trying to get shit in order so these bitches can take their rides tomorrow," Slim said through the phone receiver.

"What's the problem with the three cars we been using?" Des asked, switching the phone from his left ear to his right.

"Khadijah somehow can't find the keys to one of them. She didn't have the time to really look for them, though, because she was trying to get out to see Ahmeen earlier. The other two need tune-ups, but my girls gotta hit the road tomorrow. I need you to give me another car to loan out."

"I'll be there," Des said, hanging up the phone and then dashing out of the house, glad to be away from the real-life drama being played out on CNN.

Although he was relieved to be away from the Hurricane Katrina madness, as he drove he couldn't help but think of the behind-the-scenes hustling and come-ups this catastrophe presented.

When Des arrived at the shop, he could tell that Slim was irritated. "What's da deal?" Des asked, giving Slim a pound.

"Just tired of these bitches, that's all," Slim responded as he plopped down on the sofa in Des's office.

"You?"

"Naw, bad day, but they ain't gon' faze me."

"You ready to change your grizzle?" Des asked.

"Yo, it's whatever with me; as long as I ain't selling my asshole or my soul, I'm down."

A small grin came across Des's face. "I'm about to change the game."

"Nigga, what you saying? We've been innovating the game for years," Slim said, sucking his teeth.

Des looked in his eyes. "Not like this, we haven't." The wheels were spinning in Des's head now.

"What do you have in mind?" Slim knew when Des had that look in his eyes, it meant one thing and one thing only . . . money!

Des paused for a minute, figuring he'd allow Slim to brace himself for the blow he was about to throw his way. "You ready to be one of my deacons?"

"Man, you lost me on that one," Slim chuckled, a puzzled look on his face.

"I'ma 'bout to preach the gospel." Des flashed a devilish grin.

"Huh?"

"We are about to start a church, and I need you to be one of my deacons."

"Shit, nigga." Slim began laughing. "If the money right, I'll be God himself." Slim sat on the edge of his seat. "Fill me in on the details."

"Okay, but first, cut that blasphemy out. You know it ain't but one God, and that's me."

$$\text{\$ \$ \$}$$

Later that evening, once Des had had a chance to run his idea by his wife, Yarni wasn't as accepting as Slim about the idea.

"Have you lost your mind?" Yarni screamed. "You know you haven't been called into the ministry. Why would you play with God like that?" Yarni stormed around the bedroom before turning to Des and calmly saying, "Des, you've gone too far. I can't be a part of this."

He walked up to her and wrapped her in his arms. "Baby, I'm doing this for us. How much more legitimate can I be than to be in the ministry? Who knows, God might even rub off on me," he joked.

"That's not funny," she said seriously, turning from him. "You can play with people, Des, but don't put God in your mess."

"I'm sorry," Des apologized. "Look, I didn't realize you would be so bothered by this. If you don't want me to, I won't start this church." He kissed her and walked to the bed, where he sat down and dropped his head in his hands. "I just wanna make a good life for you and Desi," he said quietly. "Baby, hustling's all I know. This is the closest to being legit that I can get."

Yarni sighed and sat beside him. No, she wasn't in favor of Des using the church for financial gain, but no matter what, she had always been down for whatever when it came to her Des, and nothing in her heart, nothing in her soul, would allow her to stop now. "I don't agree with what you're doing, Des, but I always have your back. Promise me it won't all be about the hustle. Promise me you'll do good work, too," she said.

"I promise," he vowed, really meaning it.

$$$

Des was never one to marinate on an idea, so he quickly put together a plan for the new church he was starting. Over the next month, Des hired a street team to visit beauty salons, barber shops, community centers, and all points in between, to hand out flyers about the new church. He wanted to appeal to people from all walks of life—encouraging them to come out and save not only their own lives but also their community. He knew people were going to be angry, hurt, and upset because of how the residents of New Orleans were being treated, and they would want answers. Or better yet, a savior. Everybody sitting at home watching the uncalled-for, preventable tragedy felt useless and wanted to be able to do something to help, or at least to make them feel they were making a difference so that they could sleep at night. Well, Des was providing them with that opportunity in the Good Life Ministry.

CHAPTER 21

Pimping from
da Pulpit

Des held his first church meeting on a Thursday evening. He made sure that a tour bus, a limo, and a few of the luxury cars from his dealership were parked outside in front of the meeting hall to draw the folks in. It worked, and folks were drawn to the hall like gold-diggers to a Jay-Z after party. He had more than a thousand people come out. He showed up in a custom-made suit that he'd initially had created for a Mary J. Blige concert. It was a deep, dark violet color that shimmered with each step he took. The Gators that adorned his feet were just a shade darker than the suit, and they had a charm on them that complemented the solid gold cuff links Yarni had given him as a Christmas present one year. He limited his jewelry to a modest bracelet sporting a twenty-carat diamond set in platinum, and his wedding band. He didn't want to overdo it and look like Richard Pryor in the movie *Car Wash*.

Des ran his fingers along the brim of his hat, which was the same shade as his shoes, and made his way up to the stage. He tapped the mic and then cleared his throat. It was showtime. Looking into the crowd, he wondered if he had bitten off more than he could chew. By no means was Des shy, but public speaking was something different.

"Good—" Des started, until the mic made a loud, high-pitched humming noise that cut him off. Des's eyes met Yarni's, and she nodded her encouragement for him to continue. She hadn't been too keen on his idea to start a church, but, as always, she was there supporting him.

Des cleared his throat again and looked at Yarni, who gave him a wide smile. He grinned in return and grabbed the podium as he looked out over the congregation. Everyone he cared about had come to support him: Slim, Uncle Stanka, Rico and his family, Khadijah, Lava, Bambi, and Lynx were there along with his mother, Yarni, and Desi. It was the first time they had been together since Nasir's funeral, and he felt good that it was all because of him.

"Good evening. I don't want to take up much of your time, so I'm going to get right down to the point." He took a deep breath and swallowed. "We all know what's going on in New Orleans, and I'm sure your hearts go out to those people, our brothers and sisters. I know mine does. Some of you have donated money just as my wife and I have. But we've all been watching the horrific scenes at one point or another—the bodies floating in the contaminated, putrid waters—on newscast after newscast. If you didn't know any better, you'd think you were watching a documentary on a third-world country." Most of the people were nodding. "In fact, the surviving victims, the ones strong enough, courageous enough, and lucky enough to survive, got to suffer the misfortune to be labeled 'refugees' by the leaders of our country." He glared into the sea of faces. "The richest country on Earth."

"Come on, tell it, brother man," shouted one man, standing up.

Another lady said, "You ain't never lied."

Des walked to the left of the stage and then stopped. "See, when you get tired of the disaster and misfortune, you can get up and turn your tube off and tune in tomorrow." He walked to the right. "But these people can't, because it's reality for them, even if it seems surreal to us. They can't play magician and say, 'Poof, be gone.' " Des looked over at Yarni for some more encouragement, and she gave a smile of approval to boost his confidence and held up their daughter, who smiled, which encouraged him even more.

"What if it was our city? Your city? What if water rushed through Broad Street, destroying everything in its path? What if it was your grandmother floating down Marshall Street?" The whole entire place was quiet, and every eye and ear was tuned into Des, anticipating his next words. "What if the government and city legislature were refusing, or were slow, to help, claiming they didn't know what to do?"

People stood and began to clap.

"Is it that they don't know what to do, or is it that they don't care?" More than half of the people were on their feet, cheering Des on. "Now, I'm not here to bash or point any fingers, or dog out our president and this country's leaders—if anything, we need to pray for them to make the right decisions from here on out—but what I am here to do is to enlighten and attempt to make a change. We got to help to protect ourselves because no one else is going to do it for us. The government has shown us what they think of us, and my momma always said that if a snake bites you one time, it's the snake's fault, but if he bites you again, it's your fault. People, what we've got to do is take heed and have a plan since our leaders don't. We must protect ourselves so that we don't get caught with our pants down again." Des stomped his foot to emphasize his point, just like the preacher at Nasir's funeral.

"We have to take matters into our own hands. We have to protect our own. In our community the family has been divided, but we've got to break the curse. We've got to have each other's backs, build our own communities, our own cities, and most of all protect what we got until we get what we need. See, in our communities no one will starve because they're hungry. We'll feed ours and clothe ours. No one will be sleeping outside or thrown out of their houses, because we're going to have our own funds to provide shelter. If someone is sick, they'll see a doctor. If someone needs an attorney, they'll get legal assistance. If someone needs a babysitter, we'll have day care available for their children. We have to love and care about one another. If we don't, who will?

"I'm willing to sacrifice and work hard, but I can't do it alone. You see, strength doesn't come alone. You need preparation and unification. And that's what I'm looking to blueprint and build—a community, a civilization—and I want you all to join me in the movement. Today you have a chance to be one of the original founding members of the Good Life Ministry."

He looked around the crowd and realized that all he had to do now was reel them in, they were buying his performance hook, line, and sinker. "You see, if you do, it's great, but if you don't, it doesn't matter, because this is what I've been called to do. I've done a lot of things in my past that I'm not proud of, but God knows my heart, and he knows I'm an upright man now."

Des raised his voice for theatrics. "I know I've been changed! But I don't want to be alone in this transition. So, change starts today for all of us as I embark on this mission, this movement—a life-changing and lifesaving movement . . . with you. I need your help." He looked around and made eye contact with various people in the audience, including Slim.

The sermon was so convincing that even Slim was engrossed in the rhetoric, standing on his feet and cheering with the rest of the crowd.

Des was on fire, and looking out into the congregation to find most of the people standing on the same accord with him was the fuel he needed to continue. "See, we're not going to dis-criminate, because God doesn't discriminate against any man or woman—he embraces all—so if you're ready for change and ready to stand for something, it doesn't matter where you were last night or what you were doing. If you were smoking crack or sleeping with somebody's husband or wife, it doesn't matter. If you're lost or brokenhearted, come as you are. That's right, you can come as you are, but I promise you won't leave the same. Change is what I'm looking for, hard workers who want to see a change and make a change."

He paused for a minute and wiped his face with the purple handkerchief he pulled from the breast pocket on his suit. "If this describes you, then all I want you to do is three things." Des held up three fingers. "First thing is," he said, holding up his index finger, "sacrifice: time, talent, or treasure. Second,"—he held up a second finger—"sow a seed so you can reap the plenti-ful harvest—just a dollar or two," he said, when he saw people rolling their eyes. He looked around as he now held up his thumb, index, and middle fingers. "Finally, commit to bringing five people with you on Sunday when you return. If you have to pick them up or give them cab fare to get them here, make it your business to bring five people back.

"It starts here. You decide if you're in or out." Des looked up as he saw Slim walking up to the front, dressed to the nines in his silk suit. Slim handed him a check.

"Thank you, brother," Des said to Slim, then spoke into the mic. "Brother Tyrone Walls just pledged twenty thousand dollars to our ministry." He held up the check.

Stanka followed with a thousand dollars in cash. Des was surprised when he saw Bambi walk up and hand him a five-thousand-dollar check. "Brother Pitman, would you please come to the front with a basket for us?" Des asked his father-in-law.

Lloyd walked to the front with several oblong wicker baskets in his hands, and people lined up and began dumping money into them, filling basket after basket. The green was getting as thick as a well-manicured lawn. Des stood nearby wearing a politician's smile, shaking plenty of hands and pinching plenty of babies' cheeks, assuring people that making an offering to his ministry was the right thing to do.

Indeed, he had found his calling. There was a new pimp on the pulpit, and things up there would never be the same.

CHAPTER 22

A $hitty Mess

"Attorney visit for Samuel Johnson," Yarni said as she handed the sheriff her business card.

The sheriff punched some buttons on his keyboard and shook his head as he stated, "You probably don't want to see him. He's in solitary."

Yarni wasn't surprised. She knew her client's temper—after all, she had witnessed it the first day she laid eyes on him in the courtroom.

"You can go to his cell to see him if you dare, but it will be at your own risk."

"I'll try my luck," Yarni said confidently.

"Let me call for someone to take you back." The officer pulled out his walkie-talkie.

Yarni stood to the side as she waited for her escort to show her the way to Samuel.

"Why is my client in solitary?" Yarni asked, walking back up to the desk.

"He was trying to escape. Not to mention, while he's been back there, he's been very disruptive and highly disrespectful to the officers." The officer shook his head again.

"Really?" Yarni said as if she was shocked.

"Yeah." The guard nodded. "He's been throwing urine and feces at the kitchen crew and the guards. So that's why I told you, when you go back there, you go at your own risk."

Just then another guard arrived to escort her back to the segregated housing unit. "Thanks for the warning," Yarni said, flashing a tight smile to the officer at the front desk.

Yarni made her way down the long hall of the old jail where Samuel was being housed. The inmates called it the dungeon, and Yarni could understand why. Although there were lights on going down the hall, the building still had a dark and dreary feel to it. The hall was about a hundred feet long and lined with cells on both sides. Her four-inch heels echoed off the walls, triggering the inmates like wild dogs, alerting them that a woman was in the building.

"Hey, baby," one yelled out.

"Guyd damn, she phat as duck butta. Whoa," an inmate yelled as she continued her stride, trying hard not to switch. But she couldn't control it; after all, this had been her strut for almost thirty years.

"Hey, pretty momma, you the new shrink?" another inmate called out.

"If so, my head hurting," another one jumped in, grabbing his crotch and massaging himself as Yarni walked by.

She ignored them all. This wasn't the first time she had

walked what she considered to be her version of the long green mile.

As Yarni made it to the very last cell, the men in the segregated housing unit became more and more excited. It was the highlight of the year, maybe even the decade.

Yarni hadn't made eye contact with any of the prisoners. She'd kept her head held up straight, never looking to the side until she reached Samuel's cell. She saw him lying on his mat, looking up at the ceiling. Feces were all over the walls. The smell of waste assaulted her nostrils.

"Hey, Johnson, you got a visitor," the deputy announced.

When Samuel looked up, he thought he was dreaming; Yarni stood there in her all-white pantsuit. It was like an angel was standing before him. But as he looked her over, he realized that angels didn't wear Manolos and carry Marc Jacobs handbags.

"You look a shitty mess," Yarni said bluntly.

"Why the fuck you here?" he shot at her, his voice dripping with venom.

She could sense the hostility in his tone but didn't let it intimidate her. "Last time I checked, I was your attorney."

The guy in the cell across from Samuel overheard her comment and said, "You can be my attorney any day."

"Well, that ain't what da fuck your co-worker or boyfriend or whoever the fuck he is said when he was here last week." Samuel was so worked up, spittle flew out of his mouth as he snapped at her.

"What did he say?" she asked curiously.

Samuel returned his gaze to the ceiling. "That he had a get-out-of-jail card for me, but you, Florence Nightingale, chose not to accept the evidence under his terms. So he's sure that I'ma do forty or fifty years—that's with good behavior, of course." He finally let his eyes meet hers. "And does this shit look like a place where they keep inmates who display good behavior?"

"Hey, hey, my bed is on fire," the guy across the hall screamed. When Yarni turned to look at him, he had his dick in his hand and was jerking off. "Yeah, yeah, yeah, awww baby," he said, his tongue hanging out of his mouth.

Yarni couldn't believe she had fallen for such a juvenile trick, but then she thought about the juvenile dick he had exposed and shrugged. She quickly turned around and continued her conversation with Samuel. "And you fell for that bullshit?" Yarni asked, but didn't give Samuel any time to answer her. "Look, pull yourself together. I'm going to get a guard to bring you some cleaning supplies. You get this cell straight and get yourself cleaned up, then I'm going to meet you in the attorney visiting room, if you still want to see daylight in the next couple of months." She spoke firmly, then walked away.

An hour later, Samuel entered the attorney visiting room, showered and shaved. When Yarni stood up to shake his hand, she gained an instant appreciation for Irish Spring soap.

"What's going on with you? Why the hell are you trying to escape?" she asked him.

"I had to," Samuel explained. "I didn't have no choice. I wasn't trying to leave here in a box forty years from now."

"So now you got an escape charge to go along with the shopping list of offenses levied up against you," Yarni said, throwing up her arms.

"They gave me an institution charge, not a street charge."

"But you just jumped to conclusions without even talking to me," she chastised.

"Your partner said that my momma should put a fork in me because I was done. The evidence he had was the only way I would walk, and you fucked that up for me." Samuel was as cold as a steel bleacher at a playoff football game in Green Bay.

"First, let me explain something to you. *I'm* your attorney," she said, pointing to herself. "You listen to me and to no one else. If I didn't say it, then it ain't so. Now, I gave you my word, and it's the law. Don't ever let anybody knock you off your square and control your emotions or actions. Marvin is just pulling your chain."

"Well, Sledge da Great ain't here, so what are we going to do?"

"Did he say what the evidence was that he had?"

"Something about a deposition from a witness that could kill my whole case."

"Did he say who the witness was?"

"You don't know?" He slouched down in his chair. "Ain't this a bitch?" he said, throwing his hands up.

"No, I don't know," Yarni admitted, "but I'm going to find out."

"Can't you call him?"

"Fuck 'em, I'd rather call Satan from hell first."

"Problem?"

"It's very complicated, but as I gave you my word before, I'm going to work my ass off. Just trust me."

"You want me to trust you, but you keep talking to me in circles and not letting me know why the evidence I need ain't here." He hit the table, and Yarni jumped, the noise startling her. "You waltz in here and tell me everything's going to be okay, but what you fail to realize is that I'm the only person suffering and facing life in prison."

At first she was letting him get his rocks off, but now he had struck a nerve. "You want to talk about suffering and going through it?"

"You can't relate when you ain't the one sitting here twenty-four hours a day, having to protect yourself at all costs, and most of all, having to depend on another motherfucker who tells me she got my back, while at the end of the day, she let the missing link slip through her fingers."

"You want to talk about protecting yourself?" She started on a roll. "Let me share something with you." She reached for her Marc Jacobs purse and retrieved the photos that Bambi had taken of her face the night that Marvin tried to rape her. "Look at these. This is why I don't have your deposition." She slapped the photos on the table as she stood and leaned in closer to meet his eyes. "Because after hours of working on your case, I wouldn't let Sledge da Great touch me. When I resisted, he tried to take it, and I fought like hell trying to protect what was mine. Then I couldn't dare tell my husband who did this to me." She snatched the photos and held them up. "Because he would've run out and done God knows what to Marvin. I would have been left fighting yet another case for him. But he would have told me to forget about your ass, and I gave you my word that I would do everything in my power to get your selfish ass off. So don't you sit there and cry about no one enduring the struggle with you. Because I've gone beyond the call of duty for you and this case, and to top it off"—she raised her voice—"for mother-fucking free."

Yarni pulled herself together and continued in her normal speaking voice, which allowed her blood pressure to go down a bit. "And you know what?" she asked.

Samuel was almost afraid to ask. "What?"

"I intend to win."

Her client sat there with a look that said he was impressed. "A'ight, warrior."

"Now," Yarni said as she sat down and pulled out a notebook and pen, "I need to go over everything again with you from start to finish; tell me anything that you can think of to help me."

They covered all they could. As she listened and took detailed notes, her thoughts kept going back to one thing: that file. She knew she needed it, and she knew who could get it for her.

CHAPTER 23

Bulletproof
and Blessed

es sat in the pulpit of his newly renovated church, the Good Life Ministry, taking in the ever-growing crowd of pew viewers. He couldn't help but smile as he wondered why it had taken him so long to come up with this move. It was by far the best idea he ever had, and he was glad to add it to his résumé as hustler. He bowed his head as though in prayer before winking at Yarni and stepping up to the pulpit of the abandoned building that he once thought of buying to turn into a night-club. Ironic, since what he'd once intended to make the devil's playground was now a house of the Lord.

"So we got our place of gathering up," Des addressed his flock. "We've got a few dollars in the bank, and we've got people coming in here from the North, the South, the East, and the West. We're having communion, and things are going great. But guess what? We're not finished yet." There were a few wondering moans among the crowd. "You see, it's far easier to start something than to finish it. What if Noah never finished the ark?" Des asked his congregation. "What if he would have given up before God showed up?"

He looked over the people who were sitting in aluminum folding chairs and tried to read their reaction to his message. He caught a glimpse of the newly painted walls and smiled again. A week ago the old Piggly Wiggly sign had still been on the front of the building. Des had paid cash for the building out of his own pocket ten days ago and had donated the space to the ministry. The old supermarket had had a total face-lift. He had workers around the clock and had done what not many other churches had dared to do: build a place of worship in six days.

And on the seventh day they rested.

The floors had been stripped and the walls painted. He'd had stained-glass windows put in. Workers had built the stage on which Des was standing, and Des had ordered custom-made pews that had yet to arrive, but the people weren't complaining about the folding chairs. In fact, they seemed really comfortable, like they were at home, kicked back in their favorite chairs. He briefly wondered if he could have kept the money for the pews for himself, but he knew in the end it would be money well spent.

Des paced around the pulpit. He had been so busy admiring his new space that he couldn't recall what he'd just said, but obviously it was something to which the people could relate because they were up on their feet applauding.

"You can speak life or death into your life." Des looked around and realized he had gotten off track when he noticed the confusion on the congregation's faces. "I said you can speak life or death into your life. What I mean by that is, what you speaketh is what it shall be. If you roll out of bed and say, 'Daggone it, this is going to be a messed-up day,' then guess what? Prepare to shovel shit."

The people began to react, once again applauding. "Tell it, brother," one man yelled, striding up to the pulpit and shaking Des's hand. Des nodded.

"However, if you sit up in the bed, thank the Lord for waking you up, and say, It's going to be a great day, then you've made the first step to do just that. What I am saying to you, my people, is that no matter what folks say about our movement and our revolution, you have to be equipped, regardless of what your circumstances say. You gotta speak greatness into existence. Walk in the greatness." Des came out from behind the pulpit and began to take huge, confident strides up the center aisle. Members of the congregation cheered him on. "When someone says, How are you doing? You say, I walk in greatness." He took another step, and a couple of people lined up behind him, mimicking his words and his movements. "When someone asks how you doing, you say, Life couldn't be greater." He took another step. "When people ask, What are you doing, brother? Where are you going? You say, I'm going into deep waters, because big blessings don't come in shallow territories."

"Amen," someone said, placing his hand on Des's shoulder.

"I know that's right," a woman said, wiping tears from her eyes. "I walk in authority with the Lord!"

"That's right, my sister." Des shook her hand and agreed. "See, sometimes the blessings God has in store for us, the streams we're fishing in won't accommodate them. That's why big fish don't stay in shallow waters. Stay away from relationships with shallow folks doing shallow things talking shallow stuff." He took another stride, moving closer to the door. "The closer you get to the prize, the farther away you move from where you started. Before you know it, you are swimming in deeper water, and you can't see any land, and the ships you are passing are getting bigger and bigger, and the blessings . . . well they're bigger and bigger, too, because you have launched into deeper water."

"Preach, brother!" someone yelled.

"You take one step and then another, and soon you are in deeper waters," Des said. He was now at the door of the church. "Remember, you can't get deep blessings in shallow waters. Now let's go out and be a blessing to everyone we meet," Des said, opening the door.

The members were on fire as they left, and they let Des know just how much by dropping money in the collection baskets he had conveniently placed at the entranceway.

$$\$\,\$\,\$$

"Man, I can't believe how much money we've been making." Slim smiled as he and Des used their old drug money counter to total the church's offerings and the earnings from their other various hustles.

"If I'd known a decade and a half ago that the word of God could be so prosperous, I would have never seen the inside of a prison," Des said to Slim, a blunt bopping up and down on his lips as he talked. "Pass me that bottle of cognac."

"Amen to that," Slim cosigned, passing the Remy to Des.

Des laughed as he flipped through bundles of cash. "Yeah, I guess in some weird way, we owe it all to Nasir," he said, thinking fondly of his nephew. It had only been a few months since he died, but Des had been so busy that he hadn't had time really to miss him. He made a mental note to check on Lava.

"We've got to get all our street money cleaned up while the getting is good. The IRS ain't going to buy that we made all this paper in the name of Jesus," Des said, shaking off thoughts of his nephew. He took a stack of money and placed it in his safe.

"Got any ideas, Rev?" Slim asked, grabbing a few more stacks and putting them in the safe as well.

"My man Ahmeen has been trying to get me to go down to South America to holla at his brother Loo. That's what he does down there," Des said, thinking about his ex-cell mate.

"That's a good look, if we can pull it off."

"I'll get at Ahmeen again to make sure everything is on the up and up. I'ma let Khadija know that I need to talk to him when he calls." Des locked up the safe and grabbed the rest of the money to take to the bank as they prepared to leave.

$$\$\$\$$$

As Slim and Des exited the church, reporters awaited them outside. Because the church had been attracting attention, there had been a lot of media coverage.

"Reverend Taylor, why are your deacons sitting in your church armed with guns?" a reporter asked, shifting her microphone so that Des could answer.

"Why does the president of the United States have armed guards following him everywhere he goes?" Des fired back.

She smiled. "But you're not the president," she reminded Des.

He looked around with a million-dollar smile. "No, not yet. All in God's perfect timing," he said.

"You are actually aspiring to be president of the United States?" she asked.

"Yes, we are in America, the land of the free, where you can be anything you want to be, right? What God has for me is for me, and no one can take that away, not even you, my sister." He changed the subject since he could see the reporter was speechless. "Actually, to answer your original question, we don't have metal detectors nor do we require the people who come in to be searched." He looked into the camera. "Here at the Good Life Ministry, we welcome everyone, from anywhere and everywhere. With that being said, we would pray that everybody comes with a good heart, but knowing the things I know from serving ten years in prison for a crime that I was later pardoned for, I can't take any risks. I'm not a gambling man anymore, which means I can't roll the dice on the safety of my people."

"Why do you wear a bulletproof vest under your robe?" she asked.

Des laughed to himself. He had mentioned this fact in his sermon one day, and obviously word had spread. It still amazed him that people actually listened to every word he spoke and quoted it like it was the gospel truth. He guessed that for many of them it was.

"I know that a lot of people are unhappy with all the great things we're doing here, along with the unity and peace among my large congregation. I've been framed for two separate crimes that I didn't commit. It's evident that I'm a walking target due to the political work I'm doing in the community." He kept bullshitting. "History has a tendency to repeat itself, and I wouldn't want to be caught at a vulnerable time as so many who came before me have." And with that final thought, Des decided to end the conversation. "Thank you and may God bless you." He smiled and walked away, but the reporter was hot on his heels, almost leaving her cameraman behind.

By the time her camera guy had caught up, Des was getting into his Rolls-Royce.

"Is your car bulletproof?" the reporter asked.

He nodded his head to affirm it. "Bulletproofed and blessed by God."

CHAPTER 24

The Blessing
in Disguise

When Yarni returned to her office, her assistant Layla followed behind her. "There's a Ms. Briggs here to see you," Layla informed Yarni. "I asked her what it was in reference to, but she wouldn't say."

"Who is Ms. Briggs?" Yarni questioned.

"I don't know. However, she's been waiting over three hours, and she's demanded to see you. She said she would wait all day if she had to, until her bus leaves at seven tonight."

"Is she a client?" Yarni asked.

"No. She says it's business, but close to your heart."

"Maybe a potential new client, huh?"

"No, I asked so that I could get the preliminary info from her."

Yarni shrugged. "Give me five minutes and then send her in."

Yarni sat at her computer for a few minutes checking her e-mail. Layla announced the visitor, and Yarni stood up to greet her. "Yarnise Taylor," she introduced herself while extending her hand.

"Malinda Briggs," said the small light-skinned lady whom Layla had shown into Yarni's office. She reached out to shake Yarni's hand.

Yarni took in the woman's appearance and hid her shock. The woman looked as though she had been sleeping in the same clothes for at least a week, and her black hair was tangled, matted, and hard, like an old wig from the seventies. Yarni desperately wanted to show the strange woman a mirror, wanting to believe a sensible person wouldn't have come outside looking crazy on purpose.

"Have a seat?" Yarni offered, motioning to a chair in front of her desk.

The frail lady studied the diplomas and photos on Yarni's wall. As she looked around, Yarni stared at her, wondering why the woman needed to see her so urgently.

"Wow, you're a very smart sister," Malinda said, impressed with Yarni's accomplishments.

"That's what they tell me," Yarni said modestly.

"I wish I was smart, but I dropped out of school." The woman continued to study the photos.

"You know, you can always go back. There are so many programs out there now," Yarni said. She sat down, wishing the woman would hurry up and get to the point of her visit.

"It's not that simple." She glanced at Yarni, and Yarni used that as her cue to cease the small talk.

"So what can I help you with, Ms. Briggs?" Yarni asked, trying not to focus on the styling gel that had turned dark brown and was flaking off the woman's black hair.

"Well, actually it's not even what you can help me with. It's what I can help you with, or even better, how we can help each other." Malinda finally took a seat.

"What exactly are you talking about?" Yarni looked at her curiously.

"You know, one hand washes the other."

Yarni didn't have a clue as to where the peculiar-looking lady was going with this, but if the woman didn't state her intentions quickly, Yarni would have to ask her to leave. *There aren't enough hours in a day for this foolishness,* Yarni thought.

"Yes, Ms. Briggs, I've heard that saying, but can you be more specific?"

"It's about your husband."

"What about my husband?" Yarni asked, as alarms started going off in her head.

"It's simple." Ms. Briggs rolled up her sleeves, and Yarni noticed the track marks on her arms from years of shooting dope. "I can look out for him if he looks out for me."

"Look out for you?"

"Yes, that's what I said."

Yarni was seconds away from pulling off her pumps and whipping the woman's ass. "You coming up to my place of business questioning me about my husband? Sweetie, you got about ten seconds to state your business." She rolled her neck, crossed her arms, and began tapping her foot as she looked at her watch, silently counting down the seconds before she beat the hell out of the woman.

Ms. Briggs was visibly shaken by Yarni's sudden change in demeanor. "Look, you don't understand. I'm not here to harm you or your husband. I'm here to help."

"Then, you need to make me understand," Yarni snapped,

glaring at the woman. "Start talking, because my patience is wearing real thin."

"I can understand that, but I don't know where to start."

Yarni could hear the D.C. dialect in her voice.

"From the beginning always works." She tried her best to hide her annoyance and remain professional. Although she wanted to give the woman only a few more seconds of her time, her gut was telling her to hear the woman out. She sighed and sat back to hear what Ms. Briggs had to say.

"Well, first let me just say that I'm ninety-three days and twelve hours clean."

"Congratulations," Yarni said.

The woman took a deep breath. "Before I went into the program, I was at my lowest point. I didn't have anywhere to shoot up anymore, so I was having to use the veins in my pussy. That's how bad things had gotten for me. And I was doing any and everything to get my shot off," she admitted.

"I can imagine, but what does this have to do with my husband?" Yarni said, holding her breath, hoping Des hadn't been the one giving her the drugs. That thought went out of her mind quickly because Des hadn't been on any small-time nickel-and-dime hustling since he was twelve years old.

The ninety-day clean ex–dope fiend stared off in space as she told Yarni, "One night, I had just finished sucking off one of my faithful clients in his car. Once I got out, I never left the alley. I was so anxious to get my works out and get high that I dropped my shit. I got down on my knees and was looking for it, and I began to cry when I couldn't find it. I was desperate. I would've done anything to feed my hunger at that moment. I saw this woman when I was getting in the car but paid her no mind." She looked up at Yarni. "She knew what was up; she asked me if I was sick. I told her yes, and she asked me if I wanted to make a thousand dollars."

Tears formed in her eyes. "I asked her did I have to kill anyone."

Yarni sat up in her chair to lean forward on her desk as her interest piqued.

"She said no, but close."

"So what did you do?" Yarni asked, beginning to feel compassion for this stranger.

"She told me to say that I saw a man come out of a building at the end of the alley and take off a mask. Then she handed me this photo." Ms. Briggs pulled out a photo tucked into the outside pocket of her fake Coach bag and handed it to Yarni. It was torn in half. It was a group prison photo containing eight inmates, and Des's face was circled with a black Magic Marker. The hairs on Yarni's neck stood up. "This is the man she said I needed to identify to the police." She pointed to Des in the photo. "Handed me a hundred-dollar bill and told me once I identified him, then I would get two hundred fifty more, and then two hundred fifty more once I saw the sketch artist. Then the rest after I took the stand. Shoot, at that time, I ain't have shit to lose, so why not? It was an offer that I couldn't turn down."

Yarni sat back, stunned, as she took in what this woman was telling her. She had always known that Des had been framed for the murder, but hearing this woman confirm it shocked her speechless. She got up from her desk and began pacing.

She couldn't believe this runny-nose bitch was sitting in front of her confessing to being an accomplice to the false persecution of her man. Yarni felt like going in her drawer and pulling out her pistol. A quick vision of her being escorted out of Sunday-morning service in handcuffs, wearing her big-brimmed pastor's-wife hat, came to mind, and she quickly decided to put aside her hustler's wife mentality. After getting over the initial shock, she realized God had sent her a blessing in disguise.

"Do you know who the woman was?" Yarni asked.

The woman looked down at the floor and shook her head. "No," she said softly. "Like I said, I had never seen her before that day, and she always manages to find me afterward."

"She didn't tell you how to contact her?" Yarni asked, stopping her pacing to swing around to look at the woman.

"No," the woman repeated. "She's been contacting me."

"And you never thought to get contact information from her? How stupid can you be?" Yarni asked. "How can you just play with someone's life like that? Do you know my husband is facing a long prison sentence because of you?"

The woman sitting before her was bent and broken, so Yarni reined in her emotions. "I'm sorry," she said. "You did the right thing by coming to me. How did you find out about me, anyway?"

"I've been seeing your husband on television lately. I started to go to him, but I didn't know if he would believe me. Then I saw this profile someone done on you, and they mentioned your law practice, so I thought I should talk to you." Tears formed in her eyes. "I am so sorry for what I did, but you have to understand, the drugs had a hold on me. . . ."

Yarni walked over and placed one hand on the woman's shoulder. "I know," she said. "I'm not mad at you. I really appreciate your coming to tell me what's going on. You've helped me more than you know."

Yarni began pacing and thinking again.

Who would possibly go through this much trouble, to such extremes to have Des set up? "Where is this woman now?" Yarni fired quick questions.

"I don't know. Like I said, she always finds me. Even when I was in the program, she would pose as a family member to get messages to me."

"What does she look like?" Yarni asked.

"You know, I was always high, so I really can't give you a description."

"I mean anything." Yarni was all but begging her for something to help her locate the woman who was setting her husband up.

"Well, there is one thing," she paused. "She had a tattoo on her right arm that I could never get out of my mind."

"Tattoo? Of what?"

"A red heart with a knife going through it, and a black snake wrapped around the heart." She shook her head and looked up at Yarni with fear in her eyes.

"Were there any words or a name?"

"Yes, I almost forgot. Her man's name is on it."

"What is it?"

"Under the tattoo it has: Treach E. Rouss's Bitch."

Yarni's mind raced, but she knew she had never seen a tattoo like that before. She would have remembered something so odd. "Why now?" Yarni looked in the woman's face and asked.

"Why now what?"

"Why would you come forward now?"

"Because I wasn't in my right state of mind when I did that shit, and it's been on my heart heavy, especially when I was in the program. Plus, I figured if someone would pay me a thousand dollars to say that a man done it, then someone would give me five thousand to clear the man who didn't do it."

Yarni got her emotions under control and put her lawyer hat back on. "Listen, don't worry; we're going to take care of you. I have to get my husband's attorney on the phone, and then I'm going to record a statement from you."

Ms. Briggs nodded. "How long is this going to take, because my bus leaves at seven."

"Don't worry about your bus," Yarni said calmly. Little did Ms. Briggs know that if she tried to get up to leave the office, Yarni would have taken off her Prada belt and hog-tied her.

Yarni got Harowitz on the phone to tell him about the new evidence. Des's attorney felt optimistic that this would put a serious chink in the prosecution's case. With the primary witness recanting her testimony, it shouldn't be hard to clear Des's name and get the charges dropped.

After recording the statement and getting Malinda Briggs back off to D.C., Yarni put in a few calls to try to find out if there was any info on Treach E. Rouss. As she was making the calls, Harowitz called her back and said that in the beginning of the investigation, another witness had said that a woman had killed Richards. But since Des was only a few miles away when it happened, and since he had missed his appointment with the attorney, not to mention his past record and the new eyewitness, he had become the prime suspect.

Yarni said a prayer that night and was hopeful that Des's unfortunate run-in with the law would soon be over and done with.

CHAPTER 25

The Little
Whorehouse in
South America

"*B*ueno dias, señor,*"* the owner of the whorehouse greeted the man. "*Tengo el cualto prepardao coono tegusta.*" He let the man know that he had his favorite room prepared for him.

"*Gracias, Señor Miguel,*" the man replied.

Larry Fondsworth had migrated from Texas and had been living in South America for the past few years. Lootchee, as he preferred to be called, had been a millionaire ten times over before he ever left the States. Back at home, he was well respected in the business community as well as with the local politicians. But little did any of them know, he obtained most of his riches illegally. Everything was good in the hood for Lootchee—until the day his fiancée found out that he wasn't the man he was pretending to be.

She had stumbled upon boxes of drugs, money, and stolen

property that he had shipped in her name to a house he had purchased for her. Feeling betrayed, hurt, and brokenhearted, she tricked him into believing that the Feds had picked her up and were asking questions about him. That's when he cut all ties with her, anybody who knew her, all of his associates, and most of his friends, and fled the United States. If the Feds were coming for him, they would have to look long, hard, and deep in the jungles of South America. He found out later that his fiancée had made up the whole story, and, to add insult to injury, that she had stolen all the money, drugs, and property that he'd had in the house and headed back to her home state of Virginia.

Lootchee vowed to get back at his fiancée and never to trust another woman again. Things didn't work out too bad for Lootchee, though. He had met a few shady bankers in South America, had reacquainted himself with some of his old buddies, and was now making more paper than he could count—as if he needed any more—laundering money.

Yeah, life was sweet. He'd found a new home. And to top it off, he was getting the best pussy and head he had ever received in his life from an American hooker named Unique, who was working in a brothel that he visited three times a week.

"Tu mujer redresara tronot," Miguel said, informing Lootchee that his girl would be in shortly.

Lootchee, always in a hurry, said, *"No tengo para estar esternado,"* reminding Miguel that he didn't have a bunch of time to waste.

"Ella es la major mujer trabajando aquí." Miguel told Lootchee that Unique was the best girl that he had working for him.

"Yo se que ella es la major mujer pore so mengo aquí cada día."

Lootchee smiled, letting Miguel know that that was why he came three times a week and spent so much money there.

The place of business was an old two-story house, but it had been completely refurbished. There were twelve rooms, and at any given time, about twenty to twenty-five women worked there. Miguel made sure that all of his girls had monthly check-ups, even the ones who were being held against their will.

$$\text{\$ \$ \$}$$

Lootchee sat on the edge of the bed and cut on the twenty-inch, fuzzy, color television in what was supposed to be the VIP suite. It was the only room that had a door that actually locked and a private bathroom. It was also the sweetest-smelling room in the house; it was flooded with air fresheners to cover the smell of sex that had taken over the whole house.

Finally, Unique entered the room, and when she did, she set a little shopping bag on the dresser, on which most of the handles were broken. She knew the routine: She went in the bathroom, took a shower, and put on the lingerie and perfumed lotion that Lootchee always brought with him.

She came out of the bathroom wearing hot pink boy shorts and a matching camisole. It was undeniable that Unique was beautiful. She was light-skinned, with hazel eyes, and her body was tight. Every time Lootchee laid eyes on her, he knew she could be making big money in the States. The Luke dancers—or no stripper he had ever met, for that matter—could fuck with Unique. Every curve on her body was perfect, and what she did with her body parts kept him coming back for more. She performed tricks with her mouth and box that would have made most magicians proud. He was surprised that some other rich man hadn't come through and paid her debt to Miguel and made her his own personal love slave. That thought had crossed his mind before. Unique always begged Lootchee to do just that, but he wasn't up for making a whore into a housewife.

As Unique made her way over toward her client, she didn't speak. Instead, she went straight to work, undoing his pants, pulling out his dick, and dropping to her knees to please him. After he exploded in her mouth, she took the excess that was dribbling down her chin and rubbed it onto her breasts, which she knew turned Lootchee on. Knowing she had his attention, she started undressing him. Once she had him naked and hard again, she started her performance while working him overtime, both mentally and physically. She knew he was her only way out of the predicament that she was in. Lootchee had made it clear that he wasn't buying out her contract with Miguel, but if she could keep him coming back for about two more years, his tips would be more than enough to pay her debt.

Unique started licking between Lootchee's toes, and he started to tense up. "You like that, baby?" she asked with a smile; she knew that she hadn't lost her touch.

Lootchee could only manage a tight smile as he sucked in a deep breath. She got up and walked over to the bag she had brought in with her.

"What's that?" Lootchee asked suspiciously, rising up off the bed.

She gave him a sexy smile before heading over to him and pushing him back down. "Relax," she whispered in his ear, "let me love you."

She began round two of her unique—no pun intended—blow job, one she had never given him before. He knew she was taking him to a place in ecstasy that no woman had ever taken him.

Lootchee closed his eyes, still on guard. His eyes snapped open when he felt her anchoring his hands to the bedposts with two scarves.

"What the hell?" he asked, knowing that he was too far gone.

"Relax, baby," she said smoothly, ignoring his alarm. She reached into the bag again and pulled out a whip. "I hear you've been a very bad boy." She pranced back and forth in front of him, smacking the whip in the palm of her hand. "I'm going to have to do something about that." Without warning, she flicked the whip, and he felt it sting his thigh.

He looked at her, trying to figure out her game. Normally he would have been furious, but he was getting turned on in spite of himself. This was the only time he would ever let a woman have her way.

"Oh, yeah, you've been really bad, and I'm going to have to punish you." She began spanking him, and as much as Lootchee thought about protesting, he couldn't. There was something about the sensation that was turning him on in a way he never had been before.

By the time Unique finally straddled him, he was coming all over himself, erupting like a volcano. She smiled and bent down to take a sip. Before she could drink her fill, Lootchee's phone rang, interrupting the moment.

He sighed, annoyed that he had forgotten to turn off his phone. Why did motherfuckers always have to call when he was taking a shit or getting his nut off? He raised his hips to get Unique off him and then went to reach for his phone. It took him a second to realize he was still tied to the bed.

"Untie me," he ordered.

Unique did as he asked without question. Lootchee quickly grabbed the phone, trying to catch the call before it went to voice mail.

"Hello," he said gruffly, trying to keep calm as Unique used her tongue to tease his nipples.

"This Larry?" Des asked on the other end.

"Yeah, who dis?" Lootchee asked, pushing Unique away, but she stopped only for a moment before going down on him.

Des ignored the question. "Your brother and I were roommates, and he told me only good things about you. I'll be there in a few days. Hopefully we can play a few rounds of golf," Des said.

"No doubt, that's what I do, but how many holes are you talking?" Lootchee tried to pull away from Unique, but he couldn't.

"Well, you know traveling makes me kinda hype. I hope you can handle all the energy I got."

"I work out every day, so I'm looking forward to it. When you getting in?"

"Next Friday. Me and a couple of my deacons and doctors from my congregation will be at the hospital in the village."

"Call me when you get in, and I'll see you then. It's all love," he said, quickly hanging up and grabbing Unique by the back of her head so she could deep-throat him. After they finished, Unique sat on the bed beside him.

"Does that affect our Saturday date?" she asked.

"No, it doesn't. Have I ever missed any of our appointments?"

"Nope.

"Then, don't ask stupid questions."

"You should really consider taking me with you," she said seductively.

"Should I?" he asked with a devilish smirk.

"Umm-hmm."

Lootchee took himself in his hand, looked down, and then looked up at Unique and said, "Convince me."

CHAPTER 26

The Best Is
Yet to Come

Des stood before the church congregation and spoke. "As many of you know, for a few months I have been fighting a conspiracy against me. Well, as of yesterday at two forty-three P.M., all charges against me were dropped. God is good!" The organist began playing shouting music, and the folks in the church began to shout for joy and get their praise dance on. "The devil is a liar," he screamed as the organist hit some notes. "See, people, he comes to steal, kill, and destroy." The organist banged on the organ between Des's words. "When some see strong people and organizations, they make it their living existence to kill the dream, the vision, in any way fit. Those people knew I was a great man, destined to do great things—to swim, tread, and navigate through deep waters. They knew I'd lead a nation of many. They knew I'd be this era's king, like King David, who killed lions and bears and protected his people. They knew my people would make a difference in this city, this country, and this world, and those prison bars were the only thing that could slow me down." Des looked up and saw Lava sitting in the congregation. Des threw her a smile.

"Having that case kept me somewhat stagnant. It was a road-block, hindering me from the missionary work that God wanted me to do. But see, God is the God of all gods. He has the last say-so in everything, and he promised he would protect me from any weapon formed against me, and he did. I'm living proof of God's promise, and it's not just me God made a promise to, it's everybody. And once you begin walking in the direction God wants you to, the promise that's hanging above your head just falls and covers you."

"Hallelujah!" a member shouted.

"I receive it," another added.

"Now, God has put it on my heart to go to South America to talk to the people in the tribes of the rain forest, to nurse our people that the governments have forgotten about."

The congregation stood, applauding to show their agreement. Had they known that Des was really going to South America to launder $5.8 million, all hell would have broken loose. "Nobody here is wanting for a thing in our ministry. Everybody's rent is paid, and nobody is starving. But can we say that about our brothers and sisters over in South America? The U.S. government is sending people to Iraq and Afghanistan, but have you ever heard of them sending medicine to our brothers and sisters over in Panama or Brazil? We are trailblazers. We have to go. We have to do what God called us to do.

"When you were left unwanted and thought you were forgotten about, someone saved you. God stepped in. For I've never seen the righteous forsaken. What about the righteous over in South America? Enough of sitting back thinking how you can spend your money on extreme indulgences. Step in and help those who feel there's no way out, no one to help them; those who have no hope, and have almost given up."

The people were on their feet applauding again, and Des couldn't help but smile, still amazed that they were falling for what he was saying.

After the service, Lava waited as all Des's followers shook his hand. Lava watched a woman give Des a pound cake. "The store was out of the chocolate I needed to get, so it isn't chocolate," the woman said apologetically.

"That's all right, Ms. Mary," Des said, kissing her on her cheek.

"But I did make a homemade coconut cake for you."

"Ms. Mary, you are such a blessing to us. Thank you." Slim took the cake from her.

While Lava waited to speak to Des, she wondered if she should share with him the news she had or keep it to herself. That's when she saw Yarni, who gave her a big hug and invited her back to the house for dinner.

Once they got to the house, Lava was so happy to be there with them that she almost cried. It had been such a long time since she'd seen them, and it felt good to be around Nasir's people. She waited for an opportunity to speak to Des alone, and she got that opportunity when Yarni took the baby to put her down for the night.

"Uncle Des, remember what I told you? It's true," Lava said in a low tone.

"What is?" Des asked.

"What I told you about Felix," she whispered.

"Do you have proof?" he asked.

"Yes."

"Then, you need to give it to me."

"My cousin saw him out at the club last night. He was drunk and high as a full moon. She went home with him, and he told her in so many words that"—she took a deep breath and began fanning herself—"that he had Nasir killed."

"Felix said that to your cousin?"

"Yes. She said that he told her that he had to put down one of his customers, who was getting too ambitious and was on to his game. He felt threatened by Nasir. She was with me at church, but out of respect I didn't want to bring her here to the house."

Before Des could respond, they were interrupted by Yarni's return.

"My poor baby was so tired," Yarni said, then began to talk about Desi.

As Yarni talked, Des thought about Felix. He always knew there was something nefarious about Felix's eyes, but he couldn't pinpoint it. He was cold and low-down. No sooner had those thoughts crossed Des's mind than it hit him—Felix had the eyes of a reptile; he was a snake. Des's gut never lied. Lava was speaking the truth.

Des knew what he had to do.

CHAPTER 27

Project Getback

es and Yarni were volunteering in the South American hospital the church had adopted. As Lootchee came around the corner to meet Des, he stopped in his tracks, staring in amazement. He thought he was seeing a ghost when he laid eyes on Yarni passing out coloring books and crayons to the children. As he watched from a distance, his first thought was "It couldn't be." Then he looked again and was sure it was *her*. He was astonished, and he studied Yarni's every move for the next ten minutes.

It couldn't possibly be his ex-fiancée, this woman's skin tone was about six shades lighter. But then again, money can buy the products to make the skin lighter. He knew if it wasn't Bambi, then it was someone closely related to her. Surely, this person could lead him to the one woman who betrayed him.

"Small motherfucking world," he uttered under his breath, a sinister grin spreading across his face. "Small motherfucking world." The grin turned into a huge smile. The last time he'd seen Bambi she was on BET, discussing the good life her party-planning business enabled her to live. It was a business he had helped her build. But at the time, he was living in what might as well have been a grass hut in South America, paranoid that his freedom would be snatched from under his feet at any given minute. At that moment he chose revenge over money. Bambi, as well as anything or anyone whom she loved or who loved her, was fair game.

Since revenge was best served cold, he stood Des up and vowed that he would fulfill the promise he had made to himself a couple of years ago, when he found out that Bambi had triple-crossed him. Fuck Des and the plane or boat he rode in on. This was the first time in Lootchee's life that MOB—money over bitches—didn't apply. The bitterness, anger, and resentment in his heart overrode his golden rule.

Lootchee's itinerary for the day changed as he quickly devised his Project Getback. But he needed a partner in crime, and only one person's name came to mind: Unique.

Although this wasn't Lootchee's usual day to visit the whore-house, Miguel was happy to see him. Business had been slow, and as soon as he saw Lootchee, he knew things were about to pick up. To Miguel's surprise, Lootchee offered to buy Unique. After haggling on the price, they agreed on thirty-five hundred dollars.

When Miguel informed Unique that he had sold her to Lootchee and she was to go to work for him, she felt that her prayers had finally been answered. Unique grabbed her few things and practically ran toward Lootchee's car, where he was waiting for her.

She ran her hands along the gleaming exterior of his Range Rover and inhaled her first breath of freedom after more than three years of living and working in the brothel.

"Today is your lucky day," Lootchee said.

"I can never thank you enough," Unique said as she got inside the car, kissed Lootchee on the cheek, and then began checking out the car before snuggling into the leather, which hugged her body like a glove.

"Don't worry. Nothing comes without a price."

"It ain't nothing." Unique shrugged, not moved by her new owner's comment. "I've been paying all my life—sometimes a little, sometimes a lot, but something tells me that this is going to cost me, sho 'nuff."

"Good that you know that."

There was a moment of silence before they got down to business. "Listen, first and foremost, your loyalty is to me," he told her.

"Of course. No doubt."

"You hear what I'm saying? I gotta have unconditional loyalty."

Unique nodded. "You got that. I promise. You got that." She ran her hand along his leg. "You got whatever you want," she said seductively, thinking that he was a completely different person when she had him at her mercy in the bedroom.

"Anything other than that, I'm going to consider treason, and I approach treasonous people with extreme prejudice."

"You . . . you don't have to worry about that," she said nervously, starting to feel the wrath of Lootchee's threatening tone.

"I'm going to pay you," he said.

She interrupted him, shaking her head. "Getting me out of here and giving me freedom is more than I can ask for."

"That's nothing. I'm going to pay you beyond your wildest dreams, but you gotta understand that if you cross me, no U.S. laws or South American president, bishop, dictator, ruler, or king can protect you."

"I get it. I'm on your team," she said without hesitation; she looked into his eyes to reassure him. "Now, what do you need me to do?"

"There's an American minister and his wife over at the hospital distributing medicine from the States. I need you to go give them your sob story and get them to take you back to Virginia with them. Once in Virginia, I need you to place yourself in their inner circle."

"Once I do that, then what?" Unique asked.

"Just keep your eyes and ears open."

"Is it anything in particular that you're looking for?"

"No. I'll know when I hear it."

"So, that's it? Listen for information?" she questioned.

"Pretty much." He looked at her.

"The way you were talking, I thought you wanted someone killed or the president's daughter kidnapped."

"What if I had asked you to do that?"

"Then, I would have played my position." She looked into his eyes again. Though her hazel eyes were beautiful, there was an ugly story behind them. Unique was a trifling, shysty, low-down dirty bitch. In her day, she had pulled off some scandalous and grimy stunts. She would have done any- and everything for money, which was how she had ended up in the whorehouse three years ago. Her then boyfriend, Took, took her on a paradise vacation, but before it was all over, she'd found herself without a passport, and the property of Miguel Villa. Took had sold

Unique to him for two chickens, a mule, and a key of coke as a way of giving her a dose of her own medicine. She was a first-class snake, and she would have done anything to get herself out of that hellhole.

"Let's play ball, then," Lootchee stated.

"The last dude that bailed me out left me here," Unique said, almost feeling sorry for herself.

"Well, we'll have to get him back, huh?" Lootchee smiled, stroking the back of his hand down the side of Unique's face.

She smiled at him. "That would be lovely, but he's in the States."

"It doesn't matter where he is. Nobody who betrays me or anybody I care about has immunity."

"Sounds real good, but you don't have to say that you care to get me to do the job. I'm going to do it."

"I know that. You're going to do what I need you to do, or you'll have to pay me a bigger debt. In return, I'll protect you and make sure whoever fucked you over gets what's due to him, plus you'll get a handsome piece of money in the process. All you have to do is play fair with me."

Her heart was set on getting back to the United States to try to get revenge on the people who had betrayed her. She had nothing to lose. She said, "There's only one thing: I don't have a passport."

"I can take care of that."

"All right, then, what else do I need?"

"We'll play this as we go along, but always know that I'll never be far away. The main thing you have to do is make them embrace you and welcome you into their world."

"Done."

As Lootchee drove Unique to the hospital, he described Des and Yarni and relayed to her all the information he had dug up on them. Unique ran over and over in her head what she would say to the couple in order to convince them to take her back to the States with them. By the time they made it to the hospital, she had her lines down pat.

"Don't let me down, baby" were Lootchee's last words to Unique as she got out of the Range Rover.

"Let you down?" Unique asked. "My job is to get you up." She winked and then disappeared into the hospital.

$ $ $

Upon walking into the hospital, Unique looked around until she found what she was looking for. In a room with several children she saw an attractive black man and a woman who looked perhaps to be his wife. They were surrounded by sick children, and the woman was reading a storybook out loud.

"All right, Unique," she whispered to herself. *Do your motherfucking thing, bitch!*

As disgusting as Unique's plan was, she really didn't give a solitary fuck. She had a job to do. And not only did she have to do the job, but she had to do it well.

Unique slowly backed out of the room and went to prepare for her grand entrance. Five minutes later the velvet curtain opened, and it was time for the performance of a lifetime.

"Help me! Oh God, help me!" Unique yelled as she fell into the room where Des and Yarni were with the children, sprawled out on the floor.

"Oh, my goodness," Yarni said, dropping the book she had been reading to the children and running over to Unique, who appeared to be in excruciating pain. "Des, go get a doctor!"

Des exited the room, passing Unique, who was clutching one arm, out of which blood seemed to be pouring.

"What happened to you, sweetie?" Yarni asked as she lifted Unique's head and placed it in her lap, getting blood on her designer dress. "Who did this to you?"

Unique just looked up at Yarni with tears pouring out of her eyes. "Just let me die. He's going to find me and kill me anyway if I live. So just let me die, please."

"Don't talk like that," Yarni comforted her and began to rock her. She looked down at the arm Unique was clutching. Blood was seeping between her fingers. "Somebody help us!" Fear took over Yarni; she did not want this woman dying in her arms. When she looked over at the kids, she realized the situation was scaring them to death. She prayed help would arrive quickly.

Des returned to the room followed by a team of help.

"Let us take her," one of the nurses said, as they proceeded to lift Unique from Yarni's arms.

"No!" Unique screamed. She then looked to Yarni, having figured out already that she could play on her emotional strings. "Don't let them take me."

"Calm down," Yarni told her. "Look, I'll go with you."

Unique looked to the team of medical personnel around her and then back at Yarni. "Okay," she said.

"Fine," the nurse said as they carried Unique out of the room, "but you'll have to wait outside of the examination room."

Yarni was satisfied with that. "Des, finish reading to the kids to calm them down," Yarni said to him. "I'll be back." She followed the doctor and nurses out of the room and was directed to wait in an area outside of the examination room where they were taking care of Unique.

A little while later the doctor and nurses emerged from the room. Yarni stood. "How is she?" she asked.

"She's fine," one nurse replied. "The wound to her arm, anyway. She's a bleeder, so the blood made it look far worse than it actually was."

"You say her wound?" Yarni questioned. "Did something else happen to her?"

The nurse's eyes lowered. "I know I shouldn't be telling you this, but we believe the woman was raped as well, although she refused an examination. It's awful how these women are made to feel ashamed of something they have no control over." The nurse shook her head. "You can see her now. She looks like she could use a friend." She smiled and patted Yarni on the shoulder.

A little choked up, Yarni entered the room where Unique was lying down with her back toward the door. Yarni spoke softly, "Hello." The girl didn't budge. Yarni walked to the other side of the bed to face Unique. Tears were streaming out of Unique's eyes.

She looked up at Yarni. "He raped me and tried to kill me" was all Unique said, and she began to cry loudly.

"It's okay," Yarni assured her. "You're okay now."

"But I'm not. The man who did this to me, he's going to kill me."

Yarni's heart went out to the distraught girl. She was angry at whoever had done this to her and wanted to kill him herself. "No one's going to kill you. Not if I can help it."

Unique let out an unconvinced chuckle and said, "What are you going to do? Stay here in South America and protect me? I heard the doctor and nurses talking about the couple from America. You won't even be around to protect me. You're a liar just like everyone else in this world who has promised to help me but done nothing but hurt me. So how are you going to protect me? Are you going to take me back to the States with you? Huh?"

Yarni just stood there, feeling helpless.

"I thought so."

"Listen—"

"No, you listen," Unique cried. "Do you know what it's like to be forced to be a sex slave in a whorehouse? To get beaten and raped, and now almost killed? Nobody's ever going to help me. Never."

Yarni's heart had been opened wide since her involvement with Des and the church. Her heart wept for the girl lying before her. She had no idea what Unique had been through, but what she did know was that she didn't want to be one of those people who turned her back on her. So before she knew it, the word *yes* fell from her lips. "Yes," Yarni repeated. "I am going to take you back to the States with me, if that's what's going to keep you alive; if that's what's going to let you know that you are worthy."

Unique had a look of disbelief in her eyes. *Damn, this shit worked out better than I expected . . . and quicker, too,* she thought to herself. Once she'd spotted Yarni and Des after arriving at the hospital, Unique had found the bathroom and gone inside a stall, but not before locating a pair of scissors and taking them into the stall with her. There she cut her arm, but not too deep. She had been subjected to enough pain in her life; she wasn't about to inflict more than she had to on herself.

Because the cut was actually more of a scrape, there wasn't much blood, but fortunately for Unique, it was that time of the month. She simply pulled the plug out and smeared the menstrual blood onto her wound. It made her gag, but that blood and its scent only made her claim of rape even more believable.

Before leaving Unique's side, Yarni promised her that she would take her back to Virginia with her and her husband, help her find a job, and get on her feet. Unique embraced Yarni and thanked her repeatedly until she walked out the door. Then Unique lay there in the hospital bed with a smile of victory on her face. Indeed, she had done her job . . . and well.

CHAPTER 28

The First Lady

Ever since he returned from his unsuccessful South America trip, Des couldn't think about anything or anybody except Felix's killing Nasir.

Des was so deep in thought, it took him a minute to realize Yarni had walked into the room.

"You okay?" she asked after studying him for a moment.

He nodded.

Yarni sighed. "Well, if I can help you in any way, let me know."

"Actually, you can," Des said, sitting up in bed. "I gotta take care of something." He looked in her eyes, and she knew that whatever he had to take care of was the source of his preoccupation. "I have to do it. I don't really want to, but it's got to be done."

"Is there some way I can help you?"

"Just stand by me, the way you always do. You can't help me

with my problem, but you can go by and see Sister Robin Lyles for me."

"Okay. Does she need prayer?" Yarni had gotten used to being part of Des's newest game. Although she still wasn't totally in favor of it, she took her first lady duties very seriously. In 1 Corinthians 7:14 it said, "For the unbelieving husband has been sanctified through the wife." Yarni's hope was that she could be sanctified enough for the both of them.

"Yes. She's been calling me saying that she's sick and needs prayer."

"Okay, baby, I got that." She kissed him on his forehead and gave him a hug.

"Once I get this thing taken care of, I can spend some time with my two favorite girls."

"Okay." Yarni said, smiling encouragement at him. She turned to leave, but just as quickly, she turned around to face Des again. She reached into the pocket of her robe, removed something, and tossed it onto the bed. "Maybe this will help you. Sometimes you need to practice what you preach." She turned and left the room.

It was a small custom-made Bible with his initials engraved on the front in gold leaf. Des looked at the Bible for a few seconds before picking it up. As he flipped through the pages, he came across Psalm 23, and read aloud, "Even though I walk through the valley of the shadow of death," and thought about what he had to do.

$$$

The next day marked the beginning of the Samuel Johnson trial. Yarni got up early and was at the jail before seven to meet with her client.

Samuel came into the attorney visiting room with a smile on his face.

"My, your spirits seem to be up," Yarni said.

"Today I get to find my destiny. It's the first day of the rest of my life."

"That's what I wanted to talk to you about." She looked sternly at him.

"Don't tell me you want to plead me out." He shook his head, looking at her in disgust.

"No, just listen. I finally got my hands on the file that Sledge was holding hostage."

Samuel's face lit up. "And?"

"I'm going to need you to listen to what I'm about to tell you."

"All ears," he said.

"First, I think I can get you off on your charges. However, I'm going to need your help—make sure we have all our avenues covered. The information that Sledge was holding should be enough, but you never know, so what I need you to do is first get showered and shaved. I need you to look good."

"What? I look good now," he said, stroking his freshly braided hair.

"Yeah"—she nodded—"you look okay, but I need you to look *GQ* good. Get the braids cut off, and shave all that hair off your face."

"A'ight," he said, somewhat reluctant.

"Your girlfriend, Angie, left you shoes and a suit up front. Put them on. Once we get in the courtroom, make eye contact with the jury, look sincere and innocent, not intimidating, especially to the younger women."

"I've never had any problem with looking sincere to women."

"Well, good. My goal was to get as many older and younger women on the jury as possible, and to strike out the white men and middle-aged women. I did the best I could, but you have to do your part."

"Good looking."

"Also, if you need to ask me something or make a comment in court, write me a note."

"Don't worry, I got you," he said reassuringly.

"So, since we're clear, I've got to get going. I've got a few things I have to do before the trial."

"I saw your husband on television. I was shocked as a motherfucker. He in the big time now, preaching and shit."

"Yeah, he's doing some great things in the community. I have to go do my first lady duties now." Yarni grabbed her bag and was about to leave, when Samuel called out to her.

"Look, I want you to know I 'preciate everything you've done for me. Regardless of what happens, I owe you. There's nothing I wouldn't do for you, for real. Nothing! I mean that shit. You went beyond the call of duty to help me, and that's real. I owe you."

"Just doing my job." She smiled on the outside, but inside his comments let her know that what she was doing was not in vain.

Yarni made her way over to Sister Robin's house as Des had requested. On behalf of Des and the church, she held a get-well gift basket, and she waited impatiently for Robin to answer the door. Someone called, "It's open," and Yarni went in. She couldn't believe her eyes when she saw what was behind the door. It was "Sister" Robin wearing a red negligee with red stockings, lying seductively on the couch, grinning wickedly. She looked into Yarni's eyes and jumped up, trying to cover herself.

"Uhhh," Robin stuttered, embarrassment all over face.

" 'Uhhh' is right," Yarni said, placing the gift basket on the coffee table. "Surprise, baby. You weren't expecting me, huh?" Yarni moved in closer, looking Robin up and down. "You were expecting my husband, huh?" Tears filled Robin's eyes as Yarni got up in her face. She tried to cover herself, but her outfit was so skimpy there was no point. Yarni laughed at the attempt.

"I'm sorry," Robin said.

Yarni shook her head. "No, you're not. You're just sorry you got caught." She circled Robin, inspecting her seduction outfit a little more closely.

"Please don't hurt me," Robin said. "I promise you it will never happen again."

"Naw, baby, I ain't gon' whip your half-naked behind. I'm a woman of God. I trust I won't be seeing you at church anymore. You need to find you another place of worship and repent for your sins. Trust me, if I see you up in my husband's church again, the next time you'll be in there, it'll be for your funeral."

She turned around to leave, then quickly swung back around, scaring Robin. "Oh, you won't be needing this." She snatched the basket off the table and left.

As she got to her car, she sat there for a minute, trying to get herself together. Why did this mess have to happen today of all days—when she was about to try the biggest case of her life? She took a deep breath and focused on the trial ahead of her before praying for God's angels to surround and protect her as well as guide her during the trial. Finally, she prayed for Desi and for Des, that God would protect him, whatever he was doing. "Lord give me the strength! Watch over my family and my friends, and give me the actions and words to win this case."

Once she had pulled herself together, she gave Des a call, knowing that hearing his voice before the trial would help her to focus. She was disappointed when she got his voice mail.

She was mentally rehearsing her opening statement when her cell phone rang. She looked at the caller ID and groaned. She did not need to talk to her mother-in-law right then. When Joyce hung up and called right back, Yarni picked up, fearing that something was wrong.

"Hello?" Yarni said.

"Am I still supposed to pick up the baby today?" Joyce asked, ignoring Yarni's greeting.

"Yes, Joyce," Yarni said, rolling her eyes.

"I still can't believe you put that baby in day care. There's no reason for her to be there. I told you I could take care of her," Joyce fussed.

"I know you could. Look, Joyce, we appreciate all you've done for Desi, but she's getting older, and she needs to start interacting with other kids more. It's not like she's there every day. You still get to keep her two days a week, and if you'd like you can see her during the weekends, too," Yarni said, trying to be reasonable despite hating the thought of having to see her mother-in-law any more than she already did.

"But there are seven days in a week. That means the people at the day care center are seeing her as much as her own family. That's not right. You don't know what kind of nonsense those people are putting into that baby's head."

"Joyce, Desi is fine. This center has a really good reputation. It's the top one in the city. We're lucky we were even able to get Desi in. It normally takes people six months to a year just to get their children in."

"Whatever," Joyce said. "So should I get her at four?"

"That's fine," Yarni said. "Look, I'm pulling up to my office, so I'll talk to you later. Thanks again." She hung up before Joyce could answer.

Before going to court Yarni went to her office to change into another suit and was greeted by a stack of phone messages. Layla was out sick, so she decided to ignore them and was just about to head into her office when the phone rang. She sighed and answered it, since Unique, who was helping out at the office since she arrived, had stepped away from her desk.

"Good afternoon," she said.

"Good afternoon to you, Yarni," a slick voice replied.

Yarni felt her skin crawl. "Why are you calling me?" she said.

"Why, I just wanted to wish you luck on your case. You're going to need it," Marvin Sledge said, and chuckled.

Yarni smiled to herself. Had the man even gone to his office? Didn't he notice that a large number of his files were missing, thanks to Bambi's contact?

"Oh, I'm going to win," she said confidently.

Sledge laughed. "If you say so. Why don't we get together afterward, no matter what the outcome of the case, and celebrate?"

Yarni pulled the phone away from her ear and looked at it. The man really was crazy. She decided she had given him enough of her time and hung up without responding. She whispered a small prayer, asking God not to allow Sledge to ruin her day, then headed to her office to change. She was greeted by a huge arrangement of sunflowers, her favorite. God surely answers prayers, she thought. Of course the flowers were from Des. Yarni didn't know if it was the sight of the sunny-looking flowers or the card that put her into an extra-good mood, which she needed after talking to Joyce. The card read:

Everything important to me begins with you.
In any state and in any state of mind,
You're my first lady!
Loving you for life,

> *Des*

That alone melted her heart and gave her an extra boost of confidence. She changed and headed over to the courtroom, where she kicked some ass; an award-winning actress could not have put on a better performance. She was so savvy; she looked like the black female version of Johnny Cochran as she nailed the case in cross-examination.

She paced the courtroom in her Ellen Tracy suit and Jimmy Choo pumps as she spoke to the prosecution's eyewitness. "Mr. Smith, you testified that on the night of the crime you were there on the street at about ten P.M. Is that correct?"

"Yeah."

Yarni nodded and continued as she moved back and forth in front of the jury. "And you further stated that you were across the street from where you saw Mr. Johnson commit these crimes that he's being tried for today. Is that also correct?"

Again, he replied, "Yeah." He slouched down in his seat, looking bored.

Yarni leaned in and asked, "About how far were you from where you claim you saw these crimes committed? Was it as far as the back of the courtroom, which is probably a hundred yards?"

He nodded. "Yeah, I guess so."

"Mr. Smith, isn't it true that normally you wear glasses, which, for the record, you are not wearing today?"

"Yeah, but I broke my glasses a while back."

Yarni pressed. "On the night of the alleged crimes, you didn't have your glasses on, did you, Mr. Smith?" She then put up a finger and said to him in a firm tone, "Remember, you are under oath, and perjury is punishable as a felony."

The witness hesitated then replied, "Naw, I didn't have no glasses on that night, but I can see fine."

Yarni smirked at him then moved to the back of the courtroom, where she had a woman stand. She then asked, "Mr. Smith, can you identify the person standing here next to me?"

The witness strained and squinted, then said, "Naw, I've never seen that person before."

"Mr. Smith, are you sure you've never seen this person before?"

Again, the witness squinted, and said, "I told you, no."

"Mr. Smith, the person in the back you claimed never to have seen before is Angie Williams, Mr. Samuel Johnson's current girlfriend and your ex-girlfriend. Do you still maintain you've never seen her before? You do have three children together."

The witness began to offer excuse after excuse. "Shoot, it's kind of dark in here. And I don't have my glasses. Maybe she changed her hairdo."

"It was dark the night you said you could positively identify my client as the shooter, Mr. Smith. But what is the real reason you fingered my client as the shooter? Isn't it true that you've been trying to get your girlfriend back so you won't have to pay child support?"

"Objection, Your Honor. She's badgering the witness," the prosecutor interjected frantically.

"I'll allow it," the judge said.

"No," said the witness. "I takes care of mine."

Angie could be heard snorting from the back of the court-room.

"And you figured that by getting my client out of the way, she'd come back to you."

Angie responded from the back of the courtroom: "Samuel could have never been born, and I still wouldn't get back with that deadbeat-dad, minute man, limp-dick motherfucker."

The whole courtroom broke out in laughter. The judge banged his gavel, calling for order.

"You no good bitch!" Smith stood up and yelled to Angie, "That motherfucker think he gonna be a daddy to my kids? Fuck that! If he didn't do that shit, I bet he know who did," he tried to explain to Yarni.

Yarni looked over at the prosecutor, whose normal arrogant expression was replaced by a sickly grimace.

"I rest my case," Yarni said. She pranced back to her seat at the defense table, trying to keep from skipping.

After closing arguments, the jury deliberated for less than an hour before returning to the courtroom.

The judge asked, "Foreperson, has the jury reached a verdict?"

The foreman of the jury stood, holding the verdict forms, and after Yarni and Samuel were asked to stand, the foreman replied, "Yes, Your Honor, we have. On count one, murder in the first degree, not guilty." Yarni squeezed Samuel's hand when she heard the verdict and was so excited, she almost missed the other counts. "On count two, tampering with state's evidence, we find the defendant not guilty. Count three, possession of a firearm, we find the defendant not guilty." The foreperson continued to list Samuel's charges, and they all came back with a verdict of not guilty.

Before Yarni could react, Samuel lifted her off the ground and swung her around, kissing her on the cheek. "You did it!" he shouted.

When he put her down, she returned the hug. "We did it," she said. "Thank you, Lord." She thought to herself how the Lord worked in mysterious ways. There was really no secret file. Marvin had made the whole thing up. Bambi had stolen every single file in his office. She and Yarni stayed up for hours going through every piece of paper there, and there was nothing, no indication of any evidence. In fact, Marvin hadn't the foggiest idea as to how he was going to win the case, and that's why he was so cocky when he made the call to her that morning. Yarni knew God knew her heart when it came to this case and he would see her through.

Yarni settled down as the judge turned to address the jury. "I'd like to thank all of you for performing your civic obligations by sitting on this jury and considering these charges in a fair manner. Your time and effort is greatly appreciated by the Commonwealth. At this time, I'm going to dismiss the jury. Members of the jury, you are free to go; however, the defendant will remain in the courtroom."

Once the jurors were completely out of the courtroom, the judge turned to the sheriffs and said, "Sheriffs, would you please restrain the defendant with handcuffs and leg irons."

Yarni looked up in confusion, trying to figure out what was going on.

The judge looked directly in Samuel's eyes and spoke to him firmly, "Mr. Johnson, you are warned that any resistance at this point will add to an already bad situation for you." The sheriffs approached Samuel and placed both handcuffs and leg irons on him. Samuel's face mirrored the confusion and bewilderment that was on Yarni's face. *What the hell is going on?* she thought.

The judge saw the rage coming upon Samuel's face. "I'm going to further admonish you not to make any statements except through your counsel. I want first to commend your attorney, Mrs. Taylor, for the fine job she did in conducting your case and bringing forth an acquittal on your behalf on all charges. Excellent job, Mrs. Taylor. Unfortunately, your client, Mr. Johnson, has some other issues that we must now deal with."

He glared at Samuel, who didn't say a word. "Mr. Johnson, I take very seriously your prior conduct in throwing a chair at one of my fellow colleagues and in assaulting your former attorney." He raised his voice again, but his tone remained as firm as a Posturepedic mattress. "So, while you could have walked free from this courtroom today, that is not going to be the case. I am finding you in contempt of court for your intentionally blatant misconduct of throwing a chair at an official of the court, and I'm sentencing you to serve two and a half years in prison with no time off for good behavior or early release. I am also finding that you committed assault and battery against your former attorney and am sentencing you to serve an additional two and a half years in prison, for a total of five years. Sheriff, take Mr. Johnson back to begin serving his sentence. Court is dismissed." He banged his gavel.

Yarni saw murder written all over Samuel's face—if looks could kill, the judge would be kissing Jesus' feet at that moment. She felt bad for Samuel, and as the bailiffs came to take him to the back, he asked, "Look, let me have a word with my attorney."

One deputy was about to say no, but Yarni shot him a look. "We're going to be only a minute."

Before either of them spoke, they made sure the court officers were out of earshot and then he said to her in a whisper, "Listen, I'm forever grateful to you. I meant what I said to you at the jail. I owe you my life, and if anybody ever fucks with you . . . it's done. We have a special bond, on some real shit. I'm indebted to you."

"No, you're not. As I said, I was only doing my job."

"Naw, but you ain't have to do that."

"Listen, go and stay out of trouble and in a couple of years, we'll see if we can get you work release." She patted him on the back. "Hold your head up, and remember, no storm lasts forever."

CHAPTER 29

Ghost Killer

elix had violated him in such a foul way that Des felt he had to bring it to Felix's front door—literally. Felix rarely left his turf when he was in Richmond, and Des wanted to make sure Felix knew that he wasn't untouchable. It was time for Felix finally to pay the piper.

After days of studying the man, Des determined that he was a big jerk-off whose main activities were sniffing dope and dropping Ecstasy pills. He laughed to himself, realizing that stupid Felix never once checked to see if he was being watched. As Des analyzed his mark, he knew that committing the actual crime would be a breeze, but the getaway route could be a problem. Finding the right route to make a smooth escape became his focus. He scoped four different possibilities in case shit got too deep—he wanted to be prepared for the worst.

The day of reckoning was finally here. Des was on his cell phone, driving around the neighborhood, keeping an eye out for Felix. He had been waiting for hours, but the way he was feeling, he could stay there for a lifetime. He had decided this was going to be his last murder, and he wanted it to be perfect.

Felix's condo, though upscale, was small, with a tiny porch attached to the front and a low, flat roof that had green weeds all over it. There were a lot of well-manicured trees and bushes that hid the front of the house from the street. Felix had probably assumed that the bushes would be a great cover for the house. Too bad he had no idea that those bushes would end up being a double-edged sword, Des thought.

Des rode past in a hoopty to check out the condo one more time. He observed Felix and his peeps leaving. Des parked up the block so he could get a full visual of the place and ate a sandwich, replaying the scene over one more time in his head. Once his food had been digested he said out loud, "Showtime."

Des drove off and parked two streets over, then began making his way to his spot on the roof. He wasn't in a rush, and fear had not penetrated his heart. He quickly walked through the alleyway he had scoped out on one of his previous visits, and once he approached Felix's backyard gate, he looked around to make sure that he wasn't being watched. He then pulled out a tranquilizer gun and aimed it first at one, then the other, of the two big dogs that were tied to a fence, sending them into a state of immobility as the drugs rushed into their bloodstream. As he walked by the dogs, he plucked the darts out of them to dispose of later.

He walked along the side of the house and climbed on top of the roof, which was hidden from view, thanks to the bushes. Three hours went by, and there was no motion at all in the house.

As he waited, his thoughts were getting crazy. Anxiety and guilt started to set in. He promised God that if he let him get away with this murder, he'd never do another one. He knew he was tripping, but he believed in his heart that this had to be done.

A black Mercedes CLK 320 pulled up. Two women got out and retrieved their shopping bags from the trunk and backseat of the car.

"You really liked those shoes, huh?" one said.

"Yeah, girl, they are so nice," the other answered.

"You know I'm going to wear them when I fuck the shit out of your brother tonight." The first woman laughed.

"I don't want to hear that shit. TMI—too much information."

"He better hurry up and come on."

"Didn't he say he was on his way?"

"Yes. He said he'd be here in fifteen minutes, but that was twenty minutes ago."

"He should be pulling up any minute now."

They went inside the house, shut the door, and turned on some reggae music, but Des could still hear them talking.

He listened in on the idle chitter chat as the girls continued to have diarrhea of the mouth, but he was distracted by the approaching sound of pounding bass. As it got closer, the entire house vibrated.

Careless-ass nigga, Des thought. He took a deep breath and got into position.

Felix pulled up in the passenger seat of a black Range Rover with his three homeboys. One of the guys got out of the backseat of the car and ran inside the house while the other backseat rider got out, stood on the curb, and lit a Black and Mild. Des zeroed in closer and realized the guy who was pulling on the cigar was Felix's brother. The thought of how it would feel to see his own brother be assassinated in front of his very eyes gave Des a boost of energy. He thought about taking him out, too, just on general principle, but decided against it, remembering his promise to God earlier that day.

He watched as Felix smoked a blunt and complained to the dude who had been in the backseat. "I wish this motherfucker hurry the hell up. Pacos, hurry up, man," Felix yelled toward the house.

"Papi, come in for a minute. Pacos is having problems," one of the women said, coming to the door.

"Mami, you just want to see me." Felix knew what she was up to, but he opened up the door, got out of the car, and headed for the house.

Des took aim. He couldn't take any foolish chances, so he waited for the perfect opportunity to shoot. He didn't want to blow it. Every step Felix took seemed to be in slow motion. As he got closer and closer, Des got more anxious. Felix finally got to the porch and opened the door. Des peeped down. Felix had one foot inside the doorway of the house. With the uncanny speed of a bolt of lightning, Des reached down and put his powerful .40 caliber to the back of Felix's head and squeezed the trigger, knocking Felix out of his shoes and into the house. Just as quick, Des was back up on the roof. The women screamed as Des walked to the edge of the roof, making his getaway while Felix's goons were busy shooting at nothing.

Des reached his car, jumped in, and laughed as he smoothly made his exit. He had been so concerned with planning multiple getaways, and his first route was what he ended up using. Felix's peeps were still trying to figure out what had happened and hadn't bothered even to start looking for the killer.

The assassination was effective because the driver in the car didn't see anything, nor did Felix's brother see anyone walk up and shoot Felix, although the autopsy would show that he got shot at close range. Felix's brother even entertained the thought that one of his homeboys might have shot him. After the dust settled, Rico was suspicious of everyone at Felix's house that night. Someone knew something, because a ghost sure as hell hadn't killed his nephew. The tension and paranoia were up. No one knew who did what or who to point a finger at. If someone could kill Felix that easily, what was to stop the killer from coming back for the others?

CHAPTER 30

Things Ain't Ever
What They Seem

Once Yarni was out of court, she called Des to tell him about her victory, but his phone went straight to voice mail again. She called her office as she navigated through traffic.

"Thanks for calling Taylor and Associates. How may I help you?"

"Hey, Unique," Yarni said into the phone, "I thought you were supposed to get off at four-thirty, but you've been staying as late as I have. You know, you don't have to do that, but we do appreciate you coming in and holding down the fort so that Layla is able to help me more."

"Don't mention it," Unique told her boss. "You and Des did so much for me, so anything I can do, I'll do. I've never had anyone to believe in me and love me with all my faults. I've done some grimy stuff, and for the first time I really feel I fit in. But besides, I don't like going home because Khadijah has that big-butt white man that she creeps with in her room, and I hate the smell of those stanking-ass cigars he smokes. It brings back too many bad memories of when I was working in South America. I just try to go home when it's late and she's asleep, and her company is gone."

"So, she's really messing around on Ahmeen, huh?" Yarni asked, somewhat surprised by the revelation. She had always suspected that there was more to Sister Khadijah than she let on, but she thought the woman was faithful to her husband to a fault.

"Yes, and with a devil at that. Seems like she ain't the perfect Muslim sister she pretends to be."

"Well, you know we all have our faults. I just never thought she would mess around on Ahmeen. Hey, it's hard when a man is behind prison walls, but she didn't have to go with a white man and have him in the house."

"Well, at first I used to see him like once every now and then, when she was letting him in late at night after she thought I was asleep, or when he was leaving early in the morning before I woke up, but he's been there the last few nights. Please don't say anything. You know I still have to live there."

"I won't. I do want you to know that you've come a long way since I met you in South America, and I am so very proud of you."

"Thanks." Unique was quiet for a second, then she changed the subject, "So how did the trial go?"

"Everything went well. We TKO'd, but Samuel still got five years on some contempt of court charges. Still, that's better than the forty years to life he was facing."

"Congrats," Unique said. "You have a stack of messages, but the most pressing is that your mother-in-law called three times. Plus, I have to talk to you about something when you get here."

Yarni sighed. Ever since she had decided to put Desi in day

care, Joyce had been getting on her last nerve, treating her like she had put Desi in a girls' home.

Just then the phone beeped, and Yarni looked on the cell phone's caller ID. "Speak of the devil. It's Joyce. Unique, let me take this call."

"Okay."

Yarni clicked over to the other line and greeted her mother-in-law. "Hello, Joyce." Yarni rolled her eyes up in her head.

Joyce started right up. "I thought you wanted me to pick up Desi. Why'd you go and get her?"

"What?" Yarni said, surprised. "Joyce, I didn't pick her up. Des must have gotten her."

"No, they said you signed her out." Joyce stressed the word *you.*

"Joyce, I don't have her!" Yarni yelled as she busted an illegal U-turn in the middle of the street and sped to the day care.

"What you mean?" Joyce asked, alarm evident in her voice.

"I don't have Desi, and I didn't pick her up. I've been in court all day and just got out ten minutes ago. Let me call and see if Des got her," Yarni said, her heart pounding.

"He ain't answering either. I tried calling him right before I called you. His phone is going straight to the voice mail," Joyce said.

"Look, let me call the day care."

Yarni hung up, but not before Joyce demanded, "Yes, you do that."

She called the day care, and the director said that Desi wasn't there and that Yarni had signed her out. Before Yarni could cuss her out, she lost the call.

Yarni didn't know what to do. Des wasn't picking up, and neither was Bambi. She called her mother in Florida, frantic, as she ran every red light trying to get to the center. Gloria calmed Yarni down a little bit, and then called her brother, Stanka, and Yarni's dad, Lloyd, to fill them in since they lived nearby and could get to Yarni quicker.

Yarni tried calling Bambi again and was relieved when her sister answered the phone.

"These motherfuckers done let my baby go with someone else," she said the minute Bambi answered.

"What?" Bambi asked, sounding confused. "Yarni, what are you talking about?"

Yarni tried to calm down. She was only a few minutes from the center and knew she had to talk fast because all hell was going to break loose once she set foot through the doors, if they couldn't produce her baby.

"Joyce called me and said Desi wasn't at day care, so I called the center, and the director said I signed her out, but I don't have her." Yarni felt tears filling her eyes. "Bambi, they don't know where the fuck my baby is."

"I'm on my way," Bambi said, as Yarni pulled into the day care center's parking lot.

Yarni slammed the car into park and jumped out, rushing through the doors of the center.

"Where the hell is my baby?" she screamed at the first employee she saw.

The woman looked stunned. "I'm sorry, ma'am. Today is my first day. Who is your child?"

"Desi Taylor," Yarni said.

The woman glanced around, unsure of what to do.

"You know what, fuck this. Where's the director?" Yarni screamed, forgetting that she was indeed the first lady of Good

Life Ministry. Parents who were picking up their children stopped to stare at her.

The director arrived a few seconds later, having heard Yarni yelling from her office.

"Please calm down," the director said. "If you'll follow me to my office, I'm sure we can straighten everything out."

"I'm not going anywhere," Yarni said, planting her feet firmly on the ground. "Where is my baby?"

The director looked around nervously at the other parents who were waiting expectantly for her answer. "We don't know where she is," she said quietly. "I double-checked our records after you called, and they indicate you picked her up." She went and grabbed the sign-out sheet from the new girl at the front desk. "Here's your signature right here."

Yarni briefly glanced at it, knowing she hadn't signed Desi out. "That doesn't look anything like my signature!" she screamed. "Where is my baby?" Tears filled her eyes, and Yarni suddenly found it hard to breathe.

"Would you like a drink of water?" the director asked, touching her arm.

Yarni swatted her hand away. "I want my baby!" she yelled.

"I'm sorry. I don't know where she is. I called the police right before I came out here. They should be here any second."

"Why would you wait until I arrived? I told you on the phone I didn't sign my daughter out. What is wrong with you? How can a person just walk up in here and take my baby? Didn't you check their identification?"

The new receptionist looked at the floor, and Yarni reached out and slapped her, stunning the woman. As she reached back to swing again, someone grabbed her hand midair.

"Calm down," Bambi said. "Let me handle this."

Before Yarni could respond, the police arrived—followed shortly by Joyce, Uncle Stanka, and Lloyd—and locked down the center, not allowing anyone else to exit until everyone had been questioned. Three hours later, there was still no sign of Desi. It was as though she had disappeared into thin air.

Yarni watched the center's security video of the few minutes leading up to the kidnapping. The woman who had taken Desi had kept her back to the camera, but there was something familiar about her. Desi hadn't seemed frightened at all by the woman—in fact, she had reached for her and laughed, which in a strange way offered Yarni a little comfort.

Bambi drove her home, and it wasn't until they were pulling out of the day care's parking lot that Yarni realized she still hadn't heard from Des.

Yarni's house became the headquarters for family and friends during the crisis. Joyce, Lava, and Uncle Stanka were there. Bambi's husband, Lynx, had his ear to the streets to see if there was anything circulating, but there was nothing. They didn't know if Des was dead or alive, because he wasn't answering his phone. The church members got wind of the abduction and organized a prayer vigil and search squad as Yarni waited for news to come in.

Yarni prayed like never before. *Lord, surround my sweet child with angels to protect her. Please lead me to my beautiful daughter and let my husband be safe and sound.*

Yarni paced the floor. *Maybe this is somehow related to that motherfucking bitch who tried to set Des up,* she thought. "Get that crackhead who helped clear Des up here. She's gotta try harder to describe that woman who paid her," she said when she finally got in touch with Unique, who had left for the day. A thought occurred to Yarni, and she turned and asked no one in particular, "Did she make up the woman with the tattoo? I swear to God, if she's behind this, I'm going to kill that bitch myself!" Yarni screamed.

Lava and a few others had dashed over to meet Unique at the office to get Yarni's files on the mystery woman who had paid the crackhead to finger Des. Unique insisted on heading back to the house in case Yarni needed her, so Layla and Slim stayed at the office to answer the phone in case a ransom call came that way.

After Unique gave the files to Lava, she got in her car and was heading to Yarni's house when she decided to pick up some food and coffee for the family. She felt bad about Little Desi. For a split second she thought it was Lootchee who may have taken her to get back at the family, but she wouldn't dare point the finger at him. She knew better. She decided to call and report in to let him know what had happened and see if he would tell her anything. She got him on the phone

"Things are so crazy here. All hell has broken loose," Unique said.

"What?" Lootchee replied.

"Yarni and Des's baby has been kidnapped."

"For real?" Lootchee said, sounding genuinely surprised.

"Yup."

"That's fucked up. It should have been Bambi's and Lynx's baby. That would have made my shit easier."

"You didn't have anything to do with it?" Unique boldly asked, knowing she shouldn't question her master.

"Fuck no, I didn't do that shit, but it sounds like a good idea to snatch that bitch Bambi's baby from her, and take all my frustrations that I have for Bambi out on the baby."

His words let Unique know he was the most treacherous man she had ever come across in her life. "Oh, okay, just wanted to check in and let you know the latest on this end, that's all," she said, trying to hurry off the phone so he wouldn't hear the fear in her voice.

"Good job. Stay focused."

"I will."

Unique hung up and wondered for a second what she had gotten herself into, but, more important, how she was ever going to get out of it.

Once Unique arrived with the food, she saw Bambi's little girl running around and felt sorry for her because she knew that Lootchee would not have any mercy on her.

She thought about all the things men had done to her in her past and didn't want the little innocent girl to be exploited like she had been time and time again. If Lootchee got his hands on her, God only knew what he would do.

Bambi rolled her eyes at Unique because she thought that Unique wanted Lynx. Back in the day, Unique had made a play for him. Unique humbly sucked up the cattiness that Bambi sent her way.

The phone rang, and everyone became quiet. Yarni ran down from her home office, where she had been praying, just as Bambi answered. "Hello. Taylor residence."

"Yarnise, this Sam. I really need to talk to you," he said.

"This is not Yarni; this is Bambi, her sister."

"How you doing? I need to speak to Yarnise, please. It's very important."

"She can't talk right now, Sam."

"What about Des, her husband? Where's he?"

"He's not here either."

"Look, it's an emergency. I need to speak to one of them."

"Now is not a good time," Bambi snapped. "We actually have an emergency going on here."

"I might be able to help. I need to speak to Yarnise."

Bambi turned to her sister, who looked at her expectantly. Steeling herself for bad news, Yarni asked, "What is it?"

"This is Sam. He said he could help." Bambi told Yarni.

Yarni snatched the cordless phone out of Bambi's hands. "Samuel—"

"I need you to listen to me carefully, and hear me out. I heard that the bitch that works for your husband came down here yesterday, to see her husband, and that she went crazy in the visiting room, and they put her out."

"What does that have to do with me? I can't be a marriage counselor right now," she said, pacing the room. Several people looked at her for a second, but when they realized it wasn't a ransom call, they went back to talking.

"She was talking about how she wanted him home, how life ain't fair, and how she been talking to Columbo."

"What?" Yarni asked, rushing back up to her office so she could hear Samuel over the noise. She collapsed in her office chair and placed her hand on her forehead, longing for a pill. She took a deep breath and tried to focus on what Samuel was saying. She looked irritated when someone knocked on the door and entered without waiting for her to respond. She waved them away but they wouldn't leave.

Unique walked in with a cup of coffee and held it out to Yarni. She rolled her eyes and reached for the cup, just to get rid of Unique, but as she went to grasp it, it slipped out of her hands, landing on her desk and soaking the pictures she had been pouring over from the description that Malinda Briggs had given.

Unique grabbed the pictures, trying to keep them from being ruined. As she pulled them apart to prevent their sticking together, her eyes widened when they landed on a picture of a tattoo. She motioned to get Yarni's attention, but Yarni ignored her and focused on Samuel. Finally Unique got on her cell phone and left the room.

"She said that she can't get information on Des to feed to the cops like she needs and that she needs Ahmeen to help her." Samuel's voice raised with compassion. "Word is Ahmeen ain't want no parts of the shit. He told that bitch that he would rather do ten life sentences in solitary than cross Des and that she ain't the chick he married and that he needed a motherfucking divorce.

"Ahmeen said that he was trying to reach you to warn you but couldn't reach Des, and Khadijah just put a block on the phone so he couldn't call. He said he didn't know who she was and what she was capable of at this point."

"This shit is crazy. I gotta go," Yarni said, her mind racing.

Just then Unique walked back in the room and wrote on a piece of paper. She held up a note in one hand that read THAT'S KHADIJAH'S TATTOO, and held the picture of the tattoo in the other.

Yarni hung up, looking at Unique in astonishment. Her gut had told her that somehow Des's case and Desi's kidnapping were related. After processing what Samuel and Unique had told her and recalling how the woman in the surveillance video looked familiar, she said, "Unique, that crazy bitch got my baby. Do you know if she's at home?"

"I just called her—that's why I left the room. She told me that the exterminator was there and not to come there tonight. I believe she probably got the baby there."

"Is this the picture of the white man she's been seeing?" Yarni searched through a file and found a picture of Columbo. Unique looked at it and nodded.

Yarni grabbed her gun and put it in her bag; Bambi, Lava, and Unique followed close behind as she headed to her car, ignoring the questions the others gathered at the house were asking. They were rolling four deep to pay Sister Khadijah a visit.

CHAPTER 31

A Treacherous Bitch

Yarni arrived at Khadijah's house and motioned for Unique to use her key to open the door. Unique put her key in the lock and turned it, but it didn't budge.

"Oh no that bitch didn't," Unique said. "She had the nerve to tell me the place has been sprayed, then she changed the locks. I can't believe this shit." She knocked on the door then pulled out her phone and called Khadijah. "Hey, open up. I need to come in and get me some clothes right quick."

Unique motioned to the girls to move back so Khadijah couldn't see them if she looked out the window. Khadijah opened the door a few minutes later, then she walked to the back of the house wearing a micro-mini flowery spandex skirt and a black tank top that displayed her tattoo. Her hair was in a ponytail, swinging from side to side as though it was glad not to be wrapped up. Khadijah had transformed from a holy woman to a hoochie momma.

"Oh, sorry about the locks," Khadijah apologized flatly. "I forgot to tell you I changed them, when I talked to you earlier."

"It's okay," Unique said, looking around for anything suspicious. When they heard a cry from the back of the house, Khadijah turned to her. "Oh, I'm babysitting little Desi for Des," she said casually before she started to walk out of the room.

"Bitch, you're telling a motherfucking lie!" Yarni screamed. "Lava, go get my baby while I take care of this bitch."

Lava ran to the back of the house and grabbed Little Desi and took her outside, where Joyce, who had followed them, was waiting in her car.

A shocked Khadijah looked like she could have been bought for a penny, but she didn't seem to be intimidated at all with Yarni up in her face.

"Who the fuck told you to fuck with my daughter?" Yarni yelled.

"Please," Khadijah said, sucking her teeth. "You ain't thinking about that baby fo' real. You only had her so you could trap Des."

"Is that right?" Yarni couldn't believe what this stupid bitch was standing in her face saying.

"You don't have time for her. Plus, you don't deserve that baby no way. While your man is being greedy getting money from every avenue, my man is sitting in prison rotting to death."

"I didn't make the rules to the game," Yarni told her.

"Fuck the game. The game is dead."

"Bitch, and so are you." Yarni spit on Khadijah right before drawing back and hitting her with the hardest backhand smack ever to be delivered. Khadijah almost lost her balance, but she stood there defiantly as if to ask, 'Is that all you got?' She wasn't prepared when Yarni countered with a right hook.

After Khadijah fell to the ground, Bambi kicked her in her face. Yarni moved Bambi out the way and commenced to fuck Khadijah up, sending blows to her head one after another. Khadijah was yelling and screaming, trying to fight back with all her might, but it was damn near impossible. Bambi held Khadijah down while Yarni beat her to a pulp. Before long, Lava tapped Bambi on her shoulder. "Let's get out of here. I have a feeling the neighbors may have called the police with this bitch doing all that screaming."

Bambi pulled Yarni off of Khadijah. "Come on."

Yarni stopped hitting her once she saw the blood and allowed her sister to lead her to the front door, but when she thought about Khadijah fucking with her husband and child, she swung around. "Fuck that. Get that bitch up and sit her in the chair."

Bambi and Lava got Khadijah up. Unique tied her to the chair, and Yarni got a good look at the tattoo. "Oh you's a treacherous bitch, huh?"

Khadijah could barely open her eyes. She sat up as straight as she could. "That's right," she uttered, with blood seeping down her face.

"Well, it takes one to know one." Yarni hit Khadijah so hard that Khadijah pissed on herself.

"Why would you do some shit like this? My sister and her husband embraced you while Ahmeen was locked up, gave you a good job, a nice place, and a car. Why would you want to do some fucked-up shit like this?" Bambi asked, spitting on her, too.

"Because she's a fucked-up bitch," Unique said. "That's what fucked-up bitches do. I should know. I've been one for most of my life."

Khadijah rolled her half-open eye at Unique.

"I asked you a motherfucking question, bitch. Now answer," Yarni demanded, punching Khadijah again.

"Y'all were so dumb and stupid, you didn't even get it," Khadijah said, disgust dripping from her voice. "Y'all so happy-go-lucky, running around spending money while y'all so crazy in love. The people offered me a shot to get my man out. I took the deal, but Des wouldn't let me get into his business; he had me doing only the peon shit. Finding you tickets to the old-school show and shit like that."

"So I called as his secretary and set up the appointment with his former lawyer, and made it his last appointment for the night. I showed up instead to make sure that Des's ass would get life. I had it all figured out," she said, as if proud of her little plan.

Yarni struck her again and took a deep breath and tried to get herself together.

"Look, this is how it's gonna go down." Yarni kneeled in front of Khadijah. "Make no mistake about it. I will kill yo' ass if I have to, and nobody would give a fuck. Your husband don't give a fuck; neither does Columbo. You're a pawn for him. You, my darling . . . you are basically on your own."

Khadijah stared defiantly at Yarni, who didn't break eye contact. Khadijah dropped her head as tears formed in her eyes. She looked to Unique for help.

"Game over, bitch. I can't help your ass. You should have thought about that when you made a big deal about me using one of your tampons. I told you, you may need me one day. Remember when you said you wasn't gon' need a ho for shit?"

"You can die right here, right now," Yarni said, pulling her gun out, putting it to Khadijah's head, and cocking it, "or take door number two. If you value your life, or what life you have left, you'll sign a deposition saying that you set my husband up. Prison may be the safest place for you, off these streets. If you ever cross me, prison won't be able to protect you from me. You gon' wish you were in hell with gasoline drawers on. So, it's up to you to decide your destiny. Lose your life right now, or spend your life in the penitentiary. Make the decision now: Breathe or die, bitch."

Khadijah's cockiness quickly fled, only to be replaced by defeat as reality stepped in. She knew that she was doomed and was going to be in prison washing the underwear of some big broad named Bertha. She agreed to take door number two. Yarni called an attorney friend of hers to take Khadijah's statement.

As they waited for the attorney to come, Unique pulled Bambi aside. "Can I talk to you on some real sincere shit?"

"I guess," Bambi said, although she could never trust Unique the way Yarni did. She remembered Unique from back in the day, before she was left in South America. She knew her freak skills were legendary and that she'd always had a thing for Lynx. Bambi nipped it in the bud a long time ago and made sure that Unique would never sink her claws in her man. Yarni shared Unique's sob story with her and Bambi wanted to feel compassion, but there was something about her. She wondered what in the world Unique could possibly have to discuss with her.

"Look, as I mentioned to your sister, I never really belonged to anything or anybody, not even my momma. Nobody ever loved me. Niggas loved me because I was cute and had a mean head game and could hook a steak up. Bitches fucked with me because I got money and attracted the niggas with it."

"I'm hearing you." Bambi looked as if she was about to say something smart, but Unique saw it coming.

"Listen and just hear me out. I promise I'm going to make my point."

"A'ight," Bambi said. "Go ahead."

"Those things I did, chasing money ain't never do nothing but get me a wet pussy, shot at, prison time, and left in a whorehouse in South America with no passport," Unique admitted.

"Damn," Bambi said, not really giving a fuck. But she decided she'd listen. Unique did have a powerful testimony.

"In between customers, I wondered why this was happening to me—what was the reason? I knew somewhere there had to be one. I feel like everything happens for a reason—there are no chance encounters. Do you believe that, Bambi—that nothing happens by chance?"

"Yeah, I guess so." Bambi wondered where this conversation was headed.

"Well, I know this might sound crazy, but today I figured the shit out."

"Why you were left there?"

Unique took a deep breath. "So that I could save a soul because I had lost mine. It was God's test."

"How so?"

"I've done enough harm in my day to enough people, and for the first time in my life, I'm going to do what's right, and that's save you."

"Save me? Save me from what?"

"Lootchee."

Chills went up Bambi's spine, and fear settled in her heart.

CHAPTER 32

Something's Gotta Give

Yarni lay with her daughter, planting kisses all over her tiny face. It had been the best day and worst day of her life. She didn't know what she would have done if something had happened to her baby. Little Desi didn't seem to have a care in the world as she slept contentedly in her mother's arms. When the phone rang, Yarni thought about not answering it, but she realized she still hadn't heard from Des. Not bothering to check the caller ID, she picked it up. "Hello," she said.

"Hey, baby."

"Where have you been?" she asked angrily.

"I told you I had to take care of that stuff today," Des said. "Is everything okay?"

"Well, your daughter was kidnapped by your personal assistant, who has been trying to set you up with Columbo." Yarni did not waste any time getting to the point.

"What? What the fuck you mean?" Des asked after a moment of silence.

Yarni ignored him, finally able to vent all her frustrations. "Yes, I spent my day on pins and needles, not knowing if our child was dead or alive. Once again, you weren't here for me. I swear, I'm tired of this shit, Des." She tried not to scream and wake Desi.

"Look, baby, I love you. We're going to talk about this when I get home," Des said before hanging up the phone.

Des sat in his car. Yarni was right. He hadn't been there for her—or for their baby. He had left soon after Desi was born, and during her short life, things had always been about him, with no real concern for his wife or his daughter. Yarni had never complained—in fact, she had always loved and supported him unconditionally—and he could tell by her tone that she *was* tired of his shit.

In all honesty, he was tired of it, too. Too much had happened—he'd lost Nasir—and if he didn't change his ways, he knew he would lose his wife and his daughter as well. He couldn't let that happen.

He started his car and drove around for a few minutes before pulling over. He bowed his head and let the tears fall, trying to cleanse the game out of his system. It was time to let it go. He had to step up and be the man his wife and daughter needed. He was pretending to be a man of God, but Yarni was right. It was time he started practicing what he preached. The game wasn't the same, the players had changed, and he was slipping. While he was out murdering Felix, his own baby's life had been in jeopardy. Ripping, running, and playing in the streets was about to come to an end for him.

He wiped his eyes, took a deep breath and began to speak to God.

If there really is a God and you're as wise as e'rybody say you are, then you already know how I get down for mine! So I'm not going to try to front on you. I got a few more . . . well, let's just say un-Christian-like things to take care of, and after that, I'm goin' to clean my shit up. Excuse my language; old habits are hard to break. Anyway, if you're not too busy, I may need a lil' help. Not with the dirty stuff, I can fin for myself when it comes to that. I just don't want to lose my wife and daughter in the process. Oh, and about that thing I've been doing with the church in your name—I'ma flip it; I'm going to hustle for you like I hustle for myself. Thanks, Big G.

After Des was done, he felt as though a heavy burden had been lifted.

When he arrived home, Yarni was waiting in her office for him.

"Baby, I am so sorry," he said, reaching out to her. She moved out of his grasp and stood with her back to him.

"You're right, you are sorry." She turned to him but couldn't meet his eyes.

"This is the bottom line: Things have got to change between us," Yarni said. "I can't live like this anymore."

"Baby, I'm about to be done with the streets, but I can never be done with the lifestyle."

"What? So you're going to continue to chase the streets?" she asked in amazement. "You're telling me the streets mean more to you than me and your daughter?"

Des shook his head. "Of course not. I'm just about done with the streets, but look at how we live." He waved his head to encompass the house.

"I don't care about this. We've made enough dirty money. We're both intelligent people, let's focus on the legit money."

"I know, but I'll always be a hustler—not drugs," he said quickly, when she looked at him like he was crazy, "but hustling to make sure we a'ight." His eyes met hers. "Legally. I promise I'm going to make some changes, but you're forever going to be a hustler's wife. You ain't leaving me."

She sighed. "No," she said, and Des released the breath he hadn't realized he was holding. "I feel God has spared you too many times, and right about now you're trying your luck with him."

"I know."

Yarni hugged him as if she didn't want to let go. She didn't want to, but she knew she had to handle her last bit of business for the day concerning Des. She let him go and took a deep breath. "I have something to show you."

She closed her eyes and inhaled more air. She knew that what she had to tell him was going to break his heart, and it was one of the hardest things she ever had to do.

"Remember when I told you I had to get someone to get the files out of Sledge's office for the Samuel Johnson case? They didn't have a bunch of time, so they just took everything he was working on for the past six months. I found out that the guy you told me about, Jarbo, was one of his clients. I also found this." She handed some papers to Des.

"I'm going to give you some privacy and time to digest this," Yarni said before kissing him and leaving the room.

Des was confused but looked at the papers. He read them over several times to make sure he was seeing what he thought he was. Apparently Rico and Jarbo, the man Rico had asked him to kill, were going to turn state's evidence on someone close to them both, and Jarbo had changed his mind at the last minute. Rico felt that maybe Jarbo would go to the person to let him know, so Rico got Jarbo before Jarbo could cause any problems. While Des wasn't named explicitly as the target in the papers, there were enough details that pointed to him as the person Rico was going to rat on.

Des took the papers and sat down on the leather sofa in Yarni's study. He was dumbfounded that his boy was about to give him up after all he had done for him. "I just need some time alone to figure out my next move," he said quietly as he crushed the papers, forgetting the vow he had just made to God and his wife.

$$\$ \ \$ \ \$$$

Before Des could fully absorb that Rico was about to turn him in to the Feds, Lynx called.

"Hey, man, we need to talk," Lynx said.

"Now's not a good time," Des said, getting ready to hang up.

"You need to make it a good time," Lynx said. "I found out who beat up Yarni."

"Who?" Des asked, sitting forward on the sofa.

"That asshole Marvin Sledge," Lynx said. "Bambi told me the other night. I've been trying to get in touch with you."

"Why the fuck you wait to tell me?"

"I've been *trying* to get at you man, but with all the shit going on, then you missing in action and the shit with Lil' Desi, it was hard to find the right time."

Des saw red. He balled his hands into fists and imagined how good it would feel to crush Marvin's skull. Marvin, too, would have to pay dues. The only question was who Des should go after first: Marvin or Rico?

$$$

Des couldn't believe Yarni had been protecting that sleazeball Marvin for all this time. There was no doubt about it, Marvin was gonna get what he had coming to him, and it wasn't anything nice, but first he had to find out why Yarni had kept this piece of information from him.

"Yarni!" Des yelled through the house. "Yarni!"

Yarni poked her head out of the doorway of the nursery, "Ssshhh. I'm trying to put Desi to sleep."

"My bad," he apologized, "but I need to talk to you; it's important."

"Can it wait just one second? The baby's almost asleep, then I'll be right there."

Des nodded his head in agreement and went into the bedroom and lit a blunt.

A few moments later Yarni walked in. "That mess stinks." She waved her hand. "What's so urgent that it has you screaming through the house, baby?"

Des took a pull then put the blunt out and looked at his beautiful wife standing in front of him. As far as he knew, his wife had never lied to him. "Why are you protecting him, Yarni?" he calmly asked.

"Protecting who?" she answered his question with one of her own. "What are you talking about, Des?"

"That pretty-boy lawyer from Maryland," Des shot back, "that's who."

"Who told you?"

"Is that all you got to say, Who told me? It doesn't make a difference who put me up on it; that's not the point, I shouldna had to hear it from anyone else." The more he thought about Yarni keeping something this huge from him, the more his blood boiled. "What else are you holding back on, Mrs. Taylor?" he asked in an accusing tone.

"Don't go there with me . . . Mr. Taylor." Yarni didn't know what her husband was implying, but she wasn't having it. "Did you ever stop to think that it was you I was trying to look out for?"

Des's expression showed a touch of confusion, but he wasn't going to let her get away quite that easily. "Explain to me how the man you are spending countless hours with . . . working . . . ended up beating the cowboy shit out of you?"

"First of all, he no longer works with me. But more important, I knew if I told you, God only knows what you would have done to him."

"You got that part right," Des confirmed. "But tell me why that would be a bad thing."

Yarni looked square in the eyes of her husband, lover, baby daddy, and best friend of almost two decades. "Because I love you too much, and I didn't want you to spend the rest of your life behind bars for some clown-ass motherfucker, that's why." Tears began to trickle down her face just before Des took her into his arms.

$$$

A week later, Stanka sat waiting on the hood of his 740 BMW. His mind kept retreating to days past when he used to have to take care of his favorite niece whenever she got into trouble, which seemed to be all the time. He'd known when she was born that she was going to be more than a handful. She had her mother's good looks and her father's hustler mentality—a gift and a curse, depending on how someone looked at it.

Stanka had been happy when Yarni met Des. Although Des was almost seven years older than Yarni, he knew that the man would take care of her. If he could've handpicked the man he wanted his precious niece to marry, it would have been Des.

The garage Stanka was parked in was pretty big. It could hold about eight cars easily. A few years back, it had been the auto mechanic's shop owned by his old friend Gee, before the drug task force had found out that more heroin than engine work was being done, and closed it. A junkie named Bootsie got caught boosting to support his smack habit and decided to help himself and the police at the same time, and Gee had ended up being sentenced to two hundred months by a federal judge. Stanka went to visit him at least twice a month to keep him up to speed on the latest on the streets, so he wouldn't be in a rush to play catch-up whenever he touched down again.

What's taking Des so long? Stanka thought. *This place is starting to get cold.*

Just then someone honked the horn of a foreign car twice, paused for a second, then honked again. Stanka raised the door of the old shop's entrance, and Des drove in. Stanka shut the door behind them. "What took you so long?"

"When you called, I was in Dinwiddie taking care of Rico. I got here as quick as I could," Des answered. "Where's the package?"

"In the back." Stanka never moved off the hood of the car. He simply lifted his key ring and hit the trunk button. When Des looked at what his wife's uncle had brought him, a smile took over his face.

"How does it feel riding in coach, playboy?" Des said to a tied-up and gagged Marvin Sledge. "Oh, where are my manners? I bet it's hard to talk with all that shit in your mouth, huh? I'm not in the mood for listening to no pussy motherfucka begging no way, so we gon' just let you stay that way for now."

Marvin was terrified. For the past four hours, he had been held hostage in the trunk of Stanka's car. Marvin had literally been caught with his pants down while getting a little head from his secretary. Although Marvin had pissed his pants long ago, at least he was still alive. For now, anyway.

"I'm beat," Stanka said. "What do you want to do with this piece of shit?"

Des would've liked to spend the next forty-eight hours torturing the perverted bastard, but he had more important things to do.

"I guess it's his lucky day. I'm kinda busy myself," Des said to Stanka.

Is it possible that these barbarians are gonna let me go after all? Marvin thought. If they did, he swore that he would change his womanizing ways. But not before he made these two savages pay for what they had done to him.

Des removed the .40 caliber handgun from his back and palmed it. He could smell the fear gushing out of the pores of his contorted prisoner. "Marvin, I wish we had time to really get to know each other, but I'm a busy man. You know how it is." Des spoke as if he was talking to a new acquaintance. "But there's one thing I'd like to know. How can a man go to college and law school, graduate at the top of his class, have everything he could possibly want, but be so stupid as to get himself killed over something he can't possibly have?"

The two shots from Des's mini cannon rang off close together. The first bullet caught Marvin in the middle of his forehead, killing him instantly. The second found its mark in the corner of his left eye.

"Give this trash a permanent home in the bottom of the James River with the rest of the garbage," Des snarled. "By the way, what do I owe you?"

"Consider it an anniversary present."

CHAPTER 33

Divine Intervention

riving down the street, Des had almost reached the church when the blue police lights flashed, indicating he needed to pull over.

As soon as the officer was about to get out of the car, he got a call in on his radio. A more serious offense was in progress, and he was only a quarter of a mile from the location. With Des and his traffic violation being the less important of the two situations, the officer threw his hand, signaling Des to go on as he jumped back into his car, turned on his siren, and sped off.

Recently, Des had been pondering whether there really was a God. He had never been a real religious man, even more so now that he was making so much money off his church. He believed every man created and controlled his own destiny, and that if a man was depending on the intervention of a so-called higher power rather than on himself, then he was in for a rude awakening.

As Des pulled his brand-new bulletproof Allure into his reserved parking space at the church, he smiled. The Bible said God helps those who help themselves. He cut the engine off the world's first personal protection luxury utility vehicle and looked around for Slim. It was 7:45 P.M., and Slim was supposed to meet him at the church at 8:00 to go over some business. Des hit the release button on the glove compartment and grabbed the Bible that Yarni had given him.

He put the book in the breast pocket of his three-quarter-length Ronald Isley mink jacket. He had an identical one that he had sent to an armor specialty shop to have a bulletproof lining put in, but he was still waiting for it to come back. He never underestimated the desperation of the other guy.

Feeling a chill in the air when he stepped out of his $200,000 vehicle, he pulled the jacket tighter around him. The weatherman had predicted the possibility of a dusting of snow; winter had arrived early this year.

Where the fuck is Slim? he thought.

The church took up half of the block, and the way his congregation was growing, he would need a bigger one very soon. Des didn't doubt that his congregation would be more than willing to give to the new building fund he was making a mental note of starting. Hell, some churches have had their congregation giving to a building fund for years, with no intention of ever building a bigger church.

Des cautiously made his way up to the package he saw sitting outside the church door. *Ms. Mary,* he thought, smiling, when he peered into the basket without touching it. He would know that pound cake anywhere. Ms. Mary had been giving him pound cake twice a week for the past few months. Des picked up the treat, already tasting the mouth-watering cake, then searched his key ring for the proper key to gain entry into the building.

Boooom!

He felt the pain of the impact before he ever even heard the single shot from the sniper's rifle.

The highly skilled marksman was well disciplined. He'd waited for hours in an abandoned building across the street. One well-placed slug to the heart of his mark and his job was well done. After he witnessed Des crumble to the ground, the executioner picked up the spent cartridge and made his escape.

Des opened his eyes.

If this was Hell, then he must've been here before, he thought. He reached toward the pain in his chest with his right hand. There was a hole in his jacket the size of a quarter. When he probed the inside of the jacket to further investigate the injury, he found more than what he was searching for: He found a miracle. The Bible that Yarni had given him had absorbed the shot.

Almost speechless, Des looked up to the sky. All he could think was that indeed there was such a thing as a higher power, and he was going to stop playing with God, who had spared him so many times. This time he took heed. At that moment his entire life changed—nothing would ever be the same for him. It was a new beginning.

There was no doubt about it, God was watching over Des . . . but so were the *Feds*!

Acknowledgments

· · · · · · ·

Usually acknowledgments are all about naming names, but first I have to acknowledge the one being that is behind this entire project: God Almighty.

Father, in the name of your son and my Savior, Jesus Christ, I thank you for keeping my cup running over with blessing after blessing, and for giving me the creativity within my spirit to produce work that I can be proud to share with readers around the world.

My God, you are the Creator of all things, not to mention my protector as I walked through the valley of the shadow of death during this literary journey. It was you, God, who always loved me, comforted me, showed me the way and sent me everything I needed to make this yet another masterpiece to add to the library of Nikki Turner Originals.

I don't want to take anything away from the many people who have served a great purpose in my life or who have been with me throughout my literary career—through both the ups and downs. For those in particular who, when I felt as though I was suffocating, didn't mind using their lungs to keep me moving so that I could breathe life into this project, words can't acknowledge you enough. But how I see it today (minutes before my final deadline) is that each and every one of those individuals, and you know exactly who you are, were angels on loan to me from the Father. So again, I have to thank Him for designing you, but I do also thank my wonderful angels for being obedient to God's word and instructions, and coming forth to share this with me, wanting nothing in return but to see me succeed.

Again, this isn't about naming names because I didn't want anyone who didn't see their name on the marquee to feel that their time and existence meant nothing to me. If you are one of those people who are scanning the credits for your name, then you are not one of those genuine individuals who God called to minister to me in my time of need; and there were many. You know who you are (my family and real friends) because I've told you time and time again.

There are some people who left footprints on my heart and may not have even known that they were putting in God's work. Ecclesiastes 3:1 states that "for everything there is a season, and a time to every purpose under the heaven . . ." Although it was hard for me to grasp that people come into our life for a season, then after they have fulfilled their calling we have to let them go, I've learned to not be sad, but to understand that they've done God's work and it's time for them to move on to the next project that He has for them. I've accepted that it's not about what Nikki wants, but it's about what God wants for Nikki. And I just thank God for giving me the opportunity to allow this little light of mine to shine in the lives of many.

There are a few angels in particular that I must name: my two wonderful children, Kennisha and Timmond. You two are God's biggest blessings to me. Elouise Perry, thanks for loving me as your own. Paulette Williams, in spite of Hurricane Katrina turning your world upside down you somehow kept mine on level ground. Ms. Carol, you came into my home as a nanny for my children and Biggs, but ended up loving me as your daughter, and my children as your grands. Thanks for having such a great spirit of discernment to hear what God wanted you to do. I know it's tough, and hard work, but you are so appreciated.

A special thanks to Antonio "Tone" Tarver, for understanding that our crafts are parallel. I can never thank you enough loaning me your $5 million house and personal trainer to get me mentally focused on this book. I'm always here for you. Kia, thanks for believing in my vision. Lenny, thank you for your kind words of encouragement as I wrote this book. Robinette, thanks for being the force behind me, going through all my submissions at my office. I truly appreciate your devotion to me and my dream.

Kermit Gresham of Gresham Photography of Richmond, thanks for bringing your talent to the table and allowing it to bless me and my fans. I will never forget how you did a photo shoot within forty-eight hours for this book cover. Manaya, the cover model, thanks for being the beautiful face to grace the cover of this book! Zane and 50 Cent, thank you to you both for your mentoring and for the great blurbs endorsing my book.

To my dear friend Stanford Dorsey: You have always been only a call away when my spirits are down, and within minutes you have me charged up and ready to conquer the world. I love you for the person you are and I know our friendship is one of God's special blessings.

My editor and agent, you both have been such huge support systems for me while I wrote this book. Thanks, Marc, for that night of getting all those people to call me to inspire me, and Melody, for your patience and your solidness as you stood behind this project. I can never thank you enough.

To everyone reading this, I thank God for leading you to my

books over and over again. I truly appreciate your undying support! Thank you!

And last but not least, my own special inspiration, who inspired Yarni's Des: You definitely know you are an angel in my life and you have the tattered wings to prove it from the battles you've fought for me, to see to it that I came through.

ABOUT THE AUTHOR

NIKKI TURNER is a gutsy, gifted, courageous new voice taking the urban literary community by storm. Having ascended from the "Princess" of Hip-Hop Lit to "Queen," she is the bestselling author of the novels *A Hustler's Wife, Project Chick, The Glamorous Life, Riding Dirty on I-95*, and is the editor of and a contributing author in *Street Chronicles: Tales from da Hood.* Visit her website at nikkiturner.com, or write her at P.O. Box 28694, Richmond, VA 23228.

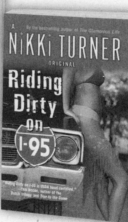
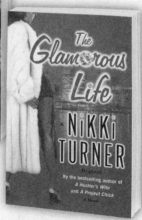